Sometimes A Warm Rain Falls

By Pierre V. Comtois

Photos by Hannah Lane

"Sometimes A Warm Rain Falls," by Pierre V. Comtois. ISBN 978-1-60264-420-5.

Published 2009 by Virtualbookworm.com Publishing Inc., P.O. Box 9949, College Station, TX 77842, US.

Manufactured in the United States of America.

Dedicated to my siblings Therese, Marie, Rachelle,
Joseph, and Louis.

And to my nieces and nephews Jeffrey, Hannah, Leanne,
Keith, James, Eric, Peter, Cecile, and Nathanael.

And to my honorary nieces Bethany, Renee, Audrey,
and Olivia.

And to the kids of Desrosiers Street 1965
(you know who you are)!

The Merrimack River, broad and placid, flows down to (Lowell) from the New Hampshire hills, broken at the falls to make frothy havoc on the rocks, foaming on over ancient stone towards a place where the river suddenly swings about in a wide and peaceful basin, moving on now around the flank of the town, on to places known as Lawrence and Haverhill, through a wooded valley, and on to the sea at Plum Island, where the river enters an infinity of waters and is gone.

Jack Kerouac
The Town and the City

A NOTE ON THE TEXT

This is the story of two people. Not Romeo and Juliet or Lancelot and Guenivere, or even Tristan and Isolde; but just two ordinary people, children actually, who lived in a very particular time and place.

It was the end of an extended period of well being for Americans that had begun immediately following the Second World War and concluded rather messily in the late 1960s. But trying to define the era only by the calendar is too simplistic because it suggests only the economic condition of the United States and not necessarily its social stability. Often dismissed by academics as "bourgeois," the "middle class values" embraced by post-war Americans actually had their origins earlier in the 20th century among the country's upper classes. Eventually they filtered downward and as more people entered a new, rising middle class, it became possible for them to acquire the things that had once been the province of the more well to do: a home in the newly expanding suburbs away from the congested city, the dream of higher education for their children, a car (or two) in the garage, etc. Although the depression years before the war had slowed the process down, it didn't succeed in stopping it. The hardships of those years in fact, helped to cement the values of family, friends, and community and when the war ended and the country's economy boomed, those values, it seemed, became universal.

So what has all that to do with the two people this story is about? I'm not sure, but I know the story would lose much of its poignancy without that middle class world to exist in. Guy and I and all our friends lived in a world that took the elements of the new suburbs for granted; the green lawns, the nearby farms, fields and forests, the small cottages and tiny local libraries, the neighborhood grocery store and the sun splashed, empty roadways that could only exist in the weekday silence of a world of single car families. With father gone to work in the family's only automobile, other family members either stayed home during the day or walked wherever they needed to go. It was a world in which there was plenty of day time and night time silence so that the sounds of birds and droning insects became an important part of the background of any suburban neighborhood. That background will be as important a character in the story that follows as any of the human ones because its unobtrusive influence helped shape the personalities of Guy and I and our friends every bit as much as our parents, the books we read, or the world at large did.

There are some today who claim that world never existed, that it was the creation of television producers anxious to present happy, sanitized programs for their viewing audiences. Well, I'll tell you right now that it was all true! In the 1960s, in the tired old mill town of Lowell, Massachusetts, before the pernicious influence of Ipods, and cell phones, and the internet, a world like that did exist; at least it did for me and my friends and I have no doubt that if it existed for us, it existed for many others too.

But like all times everywhere, that part of our history would pass as well. It ended in the late 1960s when a mass media brought the world into everyone's living room. It was at first believed that the process would unite people but the opposite happened, it fragmented them instead. The post-war world that had seemed so uniform in its values now suddenly split apart; marriages and families dissolved, places of worship emptied, and communities fragmented so that neighbors no longer even knew each other's names.

However, this story is not about those subsequent lost years; it's about the years immediately before, when two children learned about love and how to grow into adults safe from the pitfalls of the modern world. It's also my story and although some of the events detailed in the following pages have been slightly altered, they are essentially true. I *did* know someone named Guy, and Polly and Mike and Theo, but not necessarily as you will meet them here (and not necessarily with the same names!) because even though what follows is a true story, it's not meant to be a work of non-fiction. In it, I've taken the liberty of getting into other people's heads, to take a stab as to what they may have been going through and thinking about at the time, especially Guy, but I make no claims that my conjectures are accurate. Some things I was told by Guy himself and some of the others in later years, some things I deduced from my own experience living with them, and others I just used common sense in guessing at. Chapters will alternate point of view between myself and Guy and to help set the tone for each, I've headed them with selections from a diary I kept at the time and a science fiction novel Guy had been trying to write. (Guy will be the first to admit that the novel wasn't very good, but as I'm sure you'll discover, it's subject matter bears an uncanny resemblance to some of the events in this story!) I decided to do things that way in order to tell a more complete and satisfying story.

I hope you enjoy the results as much as I have.

Noël Archambault
June, 200-

PREFACE

They slipped from the house by the back door while everyone else was in the front parlor and the library.

Outside, it was cooler but still warm as the evening of July 4, 1943 drew on. The last rays of the sun stabbed through the surrounding trees as shadows grew longer, came together, and prepared to cover the world in another night.

Hand in hand, the young couple stole along the grassy path from the rear of the house into the back yard. Crickets filled the increasing gloom with a cacophony of chirping and the first bat fluttered overhead. Instinctively, the girl held the boy's arm tighter. He, of course, didn't mind. A sudden burst of laughter from the house made them stop and look back over their shoulders.

Lights burning from every window, the big house bulked darkly against the fading sky perched as it was high up on a hill outside the city. Automobiles filled the unpaved driveway and lined the street but no traffic passed on the road in front. And so, when the laughter subsided, nothing remained but the deep silence of the wooded countryside.

Turning to each other again, the two young people smiled and continued their walk into the yard.

Presently, two Great Danes, each penned in its own cage and sensing the approach of strangers, began to whine in anticipation of being visited. The couple approached the cages and the girl bent to scratch the head of one and the chin of the other, murmuring their names. After the animals had calmed down, the girl rose, her long white dress swishing against the uncut grass, and rejoined the boy.

At last, they came upon a gazebo that stood in the deepest reaches of the yard, out of sight of the house.

Neatly trimmed roses, trained to grow along its banister and columns, nearly reached to the roof. Inside, beneath its rounded cupola, the couple faced each other, hand in hand. Behind them, night had fallen and the first stars were twinkling in the sky.

"Will you wait for me?" asked the boy, nervousness in his voice.

"Yes," whispered the girl with a shy nod of her head. Then lifting her eyes to him again, said, "I want you to be careful."

"I will," the boy promised, thinking of far flung battlefields.

And then, quite spontaneously, they embraced, shared their first kiss and stood a while, in each other's arms. It was enough.

Old mill buildings along the Merrimack River

CHAPTER ONE

*In which Noël moves to Lowell
and finds the beginning of a mystery*

June 12, 1967: I admit that when Papa and Maman first told me that we'd be moving back to Lowell, I didn't take the news very well.

Papa tried to reassure me by describing the house he'd rented. It was small and cozy he said, with a white picket fence and lots of flowers. But I found that hard to reconcile with the picture of old, rotting mill buildings Maman told me about.

They tried to soothe my anxieties by telling me that Lowell wasn't that bad. After all, hadn't they grown up and married there? The only reason they'd left was because Papa's job had called him away.

Then they reminded me that I'd lived there too: for about a year after I was born.

Well, all I remembered about Lowell from infrequent trips we'd made there, were neighborhoods crowded with tenement buildings and dirty, treeless streets.

At first, the reminder that I'd been born there didn't seem to be of much help. After all, in moving, I'd still be leaving all my friends behind.

But as the time approached for us to leave it forced me for the first time to think seriously about my friends and I began to realize that I didn't have as many as I thought I did. What I had weren't real friends, but acquaintances. After I came to realize that, I wondered why that was so and I soon had to admit that it was no one's fault but my own.

I've loved to read ever since I can remember and over the years books have become my passion. And although the benefits in knowledge and pleasure that I've received from them have been enormous, I have to admit that the more time I've spent with them, the harder I've found it to make friends. At school the other kids didn't understand why I preferred to read poetry than play dolls or hopscotch or skip rope. To them, it seemed that I was just stuck up.

One of the obligations in keeping a diary is that one should be honest so I'll admit that deep down, I think I always knew that there was some truth to what the other kids thought. That could explain the mixed feelings I had when I first found out about our impending move to Lowell: on the one hand, I'd be faced with the chore of having to make new friends but on the other I'd have a chance to start all over in a town where no one knew who I was.

As time passed and the day of our departure grew closer, I actually began to feel happy about the move and the idea of possibly putting my past behind me and beginning fresh in a new town and a new neighborhood helped make the change less painful.

It was then that I resolved to take full advantage of the situation and the anonymity thrust upon me to make real friends. I've vowed to try and limit my use of proper English and not use too many big words because I'm pretty sure that they were largely to blame for my past alienation from other kids. They thought I was a snob and I have to admit that if I'd been in their place, I'd probably have thought the same thing.

Another thing I've decided is to keep this diary where, alone with my thoughts, I can be myself. Although hardly anyone keeps one anymore, keeping a diary has a very long history among heroines. All the women in the books I've read kept one including Marian Halcombe in *The Woman in White*, my favorite novel. Why, if it wasn't for Marian's diary, the hero's efforts to bring the villains to justice would have been useless!

Now, with a course of action set, I feel as if a great weight has been lifted from me and I've begun to actually look forward to my new life in Lowell.

Looking back over this entry, I'm satisfied with the way I've thought things through. I see things much clearer now. Life isn't very complicated if you set your mind to figuring it out. The future is a blank slate upon which new chapters and new adventures will be written and I intend to be the one doing the writing.

The silence of the secluded picnic area was shattered by a short, sharp cry, then the dull splash of something falling in still waters.

At a table, Lucille Archambault was just clearing away the remains of a roadside lunch when the sounds stopped her. "Noël?" she called, but there was no reply, just the dull splash of water. "Noël!" she called more urgently as she began to run in the direction of the noises.

Seconds later, she burst through the thin fringe of shrubbery that separated the open rest area from the tranquil stream that meandered down from the nearby hills. Skidding along the shallow bank, she stopped short of the water's edge. A short distance in front of her, standing knee deep in the running water, was the object of her anxiety.

Noël had frozen in mid-stride. Her short, blond hair was plastered to her head and her clothing was soaked and streaked with strands of green swamp algae. Caught, she smiled impishly with the intention of conveying an air of playful mischievousness.

It didn't work.

"What happened?" Lucille demanded. For the moment, there was only worry in her voice, not anger.

"Nothing!" claimed Noël before her mother's concern for her safety did turn into something with more serious consequences.

But it was obvious that her mother wasn't going to be satisfied with such an inadequate explanation.

"I was just trying to pick some of those pretty looking flowers," Noël tried again, pointing to a nearby tree. Fallen in some past storm, its branches were bent low over the surface of the water and clinging to them were a tangle of vines whose orange blossoms trailed into the lazy stream. One of the branches displayed clear evidence of having recently suffered a break. "I was sure the branch I used was sturdy enough to support my weight…"

Pausing, Noël saw by the expression on her mother's face that she wasn't out of trouble yet. "I was going to surprise you," she said. "With a bouquet."

"Noël, you're old enough now to be more responsible," her mother said, still unmoved. "You know better than to take chances like that."

"But Ma…"

"No buts, young lady, now you get yourself out of that mud and up here this instant," her mother ordered. "When your father hears about this, he's going to be terribly disappointed."

Lucille, knowing the value her daughter placed in her father's opinion, realized the potency of her concluding remark. Noël's standing in her father's eyes meant a great deal to her; she regarded his tall, dark form as the personification of every heroic ideal she'd encountered in her reading. He was Heathcliff and Rhett Butler, Andrei Bolkonsky and Atticus Finch and Howard Roark all rolled into one. Instantly, Noël sprang from the water to the pebbled shore, taking her mother's hand in a desperate grip.

"Oh please, Ma, don't tell him anything, please! He doesn't have to know does he?"

Her mother sighed. "What am I going to do with you, Noël? You get so wrapped up in your reading sometimes, I think you find it hard to tell that what's possible in a book doesn't always hold true in real life."

Noël heard victory in the tone of her mother's words then remembered what she had in her hand. "Don't worry about me, Ma. Anyway, at least I didn't fall in the water for nothing. Here, this is for you." She held up a single orange blossom, miraculously uncrushed. It was accepted with such tenderness that Noël almost felt that her mother believed her story about having done it all for her. *Well, maybe I did*, she told herself.

Her mother gave the flower a sniff and said, "We'd better head back to the car and get you out of those wet clothes, otherwise how'll we ever keep this adventure from your father?"

Laughing, Noël took her mother by the hand and together they returned to the rest area.

Arriving at the car, Lucille popped the trunk and pulled out Noël's big suitcase. "Ooof! What did you put in here, rocks?"

Noël shrugged, not really listening.

Lucille flicked the tabs and, lifting the lid, gasped. "Where's your clothes?"

"Huh?" was all Noël could muster. But when she looked into the suitcase, she flushed, feeling completely foolish. She was supposed to have kept a change of clothes with her for the day-long drive up from New York, sending the rest to the new house by moving van. But something must have gone wrong--definitely gone wrong, because the suitcase she had with her in the car had been filled with nothing but books. "I--I must've left them with the other boxes..."

"Noël, I specifically told you to bring a suitcase with a change of clothes with us in the car," her mother scolded. "You know how hot New England gets in the summer."

"But Ma, I'm a bibliophile." It was one of her favorite words; ever since an uncle had once laughed good naturedly at her roomful of books and said, "Well, you're the littlest bibliophile I've ever seen!" When she found out the word meant "lover of books," she immediately adopted it as a personal appellation and badge of honor.

But right then, it didn't seem like that badge was doing her any good.

"I couldn't trust my favorite books to just anybody, especially some mover I never met, so I decided to keep them with me," Noël explained. "I guess I just forgot to bring the suitcase with the clothes..."

Lucille snapped the suitcase with its incriminating contents shut and shoved it back into the recesses of the trunk. "I just don't know what I'm going to do with you," she said, almost beneath her breath. She looked at Noël's condition and shook her head. "I just hope we don't run into anyone other than your father before we can do something about your appearance. What'll our new neighbors think?"

Noël wisely kept her mouth shut.

With her wet jeans spread out in back and a dry towel wrapped around her waist, Noël watched from the front seat as her mother pulled the car out from the highway rest area and back onto the main road. A desultory silence settled over mother and daughter and Noël took the

9

opportunity to pull out her copy of Jack Kerouac's *Dr. Sax* from the glove compartment. She treated it with more care than usual, not rolling the pages or pulling at the spine, because she regarded it as almost an heirloom. She'd been helping her father pack his things a few weeks before and *Dr. Sax* tumbled out from behind a stuck drawer. Her father grunted, saying he'd forgotten all about the book. When she asked about it, he told her that Jack Kerouac had been a writer of French-Canadian background born and raised in Lowell, where they were moving. He thought a moment and added that maybe Noël would enjoy reading it to get a feeling for her new home, but warned her about Kerouac's singular prose style that might prove difficult to follow. Noël needed no further prompting. She accepted the challenge and began reading it right there.

Her father finished the packing by himself.

She did find the book tedious to read, but very rewarding. The author's rich descriptions of growing up in Lowell in the first half of the last century and his ability to weave a magical, fantasy story of the mysterious Dr. Sax and the young boy who helps him in the struggle against the sinister World Snake made of the Depression wasted city a very real place.

"Just what exactly is Pa's new job anyway?" she suddenly asked, images of dimly lit factory buildings looming against gray and smoggy skies dominating her thoughts. She shuddered.

Lucille shrugged, not taking her eyes from the road. "Just about the same as his other one. When his company announced they were opening a new division in Lowell, your father and I decided that he should take the opportunity to transfer so we could move back home."

Noël wrinkled her nose. "He's going to work in those ugly old mills?"

"They are ugly," her mother admitted, "but the one the company's in has just been renovated. The federal government has begun helping the city to develop some of its old property in order to attract new hi-tech electronics companies to come in and replace older industries. Once, Lowell used to have lots of shoe and textile factories and machine shops, but those kinds of businesses have disappeared and new ones need to be found to replace them so people can continue to work. It wasn't so long ago that your grandparents found themselves out of work during the Depression and had to go on welfare. I can't tell you how that ruined their self respect. So, I think what your father's company is doing is the right thing and in a small way, I like to think that our family's moving back to Lowell will help it get on its feet again."

Noël wasn't entirely convinced.

"Are you sure I'll like it there?" she asked, telling herself for the thousandth time that Lowell had to be better than Forest Hills; that walks in empty fields and woods had to be better than walking in a city park; that there was the possibility of making new friends who wouldn't hold her reading habits against her. But every time she started feeling better about the move, the old fears arose. Fears of going to a new town and mixing with new kids. Fears of not being accepted. More than once she tried to bury them in a good book, but it seldom worked for more than a few minutes. Even now they seemed to gather about her, unbidden, giving rise to subtle depression.

Lucille smiled. *Children always find it easy to adjust to new circumstances* she thought, *if only that held true for adults as well.* Aloud, she said, "Life never turns out the way you expect it. You'll see."

But Noël had her doubts.

The only thing she could count on was her parents with their comforting predictability. Nothing seemed to ruffle them or shake their spirits and she resolved to be more like them.

And for that, she had a strategy all worked out. When she arrived in her new neighborhood, surprises would be kept to a minimum. It was the way adults would approach the problem; certainly the way the cool headed heroines of her favorite novels did. She'd model herself on the example of Emily Dickinson, reserved and aloof. She'd study the new landscape presented by her new environment and act in a premeditated, calculated way, like the clockwork efficiency of Dickinson's poetry: "Because I could not stop for death..."

The next few hours seemed to crawl by as Noël, forcing an interest in *Dr. Sax* she didn't feel, tried to anticipate every possible challenge that might be encountered when she arrived at her new home.

Eventually however, her musings were momentarily dispelled when her mother lifted her chin and declared, "There it is."

Looking up from her book, Noël left behind a vision of Lowell whose hard edges had been softened by a writer's childhood memories and was confronted by the real thing.

And even as she wondered if she was ready for that, she saw its dim outline on the horizon, all blocky mills and tall smokestacks. From that distance, the city still held the fairy tale-like quality hinted at by Kerouac and she began to find it easy to imagine Dr. Sax skulking about its dark alleys. Then the skyline disappeared and when next it emerged, they'd plunged into the eastern fringe of the city where the crowded streets of Back Central, their fifty year old tenement buildings filled with strange people speaking in alien tongues, were located.

The sight didn't help her uneasiness.

Suddenly they were caught in a line of traffic that snaked through the heart of the city. Old, tired looking store-fronts faced the street while idle salesmen, standing in empty doorways, watched traffic as it paraded past. A gigantic painted sign over one of the shops couldn't help but catch Noël's attention. Jerry's Army/Navy Store it read in fast fading block letters, and beneath a pair of unrolled awnings the store's wares, displayed in two big windows, were hidden behind chintzy orange/yellow plastic shades to protect them from the sunlight. In the doorway between the two windows stood a short, balding man with a scowl on his face and a foot long cigar in his mouth. Noël didn't like that look. It seemed to her to reflect the mood of the city: old fashioned, set in its ways, still asleep after the long night of post-Depression disintegration.

The sidewalk in front of the store, where it was not shaded by the awnings, steamed in the early afternoon heat and the few people on the street merely shuffled by, repelled by the sickly yellow pallor cast by the plastic sheets in the windows. Those yellow sheets looked to Noël like the dead eyes of a corpse; a look of lifelessness that was shared by most of the other stores in the downtown section.

She was about to say something to her mother about the listless nature of the downtown when she detected a possible ray of hope. "Harvey's Bookland," the sign read, (rather ostentatiously Noël thought). "Used Books Bought and Sold" said another in one of the dingy windows that appeared to be crowded with dusty tomes and well thumbed popular novels. Of course, she couldn't be sure about the quality of the merchandise, but just as she was leaning over for a better look, her mother pulled the car ahead with the green traffic signal and they were soon across Merrimack Street and passing in the shadow of bulking red-brick mill buildings that rose up on either side

13

of the street. Among them, Noël was only able to catch glimpses of mysterious, litter-strewn alleys and rusty, long disused railroad tracks that curved on rotted ties to crumbling sidings.

Leaving the midtown area, they drove onto an old iron bridge that spanned the sluggish, polluted waters of the Merrimack River. Noël barely noticed the bridge's sickly green color as they pulled out onto a double-laned highway that ran along the far side of the river. On her right rose the old buildings of upper Centralville, worn down and wearing down into an emerging slum. On her left, lined up now along the opposite bank of the river, were ranged the old mills, smokeless smokestacks occasionally punctuating their monotony. Five and six stories high, rank on rank of windows giving light to their dingy interiors, even Noël could tell that it must be a depressing thing to work amid such deadening surroundings. The mills' red ranks stretched all the way down the river to the Ouellette Bridge at Aiken Street.

By this time, Noël was getting a bad feeling about her family's move to Lowell what with the slum areas, dead streets and those hideous mills. But she didn't have time to think her feelings through as her mother signaled again and the car found itself next on Lakeview Avenue. Another mile or so passed as the inner city gave way to the suburbs and she turned onto something called Fred Street, then a series of confusing lefts and rights until Noël was positive she'd never find her way to their new home if circumstances ever dictated that she should.

She was mentally reviewing the route by which they'd come when she saw something she recognized, a street sign labeled "Desrosiers Street." Its appearance received her immediate attention and she began to take a closer look at her new neighborhood.

Luckily they'd left the rougher, tenement dominated section of Centralville a few streets back and were now in a more rural part of the city. The neighborhoods here were made up of single family homes; some obviously of recent construction while others had the look of old farmhouses with their distinctive stone and mortar foundations, high peaked roofs, and generally more eccentric outlines.

Desrosiers Street was a roomy, uncrowded neighborhood with many open and partially wooded lots among the various houses. Groves of willow, maple, oak, apple, and pear trees filled the spaces in between and lilac bushes seemed to predominate among the flowering plants with a smattering of rose bushes for which the street was named. Lawns ended at the edge of the street. Apparently sidewalks were unnecessary in such a sleepy neighborhood, which suited Noël just fine.

Then the end of the street came into sight and Noël realized that Desrosiers Street was a dead end. As the car slowed and approached the end of the street, she could see further progress was blocked by a split rail fence. A line of unidentifiable shrubbery and apple trees that crowded about the fence screened a field of open, rolling pasture on the opposite side. Noël thrilled at the sight, delighted to learn that hers would be the last house on the street and that beyond it was to be only untouched pasture and woodland. Already, she began to feel a kind of proprietorship for the countryside, looking forward to the solitude it would provide her for long walks and quiet reading.

At last, the car slowed to almost a halt and crunched up the slopey end of a driveway. It passed through a white picket fence (surmounted by a mail box reading "The Archambault's") and into a sun dappled yard that was almost completely hidden by thick shrubbery. Two large maple trees shaded the front of the house and kept Noël from getting a full view of the pink colored cottage that nestled beneath them.

Entranced, Noël hardly waited until the car had fully stopped before stepping out onto the driveway. Shading her eyes against the glare of the sun and forgetting her middle was still wrapped in a towel, she walked beneath low hanging branches to the rear of the house. She was delighted to discover that the most prominent feature of the building's second story were a pair of bow windows that faced the street. A roomy porch stretched around from the front of the house to the side and a small garage, choked in untrimmed shrubbery, sat at the end of the driveway. The house wasn't one of the older ones in the neighborhood, but Noël felt sure that it was of sufficient age to possess a semblance of originality about it.

"Like it?" asked her mother, and Noël realized that she did.

"Oh yes!" she said with enthusiasm.

"Then maybe you can help me with the unpacking?"

As her mother opened the trunk of the car, Noël took one more opportunity to inspect the neighborhood. Leaning against the gate in the picket fence, she looked up the empty street but once again saw nothing and no one. In the distance however, she thought she heard the sounds of laughter and youthful voices so maybe there were other children her own age around after all.

"Are you going to just stand there, young lady, or help your mother?"

Noël whirled and ran almost without looking, into her father's arms.

A hug and a kiss later, he said, "Well what do you think of our new home?"

"I like it a lot."

"Did you get a look at your room?"

"We haven't even gotten out of the driveway yet," said her mother.

"Don't need to." He jerked a thumb over his shoulder. "It's the bow window on the right."

16

Noël's face broke into a smile of pure delight. "Mine? Why, it must be the best room in the house."

"Don't jump the gun young lady; you haven't seen the rest of the house yet."

"I don't have to; that window overlooks a perfectly beautiful front yard and I know I'll be able to see the pastures over there from it too."

"Sure and..." Suddenly her father stopped, noticing for the first time, the towel that was still wrapped around Noël's waist. "What's with the sarong?"

Noël blushed. She'd forgotten about the incident at the stream!

Her mother sighed. "You'll never believe it, Roland. But I'll try to explain later."

But Noël decided to take on that responsibility herself and in the process, salvage at least some of her self-respect. She told her father the whole story, including the part about the suitcase full of books, then waited expectantly for his reaction.

What he finally did took her completely by surprise. He smiled, then threw his head back and roared with good natured laughter.

"I'm glad someone thinks it's funny," said her mother.

But her father's good humor didn't last forever and within an hour the family was busily at work trying to get their new home in order. It took that long to get started because Noël insisted on getting back into her jeans and then conducting a thorough investigation of the house; from the sunny kitchen to her own newly wallpapered bedroom. Finally, near dusk, they stopped for a hastily made supper of sandwiches and milk. Noël and her mother had hardly started theirs when her father wiped his mouth and pushed back his chair.

"That was quick, Roland," said her mother, looking up.

Her father downed the last of his milk saying, "I want to get that shed for the trash cans finished before the skunks and possums find out we've moved in. I won't be long."

"Well you'd better hurry because there isn't going to be much light left."

Noël watched, mouth full, as her father stepped outside, the screen door slamming shut behind him. Soon, they heard the sound of his hammer.

It must have been sometime during the meal that the hammering sounds had stopped, Noël was never sure. On her way back upstairs, she decided to stop by the small sewing room at the back of the house and call to her father from the window. Pressing her face to its cool pane she could see the rear of the garage and the scatter of tools, wood, and sawdust on the ground but not her father. Then movement from the corner of the house caught her eye.

Quickly, she dashed to her bedroom window where she could see the front of the house. Her father stepped into view near the rail fence that separated the yard from the open fields beyond. He seemed to be looking around, checking to see if he were being watched. Noël blinked and just saw his leg as it disappeared after him into the bushes. She pressed harder against the window but it didn't help.

He was nowhere to be seen.

She ran downstairs as fast as she could, the back door slamming in her wake, and headed for the corner of the yard. Gasping for breath, she cast around in the increasing gloom of dusk but found no hint of her father's whereabouts. She hadn't realized how disturbed she was until a sudden flash of light startled her. But it was only the streetlight overhead switching on with the approach of night.

Her heart pounding, she stepped into the bushes where her father had disappeared and then up to the fence on the other side. Beyond it, there was only an empty sea of tall grass sprinkled with clouds of fireflies drifting on the evening breeze. Out on the horizon, where the forest began, the last, pink blush of the sun glowed in the sky. A barely discernible path formed by the grass having been shoved aside was the only evidence that her father might have passed that way. Then it was too dark to see anything more.

Shivering, Noël hugged herself against the realization that the predictability she'd always counted on in her parents was suddenly and subtlely threatened.

Already, Lowell, with its ranks of brooding, empty red brick mills, seemed to be exerting a malign influence on her life.

Shaking the feeling, she fell back into the yard and walked slowly to the house.

Dracut Public Library

CHAPTER TWO

*In which Noël discovers a new friend
and other possibilities*

July 5, 1967: Bibliophile, (bib li-o-fil),
n. from the Greek: book, + loving. A lover
of books. Book loving.

According to my dictionary, that's what
the word means. I thought that since I was
going to start my life fresh in a new home
and a new town, and begin keeping this
journal, a good place to start would be to
define myself. And what better place to

start than the most important influence in my life (outside of Maman and Papa of course)?

I must've gone over in my mind the reasons why I love books a hundred times in the past, but I've never written them out. I'm going to do that now and for the first time I'll have to be careful to put my thoughts down in such a way that they can be easily understood by anyone else who might read these pages. (Journals of course, are never to be read by anyone except the writer, but one can never be too sure of anything). Anyway, I thought a good place to start would be with the definition of a word I've grown to love. And so, this entry begins with the meaning of the word bibliophile.

On the face of it, bibliophile is such a simple word (a simple word with five syllables!), but really, it's loaded with understated meaning; lover of books. But looking at the definition here I can see that it does nothing to convey how I feel toward good books. This definition is too cool, too sterile to ever satisfy me. My love of books has always been hot and volatile-- passionate even. Can I ever express the wonderful feeling of just holding a thick paperback in my hands? I love the weight, the heft of it; to flip through a hundred onion skin thin pages (I've vowed some day to read *War and Peace*), to slap it in the palm of my hand. And the delicious smell of a new hardcover book; opening it for the first time and taking a deep breath with my nose close to the binding. How do I explain the fact that each book has its own individual identity, not because of its author or story, but taken from its particular weight and scent?

When I'm lonely or hurt, depressed or bored, Charles Dickens, Harriet Beecher Stowe, Mark Twain, and Wilkie Collins have been my dear companions. How they've transported me from my dull surroundings to new worlds and times that've filled my daydreams with wonder and excitement! Sometimes it seems that I was really with Huck and Tom on an island in the Mississippi or on the trail of the hound of the Baskervilles with Sherlock Holmes or brooding from a window alongside Emily Dickenson! Oh, how they've often come to my rescue when no one else understood me, comforted me when friends were scarce!

Well; looking back over the lines I've just written, I see that I've said it as best as I ever could hope to (and hope no one ever really does read these lines because they'll sure make me look silly!), so I think I'll drop the whole subject. But it still makes me wonder about my earliest reading experiences. How did I get to love it so? Papa told me once that I was reading along with him since I was five years old; and thinking about it, I do seem to recall following his finger as it trailed across the pages of books. But I don't want to commit myself to that because it might just be wishful thinking triggered by Papa's recollection. (And his recollections are notoriously inaccurate!)

I know for certain that by the time I was nine, *Mon Oncle* Albert had first described me as a bibliophile and I remember wasting little time looking the word up. At the time, the dictionary definition didn't seem all that sterile to me, its roots in the ancient Greek language appealed to my sense of the exotic and inspired in me a pride of belonging to a kind of select fellowship that included Thomas Jefferson and Theodore Roosevelt. But most of all, I felt closest to the Bronte sisters, Charlotte, Emily and Anne because they seemed to me to be the most like myself.

Sometimes I can't help feeling as isolated as the Bronte sisters were in their home on the English moors. But in my case, it's not as much being apart from other people as an isolation of the mind. I don't know anyone else, not even Maman and Papa, who's remotely interested in the things I am, who can talk about Jane Eyre or Mr. Heathcliffe or dwell on the poetry of Emily Dickenson. I'm sure I'd be told that I'm too young for such thoughts, but my interior life has become a lonely one and I yearn to share it with someone, but who?

Well; there's no use going there. The Brontes, I think, had the right idea. They broke the monotony of their lives by inventing stories and games and then writing them down. I've decided to do the same thing. In secret so far because I don't want anyone to know about this journal. But until I can find someone with whom I can share my interior life, I'll be more than satisfied to think of myself as simply a bibliophile. With that, I know I'm in good company.

Noël shouldered her bedroom door open and slipped carefully inside. She held a cup of hot tea in one hand and was holding the other out trying to keep herself balanced. Making her way upstairs from the kitchen without spilling any of her drink was a skill she'd mastered in her old home but one she was still getting used in the new.

Trying to keep one eye on the floor in front of her and another on her tea, she weaved her way among the stacks of books that took up most of the floor space in her room. At last, reaching her desk and setting the cup down, she took a deep breath; the first she'd taken since leaving the kitchen. Then, hands on hips, she turned to survey the room around her.

New curtains had been placed in the bow window framing the tree-shaded street outside. Inside, her mother had placed a comfortable collection of pillows in the window seat that matched the room's new wallpaper. Noël thought the soft pink and beige colors she and her mother had picked out made the room all the more cozy when it was dappled in sunlight as it was now. At this time of day, the drooping branches of the maple trees outside cast blurred shadows against the walls that moved hypnotically in the breeze. Noël had to fight off a spell of drowsiness in order to concentrate on the job at hand.

Of all the chores she and her mother had to do to make their new home livable, she'd saved putting her books away for last. Cleaning, wallpapering, and arranging furniture may have been important, but ultimately, they required little consideration. Putting her books away however, was a task requiring careful planning. First, her future needs had to be assessed: what was her reading schedule going to be like? Which books would come in most handy for school? Which books would she most likely feel like browsing through? (That was easy, the poetry books of course!) After she'd set her literary priorities, an important decision had to be made: which order should she place her books in? Author order; subject order; alphabetical order; chronological order?

She thought the situation over and decided that since she was beginning a whole new part of her life, she'd take an entirely new approach to the problem. Scanning the large book case that stood embedded in the wall by the closet, she decided to place the non-fiction books (her biographies of Jane Austen, Ernest Hemingway, and F. Scott Fitzgerald and surveys of English and American literature) on the top shelf, the classics on the middle shelves and finally her well thumbed favorites (including all of her poetry collections) on the lower shelves for easy access.

All would be in alphabetical order by author. The plan set, she took a first, tentative sip of her tea and went over to her record collection. She pulled out one of her favorites, Prokofiev's *Lieutenant Kije Suite* and set it to spinning on the phonograph by the bedside. It was the perfect mood music for both categorizing and reading; listening to it, she was always emboldened to read *War and Peace* (but never quite getting around to it).

Between sips of tea, reading passages from her books and placing them in their proper places on the shelves, she began to think back over the past few days. Gradually, it came to her that she didn't miss her old home anywhere as much as she thought she would. Try as she might, she couldn't even work up a lump in her throat for anyone left behind. Suddenly, it seemed to her that New York was an alien place she could visit but never stay. Her true home, she now felt sure, was Lowell.

Thinking it over, she wondered if that feeling had to do with the fact that it was her parents' home town. The place where they'd grown up as second generation French-Canadians, gone to school, met, and married. She remembered all the things they'd told her of their lives here, about how hard it was growing up during the Depression and the lack of employment in the city. It wasn't a question of whether the old mills were dying, but their being already dead. And then came World War II and her father going off to fight, leaving her mother behind. He didn't speak much of his experiences in Europe except to say that he'd been in Italy and France and Germany itself during the occupation. But Noël could tell somehow his reticence had something to do with the devastation he'd seen there, of the quiet desperation that the people had been reduced to.

Then, for no reason, her thoughts turned to her father's strange behavior of a few days before.

Noël suddenly realized that she'd been daydreaming, a book idle in her hands. She straightened and found its place on the shelf, not very interested anymore with the work. Her tea was almost cold when she grabbed the cup and wandered over to the window seat. She sat down with a plump, one leg tucked beneath her and gulped the sugar-sweetened dregs of her tea. Finished, she breathed in the summer scents of freshly cut grass and wild flowers that wafted in from the outdoors.

She leaned her head lazily against the window frame and peered dreamily out through the thick leafage of the maple trees to the grassy pasture beyond the end of the street. A lone hawk hovered far out over the waving grass while white puffs of clouds slid slowly across the blue horizon. A heat bug buzzed somewhere. Gradually, she began to feel the familiar pull of the outdoors. What she really felt like doing was finding a nice quiet place out there to sit and maybe read some poetry. A little Robert Frost maybe.

But just as her bucolic yearnings had reached a point where action would have been required, they were spoiled by the sound of a repetitious squeaking. It came and went with irritating regularity that positively ruined her mood.

Stirring, Noël lowered her gaze from the cloud-scudded horizon to the street below her window. Movement caught her eye from among the tree branches and presently she was able to identify the source of the sound. A young girl in a plain colored jumper and sneakers was riding a bicycle slowly along the street. When she reached the dead end, she turned about and rode back up the street. As Noël continued to watch, the girl returned, standing tall on the pedals, neck craning toward the yard. Judging the girl to be about her own age, Noël watched as she passed the house again, turned around and rode back up the street. She repeated the process a few more times. Concluding without too much difficulty that the girl was trying to collect information about the new family in the neighborhood, Noël decided to make her acquaintance.

With rising excitement at the possibility of making her first friend, Noël lifted the screen from the window and leaned outside. Presently, when the girl and her bicycle once more came into view, she called out.

"Hello," said Noël.

The sound of her voice brought the girl to a halt, her legs firmly planted on the road's surface to either side of her bicycle. She leaned low on the handle-bars peering between the bushes at the front of the house, then, stretching past her full height, craned her neck to see over the top of the hedges along the fence. Plainly, she wasn't sure where the greeting had come from.

"Hello," said Noël again. "Up here." She stuck an arm out and waved it vigorously.

The girl's head jerked over in the direction of the sudden movement and spotted her in the opening between the branches. "Hi," she said, a bit hesitantly.

"I saw you riding up and down the street," ventured Noël.

"Oh, yeah," said the girl, grinning with slight embarrassment. "I was, uh--trying to see who was moving in here."

"My name's Noël; I'm eleven years old," Noël informed the girl.

"I'm Polly--Pauline I mean, but nobody calls me that; Pauline I mean," said the girl. "I'm eleven too." There was silence a moment, then, "Will you be living here? For good, I mean?"

"Yeah, my parents lived here when they were children and decided to come back. I'm fixing my room right now."

"I live up the street," said Polly, inclining her chin in a direction that was completely hidden by the thick bushes and trees on that side of Noël's house.

Noël felt that the conversation had reached an impasse; she knew instinctively that if nothing was done to salvage it, the opportunity to make friends would be lost, and who knew when she'd get another chance?

She determined not to let it slip away from her.

"Wait there, Polly, I'll come down."

Noël turned and raced down the stairs and out the back door, wondering the whole way just what she'd say to her new friend. But she didn't have time to worry about it as she soon found herself facing Polly at the front gate. The girl had drawn her bike up onto the sidewalk and had leaned it against the fence.

"I'm Polly," she said again.

"I'm Noël. So you live over there?" she asked, pointing.

"Um hm. Is your room that one with the bow window?"

"Yeah."

"I've always thought a window like that would make for a beautiful room. I'll bet you've got a neat view of Mrs. Ginot's orchard."

"What orchard?" asked Noël, intrigued; visions of swarming bees hovering over flowering apple trees filling her head.

Polly turned and pointed up the street, past where Dean Avenue joined Desrosiers Street. "It's on the other side there, behind Jiff's house. It's an old orchard that Mrs. Ginot doesn't keep up with anymore. She just picks enough stuff for the people in the neighborhood."

"Gosh, I'd love to go over and have a look sometime."

"I'll show you whenever you're ready."

"Oh, that'll be great, but what I really need to do the very first thing, is to check out the library," said Noël, forgetting herself and her vow to turn over a new leaf.

"The library? Why on earth for? Are you in summer school?"

"Oh no, I just like to read a lot and a good library is a must," replied Noël, suddenly aware of her gaffe but deciding to forge boldly ahead anyway. "Don't you like to read?"

"It's all right I guess, but it's summer vacation for crying out loud, I've read enough while I was in school."

Alarmed, Noël suddenly imagined her first friendship crashing into flames and moved quickly to save it. "I suppose you're right of course," she began, but then couldn't help but add, "Still, I'd like to check out the local library as soon as possible. Can you tell me where it is?"

It was perhaps unfortunate that she didn't do as thorough a job of rehabilitating herself as she'd intended, but it was even more fortunate that Polly didn't seem to hold her peculiar interests against her.

"I can do better than that, I can show you where it is."

What an understanding creature! thought Noël to herself.

"Actually, there are two libraries," Polly continued in what Noël was beginning to think was a perfectly hallucinatory experience. Such a thing had never happened to her before--a friend who was volunteering to lead her to a library! And apparently with enthusiasm! "The Dracut library is closer and is a much more pleasant walk, but the Lowell library is a lot bigger."

"I'd like to see them both," said Noël, getting excited.

"I don't think you have to waste your time at the Lowell library because it's not as good as the one in Dracut."

"What do you mean? How can a smaller library be better than a bigger one?"

"I've always wondered about that myself, but it's a fact," Polly said confidently.

"What do you mean, 'it's a fact?' How do you know?"

"Well, actually, I don't know, but that's what Guy says, and Guy…"

"Who's Guy?" asked Noël.

"Oh, he's just one of the boys in the neighborhood," said Polly. She turned and pointed at the house directly across the street. "He lives over there. He likes to read too; him and Jiff."

Boys who liked to read? Ignoring the little voice inside her telling her not to get her hopes up, Noël said, "Tell me more about Guy."

Polly shrugged.

"He has twin sisters, ten years old," she said. "And he says he can always find what he's looking for at the Dracut library but never at the Lowell library." Polly shrugged again. "I don't know, I never had any reason to go to the Lowell one."

"Well then, can you show me the way to the Dracut library?" Noël decided not to pursue the subject of Guy with her new friend just at that moment. At eleven years old, it wouldn't do to display too much interest in a boy, especially if you were the new girl in the neighborhood.

"Sure, we can leave now if you want, it's still early enough in the morning so that we can get back before lunch."

"Okay, just let me tell my mother," said Noël over her shoulder. A few minutes later she was back. "Ready?"

Polly walked her bike over to Noël. "We'll cut up through my yard. I can drop off my bike and tell my mom where we're going."

Together, the two girls walked the short distance to Polly's house; a small, yellow box with a steep, sloping roof. A longish driveway rose up to the back door and except for a stand of trees in a corner of the back yard (with thick gobs of sap dripping from the bark), the property was completely barren of any vegetation. Even the grass had turned to a krinkly yellow color in the growing heat of summer.

As Noël waited on the porch, she saw that the landscape continued to slope upward and that there was no fence separating Polly's back yard from that of the house in back; a long, peach colored, ranch style house that overlooked Polly's. Against it, an open porch stood nearly fifteen feet off the ground and from which the whole neighborhood must've been visible.

Noël wouldn't know it until later, but she was actually looking at the rear of the house; the front door faced on another road that ran along the opposite side.

The sound of music drifting from somewhere inside Polly's house drew her attention back inside the porch. Through the inner door, Noël saw a big kitchen, empty at the moment, with a bounteous display of fresh fruit on the table. She tried to make out what music was being played but failed to identify it. She'd never given popular music much thought before, preferring classical instead. But as she continued to listen, she actually caught herself tapping her foot to the rhythm. She felt herself blush when Polly reappeared in the kitchen and caught her at it.

"Do you like the Beatles?"

"Beetles?"

Polly stopped in her tracks. "Don't you know the Beatles? You were tapping your foot to them."

Polly judged Noël guilty by her silence.

"You never heard of the Beatles?"

Noël shook her head. "I don't think so…"

"Boy, where've you been, living in a cave? The Beatles are the cutest, neatest guys there are," explained Polly helpfully.

"And…?"

"And what? Oh yeah, they're a rock and roll group too; they sing songs."

"Is that all?"

"There might be more, but that's all I've ever heard about them from my sisters."

"You have sisters?"

"Yeah, two of them, they're a lot older than I am. Anne's sixteen and Lisette is almost eighteen."

"Was that them playing the music?"

"Well, Anne and a couple of her friends. They're playing their Beatles' records. They've got a lot of them." She stopped, then whispered, "C'mon."

Polly led the way from the porch into the back yard where a short ladder stood near the rear of the house. Placing a finger to her lips, she climbed the ladder and clung with her fingertips to the sill of a window. Music drifted clearly from somewhere inside. Noël climbed up the opposite side of the ladder and clung to the window in the same fashion. Cautiously, she brought her eyes up to the screen and peered inside.

Three older girls were sprawled across twin beds with small, black disks scattered all around them. A boxy record player rested on the floor between the two beds with one of the black 45s revolving on its spindle.

"That's *I Want to Hold Your Hand*," whispered Polly. "It was the Beatles' first big hit and my favorite...oops." The girls inside had risen to their feet and had begun to dance to the music.

"What kind of a dance is that?" asked Noël, never having seen such strange motions before. She had to admit however, she liked the music a lot.

"The swim," said Polly matter-of-factly.

"Oh," was all Noël could muster, not entirely sure if she approved of any dance bearing such a silly name.

"Let's go," said Polly suddenly as she hopped from the ladder. "My mother is out shopping and my sister said I could go ahead and show you the library."

Polly turned and instead of heading back the way they'd come, crossed the back yard and into that of the ranch house. "We'll cut through Don's yard, it's shorter than going all the way around."

"Who's Don?" asked Noël.

"He's the boy who lives here," replied Polly. "He has an older brother and sister we sometimes play baseball with. But usually, Don keeps to himself."

A heat bug buzzed long and loud from the trees in a nearby field and when the girls stepped from the shade behind Polly's house and into the sunlight, the midday heat began to beat down upon them mercilessly. When the buzz of the heat bug finally ended, the silence that followed seemed more intense than ever. Noël wiped the perspiration from her forehead and asked Polly about it.

"Is the neighborhood around here always this quiet? Where is everybody?"

"I don't know," admitted Polly "Summer afternoons are usually like this. Mainly it's because Jiff and Don's families are invited to the Foisy's down the street. They have a pool."

It was simply a fact, but the way Polly said it, it was as if the Foisy's were in possession of the Hope Diamond or the Holy Grail.

They left Don's yard and stepped onto Burnaby Street, then moved along a series of quiet, tree shaded streets. They passed by a little white church whose steeple was a hallmark of such churches all over New England. They crossed Hovey Square where stood a heavy stone monument honoring Dracut's dead of World War I and finally, after finishing a long stretch along Pleasant Street, came to the Old Yellow Meetinghouse that dominated Dracut Center. The whole walk had taken less than a half an hour, a distance Noël deemed satisfactory.

At the moment however, it wasn't the library that was holding Noël's attention, but the imposing form of the Meetinghouse with its tall steeple and stained glass windows. As a Roman Catholic, Noël was used to the more ornate surroundings of a church whose liturgy spanned almost two thousand years. But the simpler style in architecture and design preferred by the Protestant sects that had established themselves in New England over the past three hundred years held their own kind of appeal to her. It suddenly struck her as strange that in her life, she'd hardly known anyone who wasn't Catholic. It wasn't intentional of course, simply the result of a life lived among Franco-Americans who spoke their own language, published their own newspapers, built their own schools and attended their own churches. Experiencing the new and realizing that not everyone believed the same things took a bit of getting used to. Luckily, though, having a different opinion didn't seem to matter to most people.

"There's the library," said Polly pointing to the far side of the Meetinghouse.

Nestled in a grove of oak trees, the Dracut library (its real name was the Parker Library, but as Noël would learn, no one ever called it that) seemed pretty small. There was only a single main floor fronted by a double glass door entrance. Framing the entrance were four whitewashed columns holding a part of the roof that extended out from a small dome. The main part of the building was made of red brick and surrounded by a number of tall, small-paned windows that allowed plenty of sunlight among the bookshelves inside. Later, Noël would come to realize that the architectural style of the building was very traditional in America. After the Revolution of 1776, public buildings abandoned the styles of England and embraced those of classical Greece and Rome, the cradles of democracy and republicanism. The most famous buildings in America using that style were George Washington's home at Mount Vernon and Thomas Jefferson's home at Monticello. The Dracut library, Noël decided, was most influenced by Monticello.

Noël followed Polly along a gravel driveway that wound from the street to the foot of the stone steps at the front of the library. At the top of the steps, Polly pulled open one of the leaves of the double doors. She had to use all her strength on the heavy door and Noël was still obliged to help her with it. When they stepped across the threshold into a little foyer, the closing door literally pushed them the rest of the way in.

"C'mon, we'll go downstairs first," said Polly, starting down a stairwell that led to the basement. "It's the part of the library I always use; they have the whole Nancy Drew series there. Do you like Nancy Drew?"

"Yeah, I've read them all, and Trixie Belden too." Noël didn't say that she'd read them over two years before. It was soon after that a teacher at school

35

recommended Jane Eyre, changing Noël's reading habits forever. Still, she congratulated herself for not bringing it up to Polly. Except for the slip involving the Beatles, she thought she was doing rather well in establishing herself as a normal kid.

The stairs bent around once before emptying into a large basement room that extended the length of the building. Wall to wall carpeting and the lingering scent of fresh paint indicated that the remodeling had been only recently completed. The walls were lined with metal shelves holding books both old and new (she could tell because the newer books had preprinted labels on their dust-jackets while the older ones simply had hand written decimals on their naked spines). A small desk stood in the center of the room but no one was sitting behind it. In fact, the two girls seemed to have the entire room to themselves.

"The series books are over here," said Polly, leading the way to the far end of the room where an indentation formed a small alcove. She rounded the corner and stopped short. "Oh, I should've known."

"What's the matter?" Noël was asking as she came alongside her friend and saw the boy crouching in the corner with an open book in the palm of his hand.

"Hi Polly," he said, looking up at the girls' sudden appearance.

"I should've known you'd be here," Polly said again as the boy got to his feet.

Once standing, Noël noticed that he was about her own height with very short brown hair, a step up from a crewcut. He had dark, brown eyes and was extremely thin. Aside from his being so skinny, it was his clothing that attracted Noël's attention the most. It wasn't as if they were dirty or anything. They just seemed…plain. Then, the more she thought about it, the more Noël was convinced that he was wearing an old parochial school uniform grown too shabby for classroom use. The light blue shirt still had some stitches showing on the pocket where the school emblem had once rested and the cuffs on his trousers had been let down.

"This is Noël," said Polly. "She's the new girl who moved in across the street from you."

The boy's eyes had been going from one of the girls to the other, as if not knowing which to concentrate on. "Hi, I'm Guy…Guy DeMonde."

"I'm Noël Archambault. Hi."

Guy closed the book he was holding. "So what're you guys doing here? I'd think this would be the last place you'd take a new kid to Polly."

Polly would've replied, but Noël spoke first.

"I asked her to show me the local library and she said this was the best one." Guy nodded slightly. "She said according to you it's better than the bigger library in Lowell."

"It's true. Every time I've tried to look up a book at the Lowell library, I couldn't find it, but I've been able to find it here right off the bat."

"What kind of books?" This was the crucial question Noël had wanted to ask all along, ever since Polly had first mentioned Guy. Oh sure, on first appearance, Guy hadn't been anything to place much confidence in, but beggars couldn't be choosers after all. She'd never met anyone else as interested in reading as she was except maybe some adults, let alone a boy her own age, so she felt a bit justified in hoping for the best.

Guy shrugged and appeared to think. "Well, like *The Texas Rangers*."

Noël blinked. She'd never heard of any such book. "What book is that?" she finally asked, swallowing her pride.

"It's about how the Rangers helped build Texas," replied Guy. He didn't seem to notice that he was not scoring any points with his audience.

"When I first heard about it," he continued, "I wanted to read it and went to the Lowell library to get it. Naturally, I thought the bigger library would most likely have it. I was wrong. They didn't have it, but this one did. It's happened a couple of times to me."

"Why don't you show us around Guy," suggested Polly, unaware of how close Guy had come to making the wrong impression on Noël. "You know this library better than I do."

"Okay." Guy turned and plucked another book from the shelf to go with the one he already had.

"What are those books you've got there?" asked Noël, not very interested. She could tell by their identical look that they were series books.

Guy read the titles. *"Tom Swift and His Giant Robot* and *Tom Swift and His Atomic Earth Blaster.* I've read the whole series. They're wicked good." He held out the books in his hand. "These are the last two I have to read."

Noël's interest of only a moment before was rapidly cooling. She regarded Guy's reading habits, so far as she could tell what they were, as disappointingly immature; caught in simple adventure fiction. If she wasn't beginning to feel contempt for Guy's tastes (something like the feelings of an aristocrat for a peasant), it was something mighty close.

"These six Tarzan novels here," Guy was saying, oblivious to the sudden drop in temperature, "were more books I couldn't find in the Lowell library, but here they are. C'mon, I'll show you the upstairs." Brushing past the girls, he hesitated at the stairs and said, "Oh, if you like Nancy Drew, Trixie Belden, or the Little Peppers, they're all in this room."

By this time, Noël had worked her attitude into complete indifference toward Guy's literary opinions. If he'd meant his last comment as an insult, Noël wasn't amused; but she quickly decided it wasn't. Guy seemed too naive to have meant anything more by it than being helpful and besides, weren't his tastes in reading of a similar variety?

Noël's mood began to brighten only after Guy had led them upstairs and into the main portion of the library. There, bright sunlight streamed in unhindered through the high windows sharply defining every detail of the single large room that formed the core of the little library. Dotted here and there with upholstered furniture, an unused fireplace dominated the central portion and thick rugs helped keep noise down. The book shelves, once again holding a good mixture of old and new titles, lined the walls and each corner of the room had been arranged into separate alcoves: fiction, poetry, non-fiction, and reference. Noël fell in love with the cozy arrangement immediately and just knew that she was destined to spend many happy hours browsing and reading there.

"Over here's the science fiction section," Guy was saying, hesitating only long enough for Noël to orient herself.

She followed him into one of the alcoves and cast her gaze disinterestedly along the narrow section of shelves. Some books had been arranged so that their garish covers faced outwards. Noël wrinkled her nose at blurred rocketships, distorted alien creatures, and threatening robots. One cover sported what looked to be a goat wearing a gas mask. *Ecotopia* read the title.

"Not a very big selection," was all Noël could muster in the way of commentary.

"You're right," agreed her guide. "And it's mostly of authors I never heard of, but that's what I like about it. I just pick a book that sounds interesting, and it usually turns out to be pretty good. But if I really want something bad enough, I can ask them to order it." Guy took one of the books down. "This is one they got for me." *I Robot*, it read.

Noël's opinion of Guy's reading habits was not improving.

"And over here," said Guy, moving quickly around the corner to the central section of the building, "is the history section."

The girls stared.

Guy stooped and plucked a book from one of the shelves. It was one of the older ones with the decimal placement neatly written in a fine, calligraphic hand on its binding. "This is the Texas Ranger book I was telling you about.'

There was no response from either of the girls so he replaced it.

"You're interested in history?" asked Noël.

"Mostly World War II stuff."

Noël was still trying to figure out how she felt about Guy's dual reading interests, whether there was some connection between the two, when he led them away from the non-fiction section.

This time Guy headed toward a door in the back of the room. On the other side, a narrow passage led to a washroom on one side and on the other ended at the top of a winding metal staircase.

"Down here are the stacks," said Guy with a wave.

The unmistakable aroma of old books rose up from the bottom of the stairs. Noël felt called down like Ulysses was enticed by the Sirens.

"Can we go down?" she asked, a foot already on the first step.

"Sure," said Guy and followed the two girls as they went ahead.

At the bottom of the stairs Noël found that they were in the basement again; but this time, it was a tiny room with two small cellar windows letting in a few rays of afternoon sunlight. Uncut grass webbed their dirty panes from the outside. In the room, a half dozen metal shelving units stood crammed with thousands of old books. Not a single one had a dust jacket.

"These are the oldest books in the library," said Guy. "The next step from here is a library book sale. But that doesn't mean there ain't anything good down here." He moved to the extreme rear of the room. "Here's more science fiction books."

If Noël hadn't already been won over by the library's quaint beauty, the stacks' obvious wonderland of literature would have. She knew she was going to come back for a more thorough exploration sometime soon.

"Well, how do you like it?" asked Guy.

"I love it," Noël replied truthfully.

"I can't see what's to love," sniffed Polly. "It's too stuffy and dusty down here. The Nancy Drew section has more good stuff than the whole rest of the library."

"If you don't like dust, don't take Noël to Harvey's," laughed Guy.

"Harvey's? What's that?" asked Noël.

"You wouldn't like it there," advised Polly. "It's as dirty and stuffy as Guy says. And besides, it's too far away."

"Where is it, downtown?" asked Noël, intrigued.

"Polly's right, you wouldn't like it there," said Guy.

"Why not? Because of a little dust?" But inwardly, Noël suddenly wondered if Guy wasn't as naive as she thought he was. Had he noticed the change in her attitude toward him, after all?

"This is a little dust," said Guy, running a finger along one of the shelves. "Harvey's is a lot worse and it's dark and dirty and it stinks of rotting paper besides."

"Is it a bookstore?"

"Of course. Used books. And comic books too."

"I'd love to go," said Noël. "Will you show me where it is?"

Suddenly, Guy seemed nervous. Had she been too bold?

"I guess so," he finally said. "But I don't want to go unless I have some money. How about Monday afternoon; I ought to be able to collect thirty cents worth of bottles after the weekend."

"I've got two you can have, Guy."

"Thanks Polly."

"Is that how you get your money?" asked Noël. Whenever she wanted money, if the request was reasonable, her parents generally gave it to her.

"Yeah, all I need is a quarter or so to go to Harvey's."

"Okay," said Polly, "we'll see you on Monday, okay?"

"You want to come too? Now I've seen everything."

Polly stuck her tongue out. "C'mon Noël, we'll get back just in time for lunch."

The way home from the library seemed longer than the walk up and Noël already found herself missing it. Guy however, had turned out to be a disappointment. She'd hoped he'd be a fellow bibliophile eager for dialogue about favorite books, but how could she have meaningful discussions about a great novel like *Wuthering Heights* for example with someone who thought Tarzan and Tom Swift were the height of literary achievement?

And did he say something about comic books?

"Hey, look," said Polly suddenly, saving Noël from her depressing thoughts. "There's my sister and her friends coming out of Hovey Square Variety."

It was true. The three girls had just left the little market that was located across from the grassy triangle of Hovey Square. Noël and Polly fell in behind them as they made their way back home.

"What are they doing?" asked Noël.

"I'm not sure, I...hey look, they dropped something." They continued to walk at the same pace until they'd reached the fallen object. Polly stooped and picked it up. It was a bubble gum card.

"Who's on it?" asked Noël peering over Polly's shoulder.

"The Beatles silly, aren't they the cutest?"

Noël took the card and studied the tiny images standing with guitars and open mouths, obviously on a stage. Noël decided that the figures were too indistinct to make any snap judgment. She handed the card back to Polly.

"I'm going to keep this card and put it in my pocketbook when I get one."

Noël smiled and said, "I like their music though."

Hovey Square Variety

CHAPTER THREE

An Interlude

Nick Tropoli, officer of Earth's Planet Patrol sat on a rocky islet far from shore. On the horizon, rose the glassite towers of the distant city. Beside him, his rocket pack lay cooling in the early morning sunlight.

He had arrived on Earth the day before from a six month mission to Pluto and as soon as he was finished with debriefing, escaped the cramped confines of old Cape Kennedy and made his way here, this island, which was hardly more than a rock really, just off the coast of Rocket City.

It was the place he came when he needed to do some heavy thinking.

Even though he spent most of his time in space and in charge of a twenty man crew aboard his patrol ship *Marauder*, he still considered himself to be a solitary man. He liked to be off by himself, and so, he frequently sought out such lonely places as this island, a forest, or asteroid. But even acknowledging his desire for being away from others, there was still Jane.

Jane, the girl he loved, produced in him conflicting emotions. On the one hand, he treasured his apartness and independence, but on the other, when in her presence, all those feelings melted away. When Jane was in the picture, he began making plans for the future; plans that included them both.

One of the reasons he had come to the island was to think through those feelings. But it had done no good. Away from Jane, his solitary nature took over; but even then, when the image of her face appeared in his mind's eye, things he was sure about suddenly became uncertain. He knew he would see her again and that if he did, his days of pleasurable aloneness would be over.

Nick waited another few minutes then strapped on his rocket belt and prepared to jet over to Jane's apartment.

Gateway to the Future
by Guy DeMonde

Guy was alone in the stacks.

After Polly and the new girl had left, the silence of the library again settled over the basement room. He looked up at the fading afternoon light as it filtered in through the small windows set high against the ceiling and sighed. Slowly, he passed along the tall bookcases around to the far wall away from the stairs where the science fiction books were kept. Hunkering down, he reached out and passed his hand over the old and crinkly spines. Familiar titles and old friends were there; Jules Verne and H.G. Wells and Edgar Rice Burroughs. Sitting down, back against the wall, he watched motes of dust as they drifted through the sunlight.

It was moments like this he loved the best. Quiet and peaceful, alone with only his thoughts for company.

Taking more pleasure in his own company than with that of others, it seemed to him that the drive for such moments of solitude, for being by himself, for doing things alone, grew stronger each day. Of course he enjoyed the company of his friends, watching television on Saturday afternoons with them, going to the matinee at the movies and reading comic books, but every so often, he felt an urge to go off by himself.

When that mood struck him, Guy couldn't think of a better way to spend the day than alone at the library going through the books especially here in the stacks where no one ever came. Once, out of curiosity, he checked the dates on the cards in the back of the books on the science fiction shelf and discovered that he was the only person to take them out in over five or six years. It made him feel almost as if the room was his personal domain or a hospital patient for whom he was the only visitor.

Guy prided himself in his objectivity and had decided that his occasional desire for being by himself must have developed because of his reading habits. Habits that had only recently intensified when his best friend Jiff, who'd shared his literary enthusiasms, had lost interest. Why, he'd even stopped reading comic books!

Guy's sense of isolation only grew in the summers when Jiff left him for swimming at the Foisy's who owned the only pool in the neighborhood. Since his parents weren't friends of the Foisy's, Guy was forced to settle for the lawn sprinkler or the kids' pool used by his three and four year old brothers. He smiled to himself then and looked around. No wonder he liked it here in the stacks; at least it was air conditioned. Anyway, books were more and more becoming his closest friends and he hadn't been sure if he preferred it that way.

Until today.

When Polly introduced that new girl Noël, and he found out that she liked to read, his interest had risen, but that didn't last long. He didn't fail to notice her snobby attitude. She didn't like him. But he was used to that. Girls didn't seem to care much for him anyway. He just didn't seem able to speak their language, to talk about the things that interested them. As a result, he tended to avoid them and save himself a lot of embarrassment. He slammed a fist against the books in his hand. But now he was stuck with having to show this Noël the way to Harvey's!

The shaft of sunlight coming in from the basement window had grown more horizontal in the last few minutes, telling him that it was time to head back home before his mother started looking for him to come to supper.

He stood and dusted the seat of his pants wondering what he'd do that night. Write maybe? Whenever he read a really good sci-fi novel it inspired him to try writing his own stories. He'd even sent some out to magazines, but so far they'd all come back. (He suspected it was because he hadn't been typing the stories, but he just couldn't afford a typewriter).

Guy checked out his books and emerged from the library onto the front steps, squinting against the late afternoon sun. He shaded his eyes and looked around. No one was in sight. Even the bike rack near the steps was empty. Hopping down to the driveway, he walked around to the rear of the building and dragged his bicycle out from behind the bulkhead. Straddling it, he clutched his books snugly under his left arm. Ever since his new green stingray bicycle won at a church raffle was stolen, he'd become a good deal more careful about where he left his things. Sure, he was using his old 36 inch standard bike now, but it was the only transportation he had left and he wasn't going to take any chances with it, even at a public bike rack. So he preferred to hide it in the rear of the library where no one ever went.

He shoved himself forward and wobbled unsteadily down the driveway leading to the street. It was clear of traffic and he took the corner slowly before picking up speed; riding single-handedly could be tricky but he'd long since mastered the skill.

The ride home was always better than the trip up because of the new books he always brought back and the fact that the return journey was almost completely downhill. So with the wind whipping his short hair, Guy thundered home along Pleasant Street in a quarter of the time it had taken him to climb up-hill to the library, weaving and dodging the occasional telephone pole and street sign that punctuated the sidewalks.

At last, he crossed over onto Hovey Square, swerved sharply to the left and dashed along the short sidewalk that bisected the little park. With a jerk and a cloud of dust, he skidded into the loose sand in front of Hovey Square Variety and leaned his bike against the plate glass display window. A quick check of the new comic books was definitely in order.

The store consisted of a single small room jam-packed with all the usual grocery items: the meat counter, foggy with condensation, at the back, canned goods stocked against the left wall, a free standing aluminum rack of breads and bags of chips just in front of that, the counter with the cash register along the right, and in a cubby hole formed by one of the front windows, an assortment of Aurora monster models, kites, wind-up airplanes and puzzles were displayed. But right then, Guy wasn't interested in any of that. Hanging from the end of the free standing aluminum bread rack, was a handful of wire pockets stuffed with the latest comics.

There were maybe about twelve pockets in all, each holding a single title. Guy only bought Marvel comics, disdaining the childish titles produced by its competitors with their stupid plots and primitive artwork. Nothing less than the rhapsodic prose of Stan Lee and the artistic genius of Jack Kirby and Steve Ditko could satisfy his selective tastes. He scanned the titles eagerly, knowing by heart the shipping schedules of each one. According to his calculations, this should be the week of *Spider-Man* and *Tales of Suspense,* but he could see neither title on display. Anxiously, he riffled the comics, making sure they weren't stuffed behind the hated DCs. Nothing.

Disappointed, he walked over to the old man sitting behind the cash register. He dreaded talking to him because there was something wrong with his throat. He'd had some kind of operation once that left him without a voice. Instead, he had a small metal box affixed to his throat that amplified the sounds he could make that passed for speech.

"Excuse me, but did the new comics come in today?" asked Guy tentatively, steeling himself for the reply.

It came in an almost incomprehensible electronic warble, amplified to two or three times the normal volume of ordinary speech. "...COMICS...LATE..." came the voice, sending chills down Guy's back. But what had the man said? Had he confirmed that the comics were late? Guy screwed up his courage and said, "What did you say...?"

Just then, a woman came around the end of the meat counter and stood by the man. "He said the comics are going to be late this week."

"Oh," said Guy, feeling mildly depressed.

The woman must have recognized Guy as a regular customer because she continued. "You'll have to find your comics somewhere else after next week though, we'll be closing the store then."

Closing!

Guy was shocked. He'd been visiting Hovey Square Variety for as long as he could remember. It was a neighborhood landmark. Years of visiting it, buying candy, bubble gum cards, toys, and comics by he and his friends had somehow lent the store an air of indestructibility. It was believed without knowing why, that just as it had always been here, so it would remain. Now it was to vanish, as if it had never been!

But for every action there was another, equal reaction: with Hovey Square Variety closing, where was Guy to find his comics?

"It's that supermarket across the street," the woman was saying, more to herself than to the eleven year old boy in front of her. "As soon as they opened, we lost most of our customers. We can't compete with them so we're going to retire."

Guy nodded unconsciously and walked out of the store. He looked across the Square at the sleek, single story supermarket, gleaming in its modernity, and cordially hated it. It was the reason for the loss of the only store he knew of that sold comic books. But he couldn't make himself believe that there wouldn't be any more Stan Lee or Jack Kirby or Spider-Man or Captain America. Then, with a new resolve, his depression lifted and he vowed to find another store no matter what, even if he had to search the whole city to do it.

He hopped back on his bike and shoved off down the street; in seconds he was on Burnaby Street and bumping his way into Don's yard. Then he coasted down-hill through Polly's yard and onto Desrosiers Street beyond. There seemed to be a stillness at Jiff's house which meant that his friend was probably still swimming down at the Foisy's. He didn't need to wonder about Don either: wherever Jiff went Don would be there too. It was convenient that both their parents were friends with the Foisy's, thought Guy sarcastically.

That left Mike Dozois, but he was gone somewhere with his parents visiting relatives. Mike, like Don, was a couple of years younger than Guy and Jiff, but it didn't stop he and Guy from being closer than they were to Jiff and Don. Mike lived in the house immediately behind Guy's, on Dean Avenue instead of up the street so it was easier to keep in touch.

Guy swung his bike hard through the gate leading into his own back yard and almost ended up on his face. Only quick reflexes saved him from smashing into five other bikes that lay on the ground near the shed. "What the heck's goin' on here?" he exploded, fumbling with his books.

Immediately his twin sisters, Marie and Therese (popularly known as Muddy and Trece), stepped out from the shed. Dressed identically in overalls and pink blouses, they were a year younger than Guy.

"What's the matter?" said Trece.

"I almost killed myself, that's what's the matter," said Guy. "What's the idea?"

"We're playing house and the shed is our kitchen," explained Marie.

"Well why'd you leave all these bikes lying around here for? I almost ran right into them!"

"Why didn't you look where you were going?" asked Trece logically.

"It didn't matter, I couldn't see them from the other side of the steps."

"Well, is it our fault if you come racing in the yard without slowing down first?"

"You guys are so stupid!"

"I'll tell Maman you said that," threatened Marie, making for the back door.

"Aw, you guys are just babies," said Guy ignoring the threat and heading for the house himself.

At the top of the steps he paused to look across the street and was reminded of the new girl who'd moved into the Olenbeck place. With her arrival and the closing of Hovey Square Variety, it suddenly seemed to him like it was the end of an era. As if his life had reached a turning point. When such turning points were reached in history, scholars marked them by some great, world changing event.

These two latest events seemed to divide his life in two: all that had happened before, and all that would come after.

And what of Noël? She did, after all, like to read. How bad could she be? But he couldn't forget the icy feeling she gave him. Brrrrr. He mentally shivered just thinking about it.

It was a strange mood he found himself in and he was at a loss to explain it. He didn't know if he was happy or sad. With an effort, he shook the feeling off and went into the house. After all, he had a lot of work to do planning a search pattern for a new comic book store.

A view from Lookout Hill

CHAPTER FOUR

*In which Noël makes a discovery and
finds herself taken by surprise*

August 3, 1967; A very strange thought
has occurred to me today. Boys and girls
are definitely not the same. I'm not talking
about how girls like to play with dolls and
boys don't, or how girls like to play house
and boys don't, not even how boys can
throw a baseball better than girls. This is a
lot more, oh how can I say it? More
complicated.

I know there are a lot of things that boys
and girls both like to do, and don't like to

do. They both like to go swimming, they both like to watch TV, they both like candy, they both like vacations. They both dislike school (of course, this is in general, I'm the exception to a lot of these things), they both hate to take medicine, they both dislike the same relatives.

And yet, we're so different! How can we girls look on an open field or forest and see beauty while the boys look on the same thing and see only a battleground to act out their war fantasies? Is it the way we're born or the way we're brought up? I think we're born that way because Polly told me once about Terri Larose who has seven brothers. Polly said that she and Terri went to a movie once and they both were crying at the end but that some boys who were there with them weren't moved at all. Now it would stand to reason that Terri, brought up with seven crude brothers, would grow to be like them, but that didn't happen at all. I haven't figured this all out yet, but one thing I know for sure, it's all really confusing!

But what's worse than how we're different, is how girls and boys feel about each other.

I've noticed recently that things are changing between the boys and the girls in the neighborhood. Where once we all played together, now there seems to be a growing division between our activities. I've begun to sense that invisible barriers seem to have risen between us; there are things now we girls would never talk about with the boys around and I get the feeling there's stuff they're keeping from us too.

And the funny thing about it all is that we girls find ourselves talking more and more these days about boys! Well, this is a diary and if I can't be honest here, then I might as well stop making these entries, so I will be honest: Even with all our differences (and there are plenty of things about boys that exasperate me!) I still find myself attracted to them.

We learned in class last year that opposite forces attract each other and maybe that applies to boys and girls too. It didn't make any sense to me then, and it still doesn't make sense now, but it's the kind of nonsense that's perfect to describe this whole situation.

Oh, I wish things were as simple as they used to be before I moved to Lowell! And to think that I once wrote that I had everything figured out! How naïve I was! The older I get, it seems the less I'm sure about.

It was one of those sunshiny days that was so exquisitely perfect that Noël felt she could never take it all in. She wanted to sweep it up into her arms and squeeze it to her and never let go.

The first thing she did that morning was rush to her bedroom window, lift the sash, and stick her head out beneath the branches of the maple trees. Taking a long, deep breath, she took in great gulps of air, luxuriating in the myriad smells and scents of the pollen laden atmosphere. It didn't take much after that to get her moving. She washed up quickly and dressed and let her nose lead her down to breakfast.

In the kitchen, her mother already had breakfast ready (despite Noël's belief that the hours she kept in the morning were completely spontaneous, her mother knew better).

"Bonjour, Maman," said Noël brightly.

"Bonjour, Noël," her mother said without turning from the sink.

At the table, Noël sprinkled some salt and pepper on her eggs and watched the grains form patterns on the curved surface of the yolk. A vase of fresh cut roses sat in the open window by the table and outside, a bumblebee tested the screen. Noël rolled up a piece of toast and dipped it in the egg yellow.

"What are you up to today?" asked her mother, wiping her hands on a dish towel.

"Nothin'," replied Noël around a mouthful of bread.

"You? With nothing planned?" Her mother took a place at the table and picked up her cup of tea. "What kind of spell has this house been working on you?"

Noël gulped. "Polly and I are going over to Mrs. Ginot's then maybe over into the woods."

Her mother put down her cup. "Mrs. Ginot's? I hope you're not going to make a nuisance of yourselves."

"We're not—"

"She's an old lady, you know," continued her mother before Noël could finish. "She doesn't need to be bothered by two young girls."

"We're not bothering her, Ma. She called Polly's mother and asked her to send Polly over to get some pears from her tree." Noël chewed. "She has the biggest pear tree for miles around, and apple trees too, but I don't like the apples too much, they're not ripe enough and they're all lumpy and sour tasting."

"How do you know that? Have you been eating unripe apples? They'll make you sick."

"I know, but you don't have to worry about that, I couldn't get past the first one. Anyway, Mrs. Ginot's pears are a lot better than her apples."

Lucille sipped her tea, still expecting the worst. "Hmmm," was all she said.

Noël was just draining the last of her juice when Polly's voice drifted in from outside the window. "Nooooellll," it sang.

"Be right out, Polly!" Noël stood up, wiping her mouth quickly on a napkin. "Have to go, Ma. Bye."

"Bye, dear, and don't forget; try not to bother Mrs. Ginot too much."

Noël paused at the door briefly with an "Aww, Ma," but it was drowned out by the screech and slam of the screen door. She tumbled down the porch steps almost into Polly's arms. "Are we still going over to Mrs. Ginot's?"

"Sure, she's waiting for us now."

"How do you know that?" asked Noël as the two girls started for the street.

"I've never gone over there when Mrs. Ginot wasn't already waiting for me."

"You make it sound like she never sleeps."

"I don't think she does," said Polly seriously.

They were silent for a minute as they walked and Noël found her mind drifting. She remembered the fears and doubts that had bothered her before moving to Lowell and she wondered at the ease with which she'd adapted to her new home. Why, she had more friends now than she ever had in Forest Hills. Of course, she was trying hard not to seem like a snob and she thought she was doing pretty good at it if she did say so herself. At least Polly didn't seem to think she was a snob. And neither did Denise (another girl who lived on Dean Avenue that shot out from Desrosiers Street), Theo (who lived at the far end of the street where it emptied out onto Pleasant Street) or Marie and Trece (Guy's twin sisters).

Thinking about those first anxious days reminded her of the way her father had slipped away on that first night. She'd thought about it often since then and as far as she could tell, her father hadn't done anything remotely as funny as that since. Of course she'd wondered often where he'd gone and what he'd been up to, and worried about it too, but somewhere in the back of her mind, she began to doubt the evidence of her own eyes. Maybe she imagined the whole thing. Didn't her mother always say that she was always confusing fantasy with reality? It had been getting dark that night and she'd lost sight of him when he rounded the corner of the house; and maybe it hadn't been his leg that she saw vanish into the brush. Would her mother have even believed her if she'd told her anything about it?

Then, for no apparent reason, her thoughts jumped to Guy (as they'd begun to do with disturbing regularity). Just thinking about him made her blood boil! He'd promised to show her Harvey's Bookland and never got around to it. Every time she'd asked, he'd say he had to get more money, or do some chores, or he had something else to do with his friends. She grunted at that. Practically every time she saw him, he was sitting out in front of Jiff's house reading stacks of comic books. How could he stand reading the same ones over and over again? She shook her head and determined to go downtown without him. Who needed a guide anyway?

And the other boys were almost as bad.

Jiff was the unacknowledged leader of the group. It seemed if he didn't feel like doing something, it wouldn't be done. And if he did, it would. Boys were like sheep, Noël thought with scorn, they always had to follow a leader. Jiff read the same comics and books as Guy, and watched the same TV shows.

Then there was Mike. He was younger even than Marie and Trece and hung around with Guy more than Jiff and worse, was learning all of Jiff's and Guy's bad habits.

Finally, there was Don. She stopped there. Don was an enigma. The same age as Mike, and definitely part of the boys' camp, he alone seemed to have a mind of his own. Noël couldn't say for sure of course because she hadn't met him up close yet. Anyway, from what she could tell and what she'd learned from the other girls, Don was an independent spirit who didn't believe anything until he could apply it to a practical experiment. He was always fooling around with some crack-pot idea. She'd see him in his yard sometimes from Polly's back porch fiddling with one thing or another. He was the sort of character who'd build a raft and see if it floated out on the Merrimack River. In her mind, Noël had begun to think of Don as a kind of modern day Huckleberry Finn.

That was as far as her thoughts took her when a tree branch suddenly swung and slapped her in the face.

"Oh, I'm so sorry, Noël," said Polly, rushing over to her. "I didn't think..."

"That's okay, Polly," said Noël, rubbing her eyes. "It was my fault for not watching where I was going."

"Are you okay?"

"Sure."

When her eyes cleared, Noël saw they were already in Mrs. Ginot's yard and going around to the rear of the big old farm house. The tree whose branch had struck her face was one of a dozen gnarled and rotting apple trees along the side of the house. The rest of the property was as overgrown as Noël had guessed from the times when she'd walked by on the street.

Shaped kind of funny, Mrs. Ginot's property stretched back to a stagnant swamp way down in back and then bootlegged to the right. It then followed the shore of the swamp until it drained into a pond beyond Pleasant Street. The sight always touched Noël's sense of fancy because of its state of repair: there was none!

No one in the neighborhood knew how old Mrs. Ginot was, (she was rumored to be over one hundred years old and Noël guessed it was possible to get an accurate figure from her parents, but felt the truth couldn't be as interesting as knowing someone who could've been around when Custer was still fighting the Indians!), but it was certain that her husband had died long before because none of the kids could remember ever having known him.

Once, the Ginot property must've been a thriving farm, because there was the ruin of an old chicken coop near the swamp and the rusting hulks of farm machinery littering the ground. The front of the house was nearly hidden in untrimmed thorn bushes and the yard nearest the house was carpeted in brownish, shaggy grass that clumped in unhealthy looking wads. The old orchard was still populated by hundreds of gnarled and twisted apple trees, mostly bearing green or worm eaten fruit that made it a messy business to cut across the property. The dilapidation of the house and grounds was so complete as to suggest to anyone that it had long lay fallow and uninhabited. But Noël didn't care about how it appeared to other people, she loved its weird atmosphere and imagined it as a setting for any number of stories by Edgar Allen Poe or M.R. James.

The two girls stooped beneath more branches and walked down the slope alongside the house to where the pear tree stood. It was almost a neighborhood landmark, easily being the biggest pear tree Noël had ever seen. It's wrinkled gray bark lay stretched across it much like the skin of Mrs. Ginot's face, and leaped skyward far over the house. Heavy with fruit, its branches hung almost to the ground and would have snapped if not for the pieces of two-by-fours that had been propped beneath them. Noël could see the pears, bunched as thick as grapes along every branch. But according to Polly, it was the ones higher up that were the sweetest.

A quick survey of the yard revealed that Mrs. Ginot was there ahead of them and had been there for quite some time judging by the number of pear-filled bags standing around the tree. Barely five feet tall, she was dressed in a plain cotton print dress and a blue sweater that must've been as old as she was. A polka dot kerchief was wrapped around her snow-white hair and a pair of horn-rimmed glasses jutted out from her ears to rest on her hawk-like nose. She couldn't stand without a stoop and Noël was unable to keep from comparing the way she moved with that of a crab. At the moment of the girls' arrival, Mrs. Ginot had been picking pears from near the top of the tree with the use of a long, pole-like instrument. Consisting of a kind of pulley mechanism, the pole enabled her to operate a small claw at its far end. With a skill that made it look easy, she clutched a fat pear in the steel contraption and allowed it to drop at the girls' feet. They jumped back.

"Oh, I didn't see you girls standing there," said Mrs. Ginot good naturedly. "You sure can give an old woman a fright."

Noël found herself surprised at the sound of the old woman's voice. Somehow, she had expected Mrs. Ginot to be as crabby as her appearance.

"Well, why don't you start by picking up the pears I've already got scattered around here."

The girls did as they were told and then took turns picking up the pears as they were dropped. Noël watched with fascination the skill displayed by the old woman as she handled her strange plucking device. In a few minutes, Mrs. Ginot had cleared the top part of the tree and lowered the claw. "Well, I guess that'll hold the neighbors for a while. I had to clear those branches soon or have the tree split right down the middle."

"These pears are delicious," said Polly, half way through a soft, yellow one.

"Of course they are. My apples aren't anything to brag about, but this old tree doesn't know how to make bad fruit."

"It looks so old…" mused Noël aloud.

"It's at least a hundred years old," said Mrs. Ginot with authority. "My father planted it when my brother was born and he was a good deal older than I was."

"How long will it continue to bear fruit?" asked Noël.

Mrs. Ginot smiled, and said, "Why, as long as I'm alive, of course."

Noël stared, not sure whether to believe the old woman or not.

"Well, there are eight bags full here. What I want you to do is give one to each family in the neighborhood."

"Thank you, Mrs. Ginot," said Polly, picking up and hugging one of the bags.

"Why don't we get the boys to help us carry them?" said Noël, watching her friend struggle with the bulky bag.

"The boys have already done their share," said Mrs. Ginot as she laid the pole down alongside the house. "Who do you think helped me prop those branches up with the boards? It wasn't as easy a job as it looks you know."

Noël stooped and picked up one of the bags herself, fumbling for a moment as its contents settled inside. "Quick," she said to Polly, "let's get rid of these things before the bottoms give out!"

"You don't have to tell me twice," said Polly, who was already heading for the street.

Noël followed as quickly as she could, trying not to stumble on the way.

"*Depeche vous pas!*" called Mrs. Ginot from behind them, forgetting herself for an instant. "Take your time, girls. There's no hurry."

Polly, wobbling under the weight she was carrying, made her way up the street. The first house she came to after Mrs. Ginot's was a big, two story former farmhouse. While Polly went to the back porch, Noël stopped alongside a row of hedges that bordered the street and rested in the shade of a mulberry tree. At the moment, the tree seemed full of blue jays happily enjoying a tasty dinner of fat, purple mulberries.

Inside the small porch, a door opened and Jiff Jorgenson came out. Noël couldn't hear what was said, but saw Jiff look over to the big pear tree next door and give Polly a quick nod before taking the bag inside.

"We'll drop yours over at Don's," said Polly after she'd rejoined her friend.

Briefly, Noël wondered if she'd finally get to see the elusive Don Therrien close up, but five minutes later, she'd left his house defeated again.

An hour later, the rest of the bags had all been delivered and Mrs. Ginot had treated Noël and Polly to tall glasses of lemonade. It was late in the morning when they finally left the old woman's house and wandered back toward the far end of Desrosiers Street.

"Do you still want me to show you around the woods?" asked Polly lifting her chin toward the open fields at the end of the street.

"Of course!"

"Well, then how about making some sandwiches and having our lunch there? I know the perfect place for a picnic."

"That sounds like a great idea," agreed Noël. "I'll meet you at the fence in ten minutes."

"Okay," said Polly, heading for her house.

Indoors, Noël wasted little time making a peanut butter and jelly sandwich. When she finished, she filled an empty jar with milk, took an apple from the refrigerator and put the whole thing in a brown paper bag. Exactly ten minutes later, she met Polly by the split rail fence.

Standing there, looking between the trees and out over the tall grass beyond, Noël remembered her earlier thoughts concerning her father's strange behavior on that first night in their new home. Would she now find some clue to his mysterious actions (if she hadn't imagined them in the first place!) as she and Polly passed from field to forest?

"This way," said Polly, breaking Noël's train of thought as she entered a clump of lilac bushes, their flowers all shriveled up this late in the summer.

When Noël followed, she found that her friend had stepped over one of the fallen fence rails and into the edge of the field on the other side. The grass there, in the shade of a group of maple trees fringing the fence, was fairly short, but grew taller as the field entered the sunlight. Noël noticed immediately that any trace her father may have left in the tall grass that night had completely vanished.

"Hold your lunch over your head until we cross this field," warned Polly. "There's all kinds of dust and bugs out here."

"Bugs?"

Polly laughed. "Yeah, but nothing much, just a lady bug or two. But who wants even a lady bug in their sandwich?"

Noël could only agree and follow her friend into the grass. Together they blazed a trail that left a crooked path through the grass back to where they'd started from. Ahead, a great stand of pine trees reared their pointed crowns as if to pierce the clouds that drifted overhead.

Only blackness shone beneath their low swept branches. Noël swatted involuntarily at a dragonfly that buzzed too close to her ear and the heat made her wonder how the water was in the Foisy's pool.

At last, the plain of grass ended at the edge of the forest, a stone wall topped by a few strands of rusty barbed wire separating them.

"Be careful here, we have to squeeze under this wire. I tore a dress on it once and my mother kept me in the house for a week." The two girls took turns holding the strands of wire apart with their hands and feet and so stepped easily into the pine forest on the opposite side.

"It's nice and cool in here," observed Noël, looking upward at the web of branches blocking out the sun.

"I like walking on the pine needles," said Polly.

Noël liked it too as she followed Polly deeper into the woods.

A short time later, the pine trees began to thin out and in the increasing sunlight, clumps of fern plants began to fill the spaces in between. As Noël and Polly continued on, the ferns grew in number until the pine trees dropped away and left the land completely to them. As they made their way through thick stands of the stuff, some standing as high as their heads, the two girls shook clouds of pollen into the air and watched as it settled in their hair and clothing.

"We call this fern alley," said Polly unnecessarily.

"What do you mean 'we?'" asked Noël, dreading the answer; she had hoped that this newly explored land would be their own private place.

"Oh, everybody in the neighborhood. We'll be coming to a trail pretty soon." No sooner had Polly said it, than they fell into a well beaten path that twisted deeper into the forest, now populated with a wide variety of tree and plant life that crowded the narrow trail in the rapid growth that had marked early summer.

Polly stayed on the path but turned in a direction that would take them further away from Desrosiers Street. Plenty of sunlight reached them on the open trail and the forest around them was alive with activity. Bees hummed as they flitted from flower to flower and birds called distantly from among the trees. The myriad scents of the forest were everywhere, but chief among them was an almost sickly sweet one that Noël decided she liked.

"Which flower does that scent come from?" asked Noël, flaring her nostrils as she inhaled deeply.

"I love that smell," agreed Polly, who seemed to know exactly which scent her friend referred to even though there were easily a half dozen varieties of flowers in the area. "I'm not sure which flower it comes from, but I always felt that it came from those purple flowers there. You usually find them growing in swamps."

Noël looked to where Polly was pointing. Tall stalks topped with clumps of tiny purple flowers poked up from the grass on either side of the path. None were without the protection of hovering bumblebees.

"There're some swampy spots all around here; that's why I think they're swamp flowers," said Polly. "Guy and Jiff call them Triffids. They say it's because they look like man-eating alien flowers they saw in a movie once."

Noël snorted, not sure herself whether due to pollen or contempt for the boys' cinematic interests. "I'm getting hungry," she finally said. "When do we eat?"

"Right up ahead there's a beautiful little clearing."

They walked on for another few minutes until the land began to slope upwards to dryer ground, ending at the top of a small hill, bald except for lush green grass. Polly sat down, tucking her legs under her. "Isn't this a beautiful spot? The boys call it Lookout Hill."

Noël remained standing, looking out over the tops of the trees. Their little hill rose up high enough over the forest for her to see a good ways in every direction. Only a few puffs of clouds dotted the blue sky and a slight breeze kept the sun from being too hot. To her left should have been Desrosiers Street but the neighborhood was now almost completely hidden behind the forest of pine trees they'd passed through. Behind her, to the south, the only evidence that a city existed there was Lowell's distinctive skyline of towering smokestacks, the stone steeples of its many gothic style churches and the spire of its city hall. Between the city and her position atop the little hill, Noël could see stretches of the Merrimack River as it rolled to the sea. Civilization just then, seemed very far away to her.

Turning back toward the north, Noël saw that the forest rolled out to the distant hills of Dracut which were dotted here and there with the farmhouses of people who still made their living from the earth. But if one looked hard enough, it was still possible to spot evidences of civilization closer to home.

On another hill to the northeast and across a small brook, stood what looked to Noël like an Italian villa made out of stone, it's gray bulk topped by a number of sloping, red-tiled roofs. It seemed to be surrounded by a verandah bordered in an iron railing and here and there on the upper floors, balconies stuck out into the air. Altogether, it reminded Noël of the kind of place the Borgias might've once lived in.

"What's that building over there?" she asked, pointing.

Polly stood and looked. "Santa Maria. Nuns live there, I think."

"Really?" said Noël with new interest. "I think Jack Kerouac used it as a setting in Dr. Sax!"

"Who?"

"Jack Kerouac…"

"No, Dr. Sax!"

"No, no; Dr. Sax was--oh, never mind," Noël said, realizing how difficult it'd be to explain the whole thing to Polly. "It's a convent then?" she said instead, changing the direction of the conversation.

"Yeah, and a school too," replied Polly. "I knew a girl who went there once and she told me that the classes are real small, only about eight or ten kids."

Noël nodded, intrigued. The sight of the beautiful old building on the hill, high over the surrounding neighborhoods seemed delightfully exotic to her.

Turning to the north, she spied a second structure. "How about that one there?"

Polly shaded her eyes against the sun and found the lone house Noël had indicated. Only its slope roofed second story was visible above the trees. "That's a haunted house."

"Haunted house!" Noël exclaimed. "A real haunted house?"

Noël was sure there was no such things as ghosts and haunted houses but she was big enough to admit that she didn't know everything.

"Yeah, a real haunted house," Polly was saying. "Everybody says it is. An old woman lived there for a hundred years, her and her black cat, and when she died, no one claimed the house. Oh sure, there's a for sale sign outside it, but that's 'cause the town has to try to sell it to make back the taxes the old lady owed. At least, that's what my father told me."

"Are there--ghosts?" persisted Noël and wouldn't it be neat if there were?

"Of course! Last year, the papers were full of stories about a hobo they found dead in the parlor. And..."

"Well?"

Polly looked around as if frightened, then whispered, "Mike says he saw a light there one night."

"Mike! What was he doing out here after dark?" demanded Noël. Mike was two whole years younger than she was and equipped with a fairly good imagination;

he'd be the last person to believe about an issue as doubtful as ghosts.

"No, no," said Polly, still whispering. "He didn't see it from out here. His house is kind of funny because some nights, from his bedroom window, he can see the house. And one night he said he saw a light."

"When?"

"I don't know, a long time ago. C'mon, let's eat, this subject is getting me spooked."

Noël continued standing for a few minutes more, transfixed by the mysterious house. Standing out there all alone, surrounded by trees, with only its upper story showing, it excited her curiosity. On closer examination, the white paint that covered the house was all mottled and weathered, pieces of tile had slipped loose from its roof, windows were broken and here and there, a loose board had fallen away. As the trees swayed in the gentle afternoon breeze, Noël discovered that the house even had a rounded turret at one of its corners like a medieval castle and even what looked like a tiny cupola on the roof. Then, after having stared at it for some minutes, other details began to resolve themselves and Noël thought she could see the rooflines and telephone poles of other houses beyond it.

"I think there are more houses on the other side of that one," Noël said to Polly.

"I think you're imagining things," replied Polly, biting into a ham sandwich.

Noël sat down and opened her lunch bag. "I'm sure I could see some houses on the other side. If there were, what part of the town do you think they'd be in?"

Polly thought for a moment. "I don't know, it would have to be a long way up and I've never been way up there. I don't know."

"I wonder if that house really *is* haunted?"

"Of course it is," said Polly confidently. "At least I never want to go near enough to find out."

Noël remained silent, neither agreeing nor disagreeing with her friend's sentiments.

She was just draining the last of her milk when Polly, who'd seemed nervous throughout their meal, stood up suddenly.

"I think it's time we should be getting back," she said with a noticeable tremor in her voice.

Noël replaced the empty bottle in her lunch bag, stood up, and faced her friend. "You're not scared are you, Polly? Not because we were talking about that old house?"

"Well, maybe I am. I don't know," answered Polly, hugging herself. "But all of a sudden, it feels like we're far from home."

Noël scanned the surrounding woodland, the trees swaying in the breeze creaked and moaned eerily in the silence and for a moment it seemed as though they were the only two people left on earth. "Maybe you're right," she said at last, suppressing a chill.

Polly shook herself with a nervous laugh. "Here, I took it from the bag Mrs. Ginot gave us."

Noël bit hungrily into the pear, relishing its tasty juice and together they headed back down the hill toward home.

Soon, they'd plunged back into the gloom of the forest, their feet hurrying them along much quicker than they had on the way in. Where only a few hours before, they had taken no notice of the forest's isolation, now they were both acutely aware of its solitude. Now it seemed, the call of a bird deep in the forest or the scurryings of a squirrel in the underbrush or creak of a tree made them jump and set their hearts to pounding. Noël at least, grew increasingly angry with herself for allowing her imagination to get the best of her but she couldn't help it; fear, it seemed, was contagious. And when Polly began to look over her shoulder, Noël soon began to do the same...

At last, they reached the point where they'd first stepped onto the trail. Noël recognized it by the expanse of fern plants on her left that still bore the evidence of their passage. "Wait Polly, this is where we came from."

Polly stopped and turned. "I know, but this is a short cut."

Noël suspected that by continuing on the trail, they would avoid a second trip through the gloomy pine forest; a journey she found herself relieved that they wouldn't have to make.

Following the trail, they soon found themselves on the gentle slope of a wooded hill and from between the trees up ahead, Noël thought she could see the familiar outlines of Desrosiers Street. At the sight, a weight seemed to have been lifted from her. Feeling safe at last, she began to castigate herself for the ungrounded fears and anxieties that had plagued her for the past hour.

Then, just as she was feeling like her old self again, the air suddenly exploded with noise!

Throaty shouts and blood-curdling yells rolled over the forest as the foliage on the hillside erupted with violent movement. Objects flew through the air and puffs of smoke seemed to rise from the ground all around her. From somewhere in front of her, Noël thought she heard Polly's cries of fear but in all the confusion, couldn't be sure; her first instinct was to help her friend, but instead, she fell back in fright, tumbling into the prickly underbrush on the downside of the hill. At last, she came to rest on a carpet of pine needles and lay still, trying to figure out why the world had turned up side down.

"Boy, we sure scared the heck out of them, huh?" said a familiar voice. It came from above her, on the trail.

"That was the best ambush we ever had," said another.

Noël rose painfully on one elbow.

"Just like John Wayne in *The Sands of Iwo Jima*," said a third voice, one Noël definitely recognized. With the realization, a burning anger began to grow in her.

She stood, scratched and dirty, and charged up onto the path. The first thing she saw was the smile on Guy's face that expressed the feeling of a job well done.

It didn't last long.

As soon as he laid eyes on her, it faded and Noël knew that the anger she felt must have been blazing plainly from her eyes.

"Uh, oh," she heard Guy say.

"You..." Noël stammered, for the first time in her life at a loss for words. "You...creeps," she heard herself saying. "You...stupid...idiots!"

"Okay, okay," said Jiff, holding up his hands. He was wearing the strangest headgear Noël had ever seen. A green helmet with radio antennas sticking out from the ear pieces and a blue visor that was at the moment, lowered over his eyes. There was a monkey emblem on the front of it and in his hands, he was holding a toy gun that seemed to have a dozen different functions. "Don't get all upset, huh? We were only fooling around."

Noël's eyes continued to blaze.

Guy fidgeted.

A whimpering sound came from the other side of the trail. Noël shoved her way past the boys and found Polly still hiding in the bushes. She reached in and took her by the arm. "C'mon Polly," she encouraged. "It's only the knucklehead battalion!"

"The Monkey Division," corrected Mike, brandishing a perfect replica of an M-1 rifle.

Noël saved her anger, she didn't want to waste it on someone who couldn't appreciate it. Instead, she turned on Guy.

She could see him cringe as he took the full brunt of a tongue lashing the kind of which she was sure he'd never heard in his life. Not from a girl at least. Noël heard herself, not without some amazement, as she dressed him down, and tore him apart, making him feel thoroughly foolish. She didn't ignore the others to be sure, but nevertheless found herself saving her choicest remarks for Guy.

"And furthermore," Noël continued, but was interrupted by Mike rooting around in the bushes for spent smoke grenades. She shoved, and sent him headlong into the brush with a crackle of hidden branches and a shout of surprise.

With that final show of displeasure, she suddenly felt there was nothing more to be said. She was breathing heavily, her hair was a mess and her body was covered with dirt and leaves and crawly with bugs.

"C'mon Polly," she said, aware that Guy had not uttered a word in the entire time she'd been yelling at him. He'd just stood there with his mouth hanging open. "Let's get out of here and leave these...kids...to their fun!"

Later, at home again, Noël still felt very angry but had decided that her uncharacteristic outburst had been due as much to her fears of the forest than from being ambushed by the boys. And why had she focused that anger primarily on Guy? It was something she would find herself pondering for days following the incident and coming no closer to a satisfactory answer.

Merrimack Street, downtown Lowell, Massachusetts

CHAPTER FIVE

Noël goes to heaven

Nick Tropoli hovered outside the landing deck of Jane North's apartment far above the city, unsure of his next move. She hadn't been on good terms with him since that time she accidentally spoiled a training exercise he'd been conducting with the crew of the *Marauder*.

Still uncertain on how he should approach the girl, Nick drifted around the apartment building. Slowly, he passed the kitchen window, the bedroom window, the parlor window, until he had completely circled the building and arrived back where he had begun. Circling the building had hardly taken more than a couple of minutes, but it made no difference: he still hadn't been able to figure out a good way to introduce himself.

"Hi, Jane, just thought I'd drop by—"

"Oh, Jane, I didn't know you lived here—"

"Jane, this is foolish, let's let bygones be bygones—"

"Jane, I love you and you love me, so let's stop this kidding around."

Nick smiled to himself. He couldn't be that truthful could he?

Gateway to the Future
by Guy DeMonde

Guy was still in bed.

He'd been awake for over an hour, but had delayed getting up because he had a decision to make, one he'd rather not have had to make.

Should he or shouldn't he try to make peace with Noël?

Over and over again, like a rerun of a bad TV show, the whole thing kept going through his mind. He and Jiff and Mike in the woods the day before, playing army like they always did, and hearing Noël and Polly coming down the trail. How could anyone blame them for what came next? It was at that point in the rerun that his thoughts would freeze up. At least lying in ambush for the two girls seemed like the natural thing to do at the time. Now it seemed completely stupid. Through the whole night, all he kept seeing were Noël's eyes, livid with rage and hearing her shouts of anger and ridicule. He remembered cringing at the tongue lashing she'd given him, the kind he'd never heard in his life; especially from a girl!

He groaned and buried his head in his pillow, but the same thoughts kept torturing him.

Afterwards, on the way home, he'd felt awful and hadn't talked much to Mike or Jiff. And was it his imagination or did it seem as though Noël had concentrated most her attention on him?

It was that question that kept him tossing and turning all night, making him feel worse and worse about the whole thing; even reading comic books couldn't lift his spirits. Why did he care at all what Noël thought about him? He should have just laughed it all off with the others. He was sure he would have if it was just Polly or, say, Theo.

Then, his head still buried beneath the pillow, he came to a realization. Although he and his friends had gone back to their war games after the ambush, he now felt sure that his days of soldiering were over. Was this too, a sign that he was reaching some turning point in his life?

Suddenly, with that thought, he knew what he was going to do.

Sitting up, he flung the covers away and swung his feet to the floor. The sound woke his brothers, Lou and Joe, but he didn't care. Quickly, he dressed and washed up.

Having made a decision, he felt energized. All he'd needed was a goal, a direction to take, to rid himself of the uncertainty that'd paralyzed him since the day before.

He'd once promised Noël to show her the way to Harvey's Bookland. Doing that now might be just what was needed to square things between them. He'd go right over and tell her he'd do it this afternoon, then use the rest of the morning to collect as many returnable bottles as he could find. Hopefully, he'd be able to make enough money to cover the bus ride and buy a few things at the bookstore too.

After breakfast, Guy stood out on the street, looking over to Noël's house. He couldn't tell from where he was standing if anyone over there was up yet, but figured nine o'clock in the morning was late enough for anybody.

Guy squared his shoulders and crossed the street. He pushed open the gate and if he was at all unsure if anyone was awake, the screech that resulted must surely have woken them up. He stepped up to the porch door and hesitated, suddenly confronted with an unexpected problem. Though he and his friends sometimes played with the girls, they never actually went calling for them, so he was unsure at just how he should make his presence known (that is if pushing the gate open hadn't done it first)! What to do? Should he knock or call out the way Polly did? He decided to just knock.

No answer.

He knocked harder.

Still no answer.

Swallowing, he opened the door and went inside the porch.

He knocked on the inner door and almost immediately it opened, and he found himself face to face with Noël.

There was a look of surprise on her face, just as Guy felt there was on his, but she recovered faster than he did.

"Guy? What are you doing here?" There was still hostility in her voice, but he'd expected that.

"I came over to, uh—"

"You've got a nerve! I'm still mad at you!" She made as if to shut the door in his face.

"Wait a minute!" Guy said. "I want to call a truce."

The door stopped about twelve inches short of closing. "What do you mean by a truce?" asked Noël cautiously from the other side of the narrow opening.

"Remember how I told you I'd show you the way to Harvey's before? Well I thought, if you wanted to, I'd take you there this afternoon."

He could tell that the suggestion had intrigued her, but she wasn't going to make it easy for him.

"Why should I just forget about your childish behavior yesterday and go along with you?"

It was the opening he'd been waiting for. "Because I know you're not as immature as some of the other kids around here and that you're willing to bury the hatchet, letting bygones be bygones."

Noël thought about that while Guy held his breath, then said, "Well, okay. When do you want to go?"

He'd done it! And he'd even managed to keep from admitting that he was at fault. He felt some pride in that, but almost immediately, it turned to shame. Angry with himself, he wondered why his thoughts always ended up qualifying themselves when dealing with Noël?

"This afternoon," he heard himself saying. "I have to go and look for some bottles first."

"It'll be the last time though. My father took me to the *Lowell Sun* the other day and signed me up for a paper route. They called me and gave me a route down the street. I start next week."

Noël nodded, vague approval in her look, and Guy wondered why it mattered to him.

"Okay, I'll be here or over at Polly's," she said.

Guy left feeling both happy and frustrated. He just couldn't figure out whether he liked Noël or couldn't stand her and the not knowing was beginning to drive him crazy.

A few minutes later however, his confusion was temporarily forgotten after he'd extricated his brother's red wagon from the tangle of bicycles in the shed and headed out to his first stop for collecting bottles. At two cents each, all it took was six bottles to buy three used comic books at Harvey's. For twenty cents, he could buy a used paperback. Not a bad bargain if someone counted their fortune in pennies.

He had a regular route for collecting bottles that he'd slowly built up over time. He knew all the best spots and told no one else where they were, not even Jiff or Don, because his ability to keep up with the latest comics depended on the steady supply of funds only returnable bottles could provide him.

Unlike himself, Jiff was lucky; if he needed cash, all he had to do was ask his parents and they'd give him a quarter or two. Guy came from a more old fashioned household where the idea of children getting allowances like they did on some television shows was considered outlandish. Raised during the Depression (when not only didn't children get allowances, but even when they worked, had to give their earnings up to help support their families), his own parents never got the hang of handing out money to their kids. Sometimes though, Guy could count on his mother to slip him a quarter when bottles became scarce. At those times, she'd dig deep into her purse and help him out. He never forgot that the first two comics he'd ever bought were paid for with a quarter he got from his mother. (As usual, Jiff had gone him one better and gotten two quarters from *his* mother).

But those slim times were far off during the winter season; right then, he didn't expect to come up short with his first stops being the easiest. Now and then, he could count on neighbors to let him have their empties because they didn't want the bother of taking them back to the store themselves. He was lucky, he got a total of eight bottles from Polly and Jiff's houses.

His next stop was a thick lilac bush along the sidewalk on Pleasant Street. Traffic was heavier there than on the side streets especially by foot. A lone thicket with plenty of leafage hiding its interior presented a tempting place for pedestrians to toss unwanted soda bottles and sure enough, Guy found three bottles, dirty and crawling with ants.

Up at Hovey Square, a lone litter barrel always yielded a few treasures. He found three more.

Next was the real gold mine. The line of rocks, trees, and shrubbery that fenced in the little league playing field at Hovey Square Park. The local teenagers hung out there at night, littering the ground with food wrappers and cigarette butts. Broken glass was all over the place because the big rocks were tempting targets for empty soda bottles. But more often than a person would realize, thrown bottles would miss the rocks in the dark and skip off into the bushes. It was those bottles that had beat the odds Guy looked out for. He found a bunch of them and together with three more he'd hidden beneath an old rusty sheet of metal a few days before, added up to at least thirty-six cents.

The wagon nearly full and jingling dangerously, he turned back and headed for the Alexander's Supermarket across the street from the park, acutely aware of the absence of Hovey Square Variety. He hated the new Supermarket, but yielded to its convenience. A few minutes later, his pocket heavy with change, he was headed back home.

He was cutting through Don's yard after taking the short cut down Burnaby Street when he spotted his friend on the wall at the rear of his house. He was working on something as usual, but Guy couldn't figure out what it was.

Don looked up at the sound of the empty wagon Guy was still pulling behind him.

"Hi Guy," he said good naturedly.

"Hi Don," said Guy, stopping.

Don was younger than he was, but was firmly part of the gang in the neighborhood. In fact, a lot of the "action" in the neighborhood happened in Don's yard by virtue of its size and the presence of his older brother and sister, Butch and Sally. The two of them belonged to an upper echelon of older teenagers in the neighborhood that also included Polly's brother Percy and Lewis Beaudoin, the youngest of three brothers whose home sat between those of Polly and Noël. Together, they frequently played baseball in Don's yard with the younger kids (teasing them mercilessly all the while) and sometimes getting Guy, Jiff, and Don to play games of their own invention. Games that usually involved some kind of personal risk like having Guy and his friends run back and forth along a wall while trying to hit them with a speeding sponge ball. Don's yard, with all kinds of bushes, trees, walls, and fences to hide behind and twin spotlights at the corners of the house, was also the perfect place for twilight games of kick-the-can.

"What are you working on now?" asked Guy, scratching his head.

Don stood, holding his latest creation up for display. Two huge, oval-shaped pieces of cardboard reinforced with thin strips of wood were joined together with loops of rope and strands of string. Guy didn't know what to make of it but was getting definite signals from his friend that its function was obvious.

"I give up," said Guy finally. "What is it?"

Don sighed; he was used to getting such puzzled reactions from people. But he smiled anyway, still proud of his clever design.

"A pair of wings," he said at last.

"Wings?" said Guy. "You mean to fly with?"

"Of course to fly with."

"You're gonna fly with these things?"

"I don't know," Don admitted. "But I'm gonna try. In theory it ought to work."

"Whose theory?" asked Guy, growing ever more skeptical of the plan.

"DaVinci's," said Don. "I based my design on one of his I found in a book." Don laid the wings down carefully on the top of the wall that formed a walkway along the rear of his house. "The interesting thing is that the design has never been tested. DaVinci died before he could build a working model."

"So if it works, you'll make history?" Guy believed that no one could go wrong by reading books, but he often thought they could be dangerous things in the hands of someone like Don.

"Right. By the way, do you know how I can contact the editors of the *Guinness Book of World Records*?"

But before Guy could reply, he looked up and saw Noël coming over from Polly's house.

"Hi," she said as she came up the short hill to the wall.

"Hi," said Don, turning at the sound of her voice.

"Don, this is Noël, she moved here about a month ago," said Guy helpfully.

"Oh yeah, I hadn't seen her up close yet."

"I was wondering if we'd ever meet," said Noël, looking curiously at the wings Don was still holding up.

Guy caught her look and said, "It's a pair of wings; based on a design by Leonardo DaVinci; he was a famous artist and painter."

"I know who DaVinci is," said Noël testily.

"I'll be right back," said Don, laying down the wings carefully on the surface of the wall and heading off to the cellar door in his familiar loping walk.

"Guy," said Noël after Don had disappeared into the basement, "is there something wrong with Don's leg?"

Guy shrugged. "It happened when he was born, one leg shorter than the other I guess."

"How come nobody told me?"

Guy shrugged again. "I don't know. Guess we forgot. We're all so used to it, we take it for granted. Heck, it doesn't seem to bother Don that much. He's still the best baseball player I know; you should see some of the catches he makes. He can outplay me and Jiff or anyone easy in any sport."

Guy laughed.

"When we used to have fights with the kids on Tilden Avenue, they used to steer clear of Don because they thought he had a lead shoe he could crush their feet with. Lead or not, if he used it for stamping or kicking, look out."

Just then, Don came out of the cellar with more string and Guy noticed Noël looking at the thick soled, platform shoe on his friend's foot. He noted with satisfaction that after only a glance, she apparently forgot about it.

"What are you going to do once your finished with the wings?" Noël asked. Was that worry in her voice?

"Jump from the wall," said Don matter of factly. "I'll take a running start first, then by flapping the wings, I ought to get airborne. Actually, I don't think I'll actually fly, just sorta glide." He made a motion with his hand indicating the way he thought he'd go.

Guy saw Noël shake her head. He knew what she was thinking. That Don was either crazy or brilliant. Well, Don always managed not to *sound* crazy.

"Well, do you still want to go downtown?" asked Guy, changing the subject.

"Sure, that's why I came over when I saw you. I see that your wagon's empty," she said, pointing.

"Yeah, I did all right this time."

"Where are you guy's going?" asked Don from over his shoulder, busy with the wings again.

"I'm going to show Noël the way to Harvey's," explained Guy. "She likes books."

"Her too?"

"Do you like to read?" asked Noël.

"Don's a book lover too," said Guy before his friend could reply. "Only he's not very picky about what he reads. He goes up to the Dracut Library when they have sales and scoops armfuls of stuff without even bothering to check what they're about. He ends up wasting a lot of time reading some real junk."

"That's how I got the book on DaVinci," Don protested.

Guy laughed and jumped down from the wall. "C'mon, let's go. See ya, Don."

"Bye, Don," said Noël. "Hope it's not so long before the next time I see you."

"Me too."

"He's not really going to fly, is he?" asked Noël after she and Guy had reached Desrosiers Street again. "I mean, he doesn't really expect to does he? Or even glide?"

"Nah, for Don the most important thing is the finding out. Once he finds out something from experience, he'll cross it off his list and move on to the next thing."

"But why does he bother?" Noël persisted.

Guy shrugged. "Some people take things for granted and some people take other people's word for it and some people even believe everything they read, Don doesn't."

Noël looked at him, and Guy guessed that she had taken his last comment personally. Well, if that was the way she wanted it, he wouldn't disabuse her of the idea. Whatever the reason for her sudden change in mood, conversation ended abruptly after that.

Guy obliged her, not feeling very much like talking with her anyway, he still wasn't sure he even liked her. And so, an awkward silence punctuated with small talk settled over the two of them as Guy led the way along much the same route Noël and her mother had passed when they'd first arrived in the city. But instead of crossing the river at the Lacroix Bridge farther up the highway, Guy crossed the Ouellette Bridge closer to home, making their walk more of a straight line to Harvey's than if they'd gone all the way up the highway.

For the first time, Noël was able to see the old mill buildings up close. They began at the far end of the Ouellette Bridge where she was able to see their red brick walls curve slowly up along the river's edge to Bridge Street and beyond. Here and there, their regularity was broken up by differences in height, clock towers and huge smokestacks. And from where she stood at the center of the bridge, she could observe at close range the Merrimack River as it rushed by only fifty feet beneath her.

On the far side of the bridge, she saw the dirty alleys, cluttered courtyards and rotting wooden outbuildings that lay scattered about the old mills, their presence only increasing the oppressive nature of the run down factories. Guy led the way in and out of streets that held bricked mills like grave markers of a dead generation on one side and newer, modern assembly plants on the other. There, in the name of urban renewal, other mills had been torn down to make room for the new buildings.

At last, they emerged onto a rusty pair of railroad tracks that led past the new post office, behind the high school and onto Merrimack Street, the heart of downtown. Guy hopped on to one of the rails and with his arms outstretched, walked along its narrow width like a circus high wire act.

"That's Prince's Bookstore over there," said Guy, nodding his head. Idly, he wondered if Noël was impressed at his ability to keep his balance on the rail without looking down at his feet. "Prince's is all right, but they don't have a good selection of new books. Brooks Drug Store over there, has some new books too, but nothing you wouldn't find in a supermarket. On the other hand, sometimes I find stuff there that takes me by surprise."

Noël didn't bother to reply and Guy guessed that she was probably less than impressed with any book purchased from a drugstore.

When he reached a pile of warped planks once used as a train platform, Guy hopped off the rail and led the way across Merrimack Street to where a big clock facing Scott's Jewelry Store was chiming noon. From there, he led the way through lunch time crowds onto Central Street.

"Harvey's is over there," he said at last, pointing to a long block of buildings across the street. "But before we go over, I want to check what's playing over at the Strand first."

Shortly, Noël found herself in the shade beneath a marquee that hung over the sidewalk. On it, a string of bulbs circled the title of the main feature, *Georgie Girl*. A ticket booth stood at the opening of a long passageway that led into the darkened interior of the old theater. On the walls outside, movie stills were displayed in glass cases surrounded by Hollywood hyperbole. Joining Guy, who was examining the movie stills as if they were scientific exhibits, Noël looked too and made a face. *Planet of the Vampires* and *The Crimson Executioner* were the double bill for the coming Saturday's matinee.

"Oh boy, I've gotta tell Jiff and Mike about this," said Guy.

"Don't tell me you like this stuff?" asked Noël, repulsion clearly in her voice.

"Of course; don't you like monster movies?" Guy realized how ridiculous the question was as soon as he'd said it; she was a girl wasn't she?

"Don't get me angry, Guy. This stuff is stupid and you know it. What intelligent person would want to see a movie about monsters and space ships when they could just as easily see a movie like *Georgie Girl* that's about real people and real problems?"

"I would, that's who. And Jiff and Mike too. These movies are neat," said Guy, jerking a thumb at the movie stills. "Who wants to pay a whole dollar to see a movie that looks just like real life? I want to see movies that'll give me what I can't get in real life. Why bother seeing anything else?"

"Because movies about real people try to tell us something about ourselves, about how we get along with one another—"

"Never mind," sighed Guy, beginning to realize that the two of them would never see eye to eye. "Harvey's is over there."

Noël turned, resentful at being interrupted and saw the bookstore she remembered seeing the first day she'd come to Lowell. A cheaply painted billboard sign that read Harvey's Bookland hung over a door flanked by two plate glass windows. Behind the grimy windows Noël could make out stacks of dusty books, some with jackets whose colors had been completely bleached from exposure to the sun.

Guy led the way across the busy street. At the door, they were greeted by a hand written sign: *Open*, it read. Guy pushed the door open with the tinkling of an overhead bell and immediately, the familiar, friendly scent of old paper entered their nostrils.

Noël breathed in the smell gratefully, waiting for her eyes to adjust to the gloom inside the store. Slowly, the bare, dusty planking of the floor became visible and then the crammed store itself. In the single, large room, bookshelves were everywhere, reaching all the way up to the high ceiling where their topmost contents were obscured in distance. A solitary fan whirled lazily in the center of the peeling ceiling and an ancient Coca Cola cooler sat near the entrance.

88

A rough wooden counter ran along one side of the room protecting a wall of shelves that held stacks of old comic books labeled by title. At the far end, a man and woman sat behind an antiquated cash register. The man had dark hair, glasses and a slight paunch and the woman sitting alongside him was overweight in a grandmotherly sort of way, not at all the ill-tempered proprietors Noël half-expected to find.

"Hi, Guy," said the man, munching on a sandwich, a brown paper bag lay on the counter in front of him.

"Hi, Harvey," said Guy familiarly. "I've got a new customer for you."

"Good, good!"

"How's your father, Guy?" said the woman.

"Okay, I guess."

"Still selling ice cream?"

Guy's father was known to almost everyone in town as Mister Softee. He drove around in a gayly painted ice cream truck selling banana boats and sundaes and summers for a lot of people in town had become unthinkable without him.

"Yup. Any new comics?"

Harvey waved at the wall behind him. "All these."

Guy turned to Noël. "I'm gonna look at the comics, the books are over there." Then, knowing how it would rile her, he couldn't help adding, "The science fiction section is over there."

As expected, Noël gave him a dark look then headed in the opposite direction.

She moved around a low series of counters stuffed with used records until she found herself in a little nook facing one of the tall wall cases. Little, hand-written cards indicating the subject category were all the help she could expect in finding the books she wanted because nothing was stacked in any kind of order, neither by title nor by author. As she scanned the shelves, the first thing she noticed was school textbooks. At first she didn't think it was anything that'd interest her, but she soon found to her delight that most of the books consisted of cast off novels from various literature classes. Then her heart began to pound; they were all here, all the authors she'd ever heard about and plenty more besides: Nathaniel Hawthorne, James Joyce, Rudyard Kipling, Charles Dickens and Charlotte Bronte; Mark Twain, Emily Bronte, Lewis Carroll, Aldous Huxley, Ralph Waldo Emerson and Herman Melville!

She found herself transfixed by the sheer abundance of material as her attention was pulled from one section to the next. She entered the mystery section with Raymond Chandler, Agatha Christie, G.K.Chesterton, and Dashiell Hammett; the Russians had a category all their own with Leo Tolstoy, Alexander Pushkin, and Nikolai Gogol. History, science, architecture, art, philosophy, and much, much more filled the shelves until Noël's eyes began to water and sting. She stopped looking to rub them.

It was all too much to take in on a single visit and most of the books she saw, she wasn't sure she even understood. But she appreciated, in an instinctive way, the range of human thought they represented. The thousands of years of painstaking trial and error of history.

She finally decided to concentrate on the classics section and began rummaging through stacks of books, many with their covers curled and pages well thumbed. Noël took that as evidence that the book was a good one.

"All set?" said a voice, startling her. It was Guy's.

"Don't sneak up on me like that!"

Guy chuckled. "I didn't have to, you were in another world."

"I was in heaven," she corrected, not appreciating the allusion to Guy's reading interests.

Guy looked around at the shelves around her and frowned. "You call this heaven? The science fiction section is over there."

She ignored him and turned back to her browsing.

"Anyway, we'd better get going, it's after four o'clock."

Noël stood suddenly, surprised.

"What! Already? It can't be!"

"Well it is, pick out what you want and c'mon."

There was so much she wanted, but she managed to pick out two cheap selections: Mary Shelley's *Frankenstein* and Wilkie Collins' *The Moonstone*. She paid the ridiculously low price of twenty cents for each and left with Guy.

"Do you have enough money left for the bus? We're gonna be late for supper if we walk. I completely lost track of the time in there."

"Me too. Yeah, I have enough."

Good," said Guy, then he pointed. "Look, there it is! If we run, maybe we can get the driver's attention before he leaves!"

Weaving their way between passersby, the two of them raced along Central Street and reached the stop just as the bus was revving up its engines. The driver saw them and opened the doors.

The ride home was noisy inside the bus, but they passed the time comparing each other's new acquisitions. Guy grunted at Noël's choices. "I thought you didn't like that stuff."

"What stuff?" asked Noël, holding up one of her purchases. "This?"

"Yeah. Monsters and fantasy."

"*Frankenstein* isn't a monster story, it's a classic. The sub-title says it all: *The Modern Prometheus.*"

"You could've fooled me," said Guy, willing to concede Noël the point. "Well, maybe you're right, the movies about Frankenstein are just monster stories, but from what I've read, the book is a lot more serious."

Noël seemed to look at him with new appreciation. "That's right."

"Maybe I can borrow it from you some time."

"Sure you can, any time."

Noël was actually smiling now and Guy thought that she might be on the point of deciding that she'd been too harsh in her judgment of him. After all, you couldn't tell a book by its cover, right?

"But that romance stuff, forget it," continued Guy. "How can you waste your time with that garbage?"

As soon as he'd said it, Guy knew he should've kept his mouth shut; left well enough alone. Noël's smile vanished and the temperature in the bus plunged noticeably. Guy hurried on. "But if you like stories like that, I guess that's okay." He'd intended his comments to dampen the chill, but they had the exact opposite effect.

"Oh, you're as dumb as ever," said Noël in frustration, ending the conversation.

Feeling helpless (and yes, as dumb as Noël said he'd been), Guy decided to seek refuge by looking over his own purchases.

Later, when he began to think that the bus ride would never end, it did and they were disgorged at Hovey Square. Still not on speaking terms, they followed the familiar route home and down into Don's yard. There, Guy suddenly stopped and walked over to the trash barrels by the side of the house.

"What's the matter?" Noël demanded.

"It's Don's wings, he threw them away."

Noël came over to the barrels and looked for herself. It was true. The wings lay crushed amid a tangle of rope and string and wooden spars at the bottom of the barrel. "I guess it didn't work out," she concluded.

"Yeah."

Together, they continued around to the rear of the house.

Don was there. This time, he was crouched down in the center of the yard where the grass had been beaten out of existence by years of play leaving a great, circular area of naked earth. A small plastic rocket lay on a makeshift launch pad.

"Hey, Don, what're you doing now?" asked Guy.

Don stood and turned, a new scrape prominent on his forehead, grass stains on his knees. "I'm trying to see how high I can make this rocket go. It all depends on the balance between the vinegar and baking powder."

"Oh."

"What about you're wings; they're in the barrel," said Noël, a bit injudiciously.

Don smiled and waved a hand in dismissal. "I took one jump and fell like a rock. The cardboard caved in with one flap. Maybe I'll try again sometime with stronger material. Want to help me with this?"

Guy shook his head. "Got to get home for supper. See ya later."

"Okay," said Don returning to his research.

"He doesn't sound too disappointed," observed Noël after they'd reached Desrosiers Street.

"I don't think I've ever seen him unhappy," said Guy. "He's always been perfectly content to play with us or fool around by himself. I guess you can call him a kind of Huck Finn."

Noël stopped, struck by the coincidence that Guy would use the same comparison she'd once made. She was still trying to decide if the coincidence meant anything when Guy said "bye" and left for home.

Noël stayed in the middle of the road looking after Guy long after he'd gone in. Eventually, she did the same.

CHAPTER SIX

In which Noël is reminded of an old mystery

September 1, 1967: It's hard to believe that we've been living here for the whole summer already. Where did the time go? It seems like just yesterday when Maman and I drove into the city and I saw the old mills for the first time. It's even harder to believe that all my fears about moving to a new neighborhood and having to make new friends turned out to have been for nothing. It's as if I've lived here all my life and my new friends, especially Polly, are all wonderful. Of course there's *some* people I could live without, but you can't have everything can you? Anyway, what a difference only a few months make!

And now it's starting all over again.

Already, the butterflies are fluttering in my stomach over the first day of school. I wouldn't be half as nervous though if my friends were going to go to the same school as I am but they're not. Because they belong to different parishes than our family does, Polly and Don will be going to St. Michael's school on the other side of town and Mike and Theo are going to St. Theresa's in Dracut. Jiff will be the only one of us to attend a public school, the Greenmont Avenue School up by the Dracut Library.

Guy and his sisters go to St. Louis School in Lowell, only a ten minute walk from here and (just my luck!), the same parish I live in. What's even worse is, Guy is in the same grade I am and even though I found out there's going to be two classes of the sixth grade, what do you think the odds are that Guy's going to be in the same one I am? And because I'm going to walk to school with his sisters, Trece and Marie, I'll probably have to walk with him too. Well, there's nothing I can do about it I guess, so I might as well make the best of it and hope Guy doesn't embarrass me.

Noël sat leaning against the headboard of her bed with her knees drawn up to her chin and her arms wrapped tight around them. Outside her window, a full, silver moon looked as if it were caught in a tangle of tree branches even as a few stray beams of light managed to escape into the room where they lay dashed against the floor. On the bed, amid a mess of sheets and blankets, a book lay open. Unable to sleep, Noël could sense all around her the stillness of the house.

Tomorrow was to be the first day of school.

One by one, Noël had listed in her mind all the things she could possibly be nervous about on the first day of school. She wasn't worried about her scholastic performance because she'd always done well before and even enjoyed the intellectual challenge. She wasn't even worried about the teachers because she'd attended a Catholic school before and found the nuns strict but fair. And since things had gone so smoothly since moving into her new neighborhood, she didn't expect any problems making the acquaintance of her new classmates. Then what was it that was bothering her?

She sighed, looking down at the cover of the book she'd been reading then turned back to the window. No, after eliminating all the possibilities, she'd narrowed down her uneasiness to just one thing: Guy. Sure it was silly, but how many times had she told herself that and still not been able to dismiss it from her mind? She felt sure that somehow, in some way, Guy would be the cause of some unintentional embarrassment to her. (Although there wasn't a vindictive bone in his body, Guy was like an archer who shot off arrows in every direction without ever hitting what he aimed at).

So she sat there worrying about what Guy might say about her at school and wondering if there were any way she could avoid it. Maybe she could ask Trece or Marie to help? She was still trying to think of ways to get around Guy's lack of tact when she heard the sound of distant sirens.

She crossed the floor and, running to the window, pressed her face to the cold panes. Up the street, the whole sky had turned a glowing red. Fearful but still curious, she left the window and ran down the short hallway to the sewing room at the back of the house. From the window there, she could see tongues of flame licking up over the trees in the direction of the Therrien's house.

Her throat tight with worry, she started back to her room only to run head-on into her father.

"Whoa, hold on there," he said from the darkness, his big hands steadying her.

"Pa, there's a big fire out back, I think it's the Therrien's house," Noël gasped.

"I know, I'm going out to take a look."

"Oh, let me come with you, please!"

Her father stood silent for a moment before replying.

"Will you promise to be careful and listen to everything I tell you?"

"I will."

"All right then."

"I'll be just a minute," Noël said racing back to her room. She threw on some clothes and ran out with her shoe laces still undone.

"Be careful Noël, and mind everything your father tells you," said her mother. She stood framed in the doorway to her bedroom, the glow from the window inside outlining her figure in crimson.

"Sure Ma, but aren't you coming with us?"

"I'm staying home," said her mother. "I want to make sure sparks from that fire don't drift over here and start something."

Noël hadn't thought of that. But then, she was worried that Don's house was burning down even as they spoke. "Hurry up, Pa!" she pleaded.

Hand in hand with her father, Noël led the way outside and up the street.

There, she tried to peer through the trees behind the Cardova's house to the Therrien's and was relieved to discover that Don's house was perfectly safe. But beyond it, on Burnaby Street, the flames were even more ferocious looking.

"C'mon Pa," Noël urged, racing ahead to the top of the wall in Don's backyard.

"Wait right there, Noël. Don't you take another step without me," cautioned her father.

Together, they entered Burnaby Street and immediately walked into a swarm of confusion made up of snaking firehoses, flashing lights, and everyone it seemed, for miles around. They were all milling about oooing and ahhing while the police bellowed to "Keep back folks" and "Let the firemen do their job." Barricades had been erected in a rough perimeter, blocking off both ends of the street and for the first time, Noël could see the object of the flames' hot caress.

It was the little white church, affiliated with the congregation of the Old Yellow Meeting House up by the Dracut library. Immediately, Noël felt a pang of deep regret at the destruction of the beautiful colonial style building where, she knew, Jiff had attended Sunday School.

A loud crack thundered from deep inside the building and Noël joined the crowd as it instinctively fell back with a collective gasp.

Nervous, she looked around for her father and saw him standing with some of the neighbors a few yards behind her, talking and shaking their heads as they watched the hungry flames. Looking back at the crowds, Noël decided she could squeeze through to the front of the barricades. There, she found herself standing next to Don and Mike and farther down, lit up in the eerie light of the flickering fire, she spotted Polly and Theo.

After a few more minutes of watching, Don seemed to notice her for the first time. "Hey Noël, what are you doing here?"

"Same thing as you," Noël replied. "We saw the fire from our upstairs windows and I thought for sure it was your house that was burning. I was so worried, I ran from home without even tying my shoelaces."

"You thought it was *my* house that was on fire?"

"Yeah," said Noël, tying her shoes. "How long have you been here?"

"I don't know, about an hour I guess," said Don. "I heard the sirens and my brother told me about the fire. Mike got here right after I did."

"Do you know what started it?" Noël asked, watching a shower of sparks float into the air, hoping they wouldn't go in the direction of home.

"Nope. Everybody around here thinks it was the heater or something. They say they turned it on today to check it out for the fall. Maybe something went wrong."

98

"I'll say," said Noël, her eyes watching the glowing walls.

"Ever see a fire this big before?" asked Mike to no one in particular.

"Not me," said Don in general.

"Me neither, I—" Noël's comment was cut short by a sound that began abruptly from the depths of the burning building and quickly built into a long, drawn out crack, like thunder until, in a single motion, the entire steeple began to sink into the rest of the building. Then, with a roar of flame and burning timber, it disappeared completely from view and in its place, a huge fireball reared up and exploded into nothingness. Noël reeled back at the sudden wave of intense heat that rolled over the crowd like a hot wind.

With the collapse of the steeple, the police began to push the barricades further back. This time, the crowds weren't eager to get a close look at the fire. Instead, they kept their distance.

"Wow, did you see that?" asked Don, breathlessly.

"I hope nobody was inside," said Noël.

"That's right," added Mike, "There might've been some firemen in there."

It was a sobering thought that took much of the fun out of the event and transformed it into deadly seriousness. The three friends stopped talking and gave their full attention to the desperate activity surrounding the flaming ruins of the church. In no time however, any recognizable shape the building might've had was gone as the last remaining walls tumbled into glowing ashes. Soon, all that was left was a pile of blackened debris dotted with a few remaining licks of fire. Then, even that was snuffed out by the tons of water that was poured onto the remains by sweating firemen.

A stray breeze drove a great pall of oily smoke over the crowd. When it cleared, all that remained of the church was a hissing, crackling pile of blackened rubble. At the sight, Noël sensed a collected sigh of relief and regret come from her friends and neighbors as the loss they all had suffered at last became a reality. No more would the little white church greet them on sweet summery mornings, no more would they wake to the sound of its bells, no more would the children play in its comforting shadow on slow autumn evenings.

Everyone stood silent, looking at the pile of debris but gazing beyond it to something they could only see in their souls. Noël saw it too, and if asked, could never have expressed how she'd felt in words; she and her neighbors could only feel the loss of a building that was more than the sum of its timbers, glass, and concrete. But then, despite the sorrow, Noël smiled because, for the first time since moving to Desrosiers Street, she really felt as though she were a part of her new community. Until that moment, she hadn't realized how important that had been to her.

Then someone tapped her on the shoulder.

"Noël, I'm going to stay a few minutes more to talk with the Agoulis'," her father said. "It's late and there's nothing more to see so I want you to go right home to bed now, okay?"

"Okay, Pa. How long shall I tell Maman you'll be?"

"Only about a half hour or so. Get along now."

Noël turned and saw that her friends were preparing to go too and joined them on the way back down Burnaby Street. Already, talk of the fire had begun to recede in importance as Don reminded them that the next day was the first day of school.

"Why'd you remind me?" moaned Mike.

"Are you gonna take the bus with us to school, Noël?" asked Don.

There had been some question whether she'd ride to school on the bus that stopped at the bottom of Dean

Avenue, but Noël decided that although it was a good idea for the others who attended St. Michael's, for her, St. Louis was far too close to home to justify a bus ride.

"No, I decided to walk to school with Trece and Marie," said Noël.

Don shrugged.

"Well, it's after midnight already," said Mike, looking at his glow-in-the-dark watch (it had taken him nearly a year to save the 1,000 points needed in Mallo Cup cards to send away for it). "Don't know how I'm gonna get up tomorrow."

Midnight! Noël stopped in her tracks, wondering if her father had realized how late it was? She looked back uncertainly and decided she should go and remind him.

"I'll see you guys after school tomorrow," she said. "I think I'm going to go back and get my father."

"Okay, see you," said Mike.

"Be careful," warned Don.

At the scene of the fire, Noël soon discovered that the barricades stood almost deserted with only a handful of people still watching the cooling remains; others were heading for home. There were however, still small knots of adults here and there talking with one another.

Slowly, Noël moved among the retreating crowd, searching for her father. The last she saw of him, he'd been with Mr. Agoulis, Theo's father, on the outskirts of the crowd. Finally, a barricade prevented her from getting across the street. When she'd first arrived on the scene, the crowd of people had formed a wide crescent around the burning church stretching from the end of Burnaby Street out to Pleasant Street. Now the area where the crowd had gathered had been cut in half by two lines of barricades sketching out a corridor for the departing fire engines.

Leaning against one of the barricades, Noël looked over to the other side. In the blue and red glare of the lights from the police cars and fire engines, she could see that there were still quite a few people there, among them, her father. He was standing at the back of the crowd looking around and Mr. Agoulis was nowhere in sight. But as Noël watched, she began to feel that there was something familiar about the way he was acting. Then her heart began to beat quicker as she realized that it was the same way he'd behaved that first night when they moved into their new home. He looked to her exactly as if he were checking to make sure he wasn't being watched.

Suddenly, a huge ladder truck crossed her field of vision and blocked her father from view; when it had passed, her father was gone! At first, she thought nothing of it and looked around thinking that perhaps he'd spotted her and come over, but there wasn't a sign of him. With growing trepidation, she decided to go back across the street and try to catch up with him before he got too far, but it seemed as if there was no end to the coming and going of the emergency vehicles. Tired of waiting, Noël stooped beneath the barricade and slipped into the street. She heard the shrill call of a police whistle and a "Hey you, wait…" but she ignored them and dashed out just behind a passing fire engine and lost herself on the opposite side before anybody could stop her.

Back on the Burnaby Street side of the road, she slipped through the thinning crowd, emerging on the sidewalk leading up to Hovey Square. Ahead of her, couples and small knots of people were still drifting homeward but there was still no sign of her father. Convinced that he couldn't have passed her on the street without her spotting him, Noël decided that the only way he could've gone was up the street (even though she couldn't think of a single reason why he'd do that).

She ran up to the top of the hill where Hildreth Street bore off Pleasant and disappeared in the darkness from Dracut and into Lowell. By this time of the night, the moon had slipped below the horizon and had thrown everything into darkness.

Now, only pools of yellowish light cast by the occasional street lamp dotted the road at infrequent intervals. Everything else was masked in gloom and things that were familiar in daylight, were now unsettling in the dark. Noël thought she could make out a house here and a garage there, but she couldn't be sure. For the first time in her life, she felt that the trees she'd always loved were more menacing than friendly as they gathered and huddled in threatening groups all around her.

In her growing anxiety, she hadn't noticed how far she'd gone. Time passed and it began to dawn on her that she was by herself on the street. Everything was quiet, hushed. Not a night bird chirped nor dog barked. She felt utterly alone until her eyes noticed movement farther down the road. A figure had entered one of the circles of light cast by a street lamp. Noël's heart leapt. She was sure it was her father. But no sooner had the figure entered the light than it vanished again upon leaving it. Noël ran on ahead.

Now she saw that she'd passed completely out of the area of town she was familiar with and had moved into one that was as alien to her as any foreign country, the emptiness of whose landscape continued to make her apprehensive. But just as the oppressive nature of her surroundings began to make her wonder if her decision to look for her father had been too rash, her gloomy thoughts were wiped away like strands of dust when she once again glimpsed the figure up ahead.

This time it was closer and there was no doubt in her mind; it was her father. But where was he going? Why hadn't he come home with her? What was he doing in this strange neighborhood where the residential, suburban nature of Desrosiers Street had melted away to become one of a more commercial aspect. Single family homes gave way to tenements and storefronts with their big glass windows lined the sidewalks. Trees became scarce and litter crowded against the curbs. For the first time that night, Noël wondered what time it *really* was.

Then she lost her father.

She walked on for a few minutes more, but there were too many streets, too many alleys, too many buildings he could've gone into. Gradually, she slackened her pace and finally stopped, not knowing what to think. She found herself at a deserted intersection, a lone streetlight shone over her head and a traffic signal changed from red to green for automobiles that would not arrive for hours yet. Noël decided that there were times when she'd felt less alone in a cemetery.

Standing there in the dead quiet of early morning, she felt the same emotions that had seized her the first time she'd seen her father disappear under mysterious circumstances. She didn't know whether to be curious about the whole thing or simply cry, but just then, tears came more easily. Sobbing lightly, she turned and headed back the way she'd come. Slowly, the landscape began to revert back to what she was more familiar with and the number of trees increased. She wasn't in a hurry to go home and the empty streets, disturbing as they were, fit her mood. Just then, she wanted to be alone.

Eventually, she came again to the cold remains of the church, now with only the skeletal barricades and a lone policeman to keep it company. She contemplated the blackened, steaming heap from the concealment of a nearby tree and decided that there was some kind of meaning to it that bore some relationship with what she was feeling, but just at that moment, she was unable to make the connection.

At last, the long night almost over, she turned quietly and found her way home.

St. Louis Elementary School

CHAPTER SEVEN

In which Noël goes to school and forgets herself

November 15, 1968: School is going to be a little more difficult than I thought. Things had gone so well with my neighborhood friends that I thought I could get along in the same way with my classmates at St. Louis, but it didn't turn out that way. When I first started writing this diary, I promised myself that I'd behave in such a way that other kids wouldn't think me stuffy or snobby. I worked hard to keep from using too many big words and saying how I read this or that in a book, and I did it. Friends like Polly, Theo, Trece, and Marie and even some of the boys like Mike and Don are more dear to me than anyone I knew back in Forest Hills; and now that they know me better, I think I can let a little more of my real self show without worrying much about how they'll take it.

Unfortunately, I think that experience has made me overconfident. I forgot the lessons I learned over the summer and went ahead and acted like my old careless self at school. The teachers of course, were surprised and pleased, but my classmates ended up keeping their distance. That was in the beginning though. Now that school's been going for a month or so, things between them and me have begun to improve, especially with Trece and Marie explaining me to the others.

But whether I'm accepted at school or not, I've decided that my friends there should never be more than acquaintances. I'm not sure why that should be so, but I can't help feeling protective about my position with the gang on Desrosiers Street and I don't want anything to mess it up now.

Anyway, since school started, I've fallen into the habit of spending more time by myself. I like going into the woods to read and do my homework until the sun starts to go down then walking slowly back home in the growing dusk. I don't know what I'll do when it gets too cold outside. Soon I'll have to stay in the backyard and in another week it'll be too cold for doing anything outdoors but taking walks. I remember how the woods and fields beyond the fence used to spook me when Polly first showed them to me but now, I really can't think of a better spot for peace and solitude than on top of Lookout Hill.

Sitting with the rest of the sixth graders near the front of the church, Noël had a perfect view of altar and pulpit. Behind her, the class' home room teacher Sister Domicile, a very Franco-American nun of the Assumption of the Blessed Virgin Mary, an order based out of Canada, watched over the class like a hawk. Father Beaujois had just reached the midpoint of his sermon and, as usual, it was the time of the Mass when Noël's attention began to waver.

It was Sunday morning of course and, also as usual, every other class from St. Louis de France elementary school was also present, each in its assigned position throughout the church: the lower grades up front, the middle grades at the center and the higher grades toward the back. The remaining space not occupied by students was taken up by their parents. In each class, boys and girls were strictly segregated, with the girls placed ahead of the boys on the theory that they were naturally better behaved and didn't require as close supervision. None of them, boys or girls, would be allowed out of Sister Domicile's control until they'd filed out of the church and back into their parent's keeping.

As a result, everyone, including Noël, couldn't help feeling self-conscious throughout the service knowing that their every move was being carefully observed (and if they stepped out of line, like talking or chewing the Eucharist when coming back from communion, they could expect pink demerits to be issued in class the next morning).

There were many things Noël had been taught shouldn't be done in church and one of the most perplexing was the rule against turning around. Noël was sure the rule had something to do with politeness but that didn't stop her from feeling the urge to do it every time she came to church. As a matter of fact, she was feeling it now. Somewhere on the other side of the church she knew, her parents were sitting and she felt an unbearable urge to look for them. Risking a pink demerit, she decided to chance a quick look and spotted her mother's distinctive green hat and veil. Turning back to the front of the church, she couldn't help a sense of relief at Sister Domicile's silence.

Then, before she knew it, it was time for communion.

Noël waited patiently with her class, their hands folded prayerfully under the eye of Sister Domicile and watched as the lower grades filed in order, row by row, up to the communion rail. At last, their turn came. Sister Domicile rose and moved to the first row of children, signaling them to exit their pew. Noël rose from her knees and joined the line that was moving slowly toward the front of the church. She remembered her mother's advisory to say an Act of Contrition before receiving communion, but couldn't keep her mind from wandering again.

It was Guy's new haircut that did it.

He was serving as altar boy that morning, holding out the spatula beneath the chins of communicants to prevent any stray particles from the Eucharist falling to the floor. But it was his haircut, that was just beginning to grow out, that reminded Noël of the first day of school.

She remembered being nervous that morning, with her trembling hands and the butterflies in her stomach. She was so nervous that even the feel of her new school bag and the smell of her new pencil case made her jittery. She'd experienced first days at school before, but this time it was different. This time it was a new school where the only person she knew in her class was Guy. After all, how much good could he do in helping her get to know the girls in their class? Not much good at all when the two genders were kept separate for most of the day.

The first thing she noticed that morning when she went to Guy's house, was his new haircut. As she walked to school with Trece and Marie, she couldn't seem to take her eyes off the back of Guy's head. Concentrating on his haircut kept her from thinking too much about school.

But no amount of distraction could last forever and soon they came into sight of the church steeple.

Modern by most standards, St. Louis Church was all yellowish brick and recessed stained-glass windows. Disdaining heights, rather than zooming into the air toward heaven like most churches, St. Louis instead went below ground. Inside, it was remarkably free of the clutter usually found in Catholic churches; there were hardly any statues, candles, and no elaborately carved wood or stonework. Noël had decided that she liked its bare simplicity and was especially impressed with the amount of sunshine its stained glass windows let in on Sunday mornings.

But around the corner, standing in stark contrast to the bright airiness of the church stood the massive bulk of the elementary school. It was three stories tall not including the attic and constructed entirely of dark, red bricks, much like those of the city's old mills. Devoid of ornamentation, it jutted straight up into the sky out of a schoolyard paved over in tarmac. Topped by a green-tiled roof sloped and squared like a Chinese castle, it reminded

Noël of a Gothic mansion, the kind that littered old Victorian novels.

Around the outside of the building, hundreds of children were already milling about, not doing much of anything. There wasn't much laughter. Well after all, thought Noël, it *was* the first day of school.

As they entered the schoolyard, Guy joined a group of boys leaning against the windows at the rear of the church and when Noël looked back, Trece and Marie had disappeared too. Feeling abandoned, she wandered aimlessly, careful to avoid crossing the invisible line in the schoolyard that separated the boys from the girls. Growing bored, she took out a book of poems by Emily Dickenson but only had time to read a few passages before a bell sounded bringing all activity in the school-yard to a stop. Slowly, like filings to a magnet, everyone began drifting to the rear of the school where a small knot of black-clad nuns stood together.

Noël found Guy again and followed him to where the children were beginning to divide themselves into their separate classes. It soon became apparent that each class stood in two sections, boys and girls, but as the groups coalesced, Noël found herself among a handful of students who looked as lost as she was. At last, with each sister before a different group of children, things quieted down and the single nun with the bell began to move from class to class reading off names from a list. Every once in a while, one of the children standing with Noël would reply and step forward to be inserted into the appropriate class.

Slowly, the group with Noël dwindled until she was the only one left, and feeling utterly self-conscious. She was still worrying whether or not to feel embarrassed when a name she didn't catch was called out and followed immediately by silence.

There was no reply.

When the name was repeated, she realized with a start that it was her own! Suddenly, she noticed that the sister with the bell and all the gathered students were looking at her. Vainly, she tried to find Trece or Marie for some kind of moral support, but couldn't locate them.

"Noël Archambault," said the sister again looking at her clipboard.

"Here," said Noël at last.

"Please take your place with the sixth grade." As Noël started to move, the sister added, "You'll be in 6B," gesturing to one of two sixth grade classes, among whom she noticed was an uncomfortable looking Guy. Was it because of her or his new haircut?

The nun who'd called out the names put down her clipboard and looked imperially over the assembled students. *"Bon jour mes enfants,"* she said in French.

"Bon jour ma soeur," came the dutiful reply.

"I am Sister Marie-Joseph," she continued in English, having established the fact that St. Louis was indeed a Franco-American parish.

"I'm sure you're wondering about what happened to Sister Jeanne," Sister Marie-Joseph continued. "During the summer, she asked to be sent to the missions in Africa and her request was granted. In her place, I have been named as your new principal and look forward to observing your progress throughout the year. In this regard, I have been assured by the good sisters," she nodded to her colleagues, "that they will do all they can to see that you each receive all the help you need. I'm sure that you will all give them your best effort and do it with a minimum of hooliganism." Here she fixed a cold stare in the general direction of the boys. It was a stare carefully practiced to evoke in them a vague terror. "And now, the sisters will conduct you to your classes."

Almost with the final word, the sister at the head of the first group of children raised a hand. In it was a small wooden device that she squeezed once. A single, sharp click was all Noël heard as the first class, with the girls in the lead, began to walk double file around to the front of the building. Soon it was the sixth grade's turn as its sister snapped her clicker. Noël walked with the others to the front of the school where they entered the building through one of three entrances.

Reaching the second floor, the first thing Noël had noticed about the interior of the school (and which would forever after remind her of those first, anxious days of class), was the smell.

She sniffed.

Though clean, the inside of the school clearly showed the wear and tear caused by the thousands of students who'd passed through the building over its sixty year history. At last, arriving in her home room class, Noël saw more evidence of those vanished students in the badly scratched and beaten desks and chairs which were carved with all manner of words and doodles. The desks and chairs were clearly as old as the building and would've been considered antiques in any public school, but Noël felt that their empty ink wells and pencil grooves, their cast iron legs that bent and curved in an attempt at design, all gave the school character. Taking a seat near the row of tall windows that dominated the far wall, Noël lifted the cover of her desk and peered inside. A few books lay there, neatly arranged. She left them undisturbed and while her classmates found their places, she continued her examination of the room. A thin layer of grit covered the wooden floors whose slats seemed to make it impossible to keep completely clean and outside the tall windows, the green leaves of a spreading oak tree swayed invitingly, as if beckoning those inside to come out and play.

Sighing, Noël looked away from the windows and noticed an old upright piano in the back of the room, its sheen long since dulled with time, and wondered fleetingly if the sisters gave lessons (wouldn't it be dreamy to be able to play like Mozart?) Much of the room's wall space held a number of low bookshelves lined with paperbacks (whose titles she couldn't make out) and clean scrubbed blackboards. A limp American flag stood at the front of the room and the alphabet in cursive script stretched across the room over sister's desk.

Noël noticed that sister's desk was in almost as bad a condition as the students'. It too was worn and dull with age and Noël could appreciate the cunning that went into its design: it had a low guard at the front that kept seated students from seeing what sister's hands were doing and stood on a low platform that raised it a good six inches from the level of the floor.

At the moment, the chair behind it was occupied by the nun who'd led them to class. Dressed completely in a flowing black habit, the only relief she had came from a white headpiece that held her veil in place. The whole thing, concluded Noël, made it difficult to guess sister's precise age; she could've been anywhere between fifty and seventy. A heavy crucifix hung from her neck and a light dusting of white chalk clung to the cuffs of her habit, which was the sure sign of a teaching sister.

"Bon jour mes enfants," she began.

"Bon jour ma seour," the class replied, sitting erect in their places.

"I'm Sister Domicile, your new home room teacher. In the mornings, I'll be instructing you in catechism, ancient history, arithmetic, and science; and in the afternoons, you'll go across the hall where Sister Zelia will have you for French and English grammar.

"You may have heard about me from some of my previous students and I hope you won't be disillusioned if I say that everything they've told you is probably true.

"You're all either eleven years old now or will be in the next few months and I expect you to act accordingly. You're not children anymore and I don't intend to treat you that way. I usually give at least two hours of homework every night and expect to have it finished on time. I'm a stickler for punctuality and will expect nothing less from you. All homework assignments will be signed by your parents before being handed in," she paused to let what she'd said sink in.

"Of course, there will be no speaking in class, unless I specifically give you permission, and no gum chewing."

"Now, is all that clear?"

"Oui, ma seour."

"Good. Now, I'm going to call out each of your names and I want you to take your seats in that order starting with the first desk on either side of the room. Boys to my left, girls to my right."

She raised her arms in signal for everyone to rise and Noël joined the other girls as they lined up beneath the windows on the right. On the other side of the classroom, the boys ranged themselves in front of a blackboard that separated the room's two exits. Noël hoped she wouldn't be called first and get the attention of the whole class so early. Desperately, she tried to figure the odds on how many girls in the class would have last names that began in A, but before she had a chance to conclude that she was doomed, her name was called.

"Noël Archambault," read Sister Domicile from a seating chart on her desk.

"Ici, ma seour," said Noël, stepping out a bit from the others.

"So, you're the new pupil. I hope you'll enjoy your stay at St. Louis, Noël."

"Merci, ma seour, I'm sure I will."

Sister Domicile seemed to detect something she liked in her new student. "Can you tell the class a little bit

114

about yourself, Noël? I'm sure being new to the school, the others would like to get to know you better."

Noël blushed and cleared her throat. Looking around the room, she finally found Guy seeming as if he were holding his breath.

"There's not much to tell, *ma seour*; I recently moved to Lowell from New York, and don't know too much about the area yet." She moved to the first seat at the head of the class and sat down, placing her schoolbag on the floor beside the desk. She'd forgotten the book in her hands and placed it on the desk in front of her.

"I'm sure you'll feel right at home here in no time, Noël," Sister Domicile assured her. Then, noticing the book, said, "You've brought a book with you on the first day of school?"

"Oh, yes, I like to read every spare chance I can," Noël said without thinking. "That's my real love, books. I'm a bibliophile." There was a slight rustle from the assembled students and a murmur of uncertainty, but by then Noël was focused only on someone who'd shown an interest in her book and didn't notice the disturbance her words had caused.

Sister Domicile smiled again in barely repressed good humor. When she felt herself in sufficient control, she continued. "And what book have you brought that's fit for the first day of school?"

Noël held the book up for her to see. "The poetry of Emily Dickenson. I wasn't sure how much time I'd have to read today so I thought poetry would be the most convenient."

Sister Domicile was impressed. "You enjoy Emily Dickenson?"

"Oh yes, she's my favorite," Noël replied, "I can identify with her moods of melancholy and sometimes I can even..." Suddenly, her voice trailed off as she remembered where she was.

Around her, the room had fallen silent. Then, from somewhere, she heard the sound she'd dreaded most to hear: a snicker, then a giggle or two and she realized her mistake. On the other side of the room, she saw Guy shaking his head slightly, his face unsmiling.

Noël felt like crawling under a rock but before she could, a single snap of Sister Domicile's clicker silenced the class.

"I'll look forward to working with you in the coming year Noël," said Sister Domicile in the resulting quiet.

"Merci, ma seour," Noël mumbled, sinking in her seat.

One by one, Sister Domicile named off the other students, each taking their assigned place. When at last everyone was seated, she wasted little time in plunging them into the first subject of the day.

Gradually, as the morning passed, Noël began to forget her initial embarrassment and concentrated on her studies. She decided that she liked Sister Domicile not just because of her good humored but no-nonsense style, but because of her obvious command of the material.

So, by the time the class had gone across the street to the cafeteria for lunch and then gathered again in the schoolyard for recess, Noël had begun the process of becoming accustomed to her new environment and even to sort out some of her fellow classmates.

There was Terri Larose, a curly headed blond and Nancy Bertrois who had long black hair. Both, she learned, were the brightest students in the class, followed closely by Deni Cardolet who was also the fastest runner (a quality more appreciated by the boys).

Guy hung about with his own small band of friends which seemed to be made up of boys who had stayed back with him in the fourth grade two years before; all except for Billy Beaulois, who seemed to hook up with them as naturally as a fish takes to water. Ricky Poilette was distinguished by a big, red birthmark that covered nearly half his face and was a school celebrity by virtue of living directly across the street and having special permission to go home for lunch every day. Rocky Fourchin was a tall, lanky boy who was the fastest runner after Deni.

Noël spent that first recess reading, oblivious to the sounds of play around her until roused by the bell that signaled the end of playtime. As an afternoon littered with broken French conjugations and tortured grammatical diagrams wore on, Noël began to feel the pull of the outdoors and yearned for release. Outside, an absolute stillness seemed to have settled over the city and even the trees were motionless. The only activity was the sound of heat bugs as they continued to buzz in the last warm days of summer. The world was holding its breath, only waiting for the two o'clock hour when children would pour out, as they always have, from schoolhouses everywhere into the freedom of sunshine.

Finally, the hour *did* come and the class lined up at the exit to their homeroom in the order by which their destinations would be called. One by one, street names were called out over the intercom and Sister Domicile clicked and allowed one more group of students to leave the building. At last, Noël heard "West Sixth right" and entered the corridor right behind Guy and in another moment they greeted Trece and Marie on the street.

Normally, the walk home should have been a pleasant one, but Noël was subjected to a lecture by Guy on the proper way for a bibliophile to behave at school.

"You've got to be more careful," he told her. "You've got to start slow. You should've waited a couple of weeks before letting them know you actually *like* to read and then start off with something they'll understand like the Nancy Drew books. Not Emily Dickenson for crying out loud!"

Noël surprised herself and remained quiet as Guy had spoken.

All of the details of that day had come to her in a few minutes but a nudge in her back ended them in a second. She hadn't kept up with the line going to communion and a gap had opened up between herself and Nancy Bertrois.

Quickly, she moved to catch up, reciting a fast Act of Contrition as she went. In another moment, she was replying "Amen" to Father Beaujois' question: *"Le Corps de Christ?"* Feeling the wafer resting on her tongue, she made her way back to her place, content to be with her class.

CHAPTER EIGHT

In which Guy finds himself humiliated and rescues a damsel in distress

"Help, somebody help," cried Jane North from deep in the jungle. "Help," she shouted again before giving up. Her throat was sore from calling uselessly for help and with each cry, her body sank deeper and deeper into the quicksand she had fallen into.

She looked around in desperation for anything to grab hold of, but there was nothing. The only thing was a rotten branch that had lain across the quicksand, but it fell apart in her hands when she tried to use it to drag herself out. She felt panic rising inside her, but fought it down. She was not sure which she preferred, death, or rescue by Nick, but finally decided the humiliation of the latter would be less permanent.

Meanwhile, Nick Tropoli sailed slowly over the jungle with his hover-belt; his keen eyes scanning the forest for any sign of Jane. He could not decide whether the girl was worth all the trouble she was always getting into, but every time he got her out of it, he would realize that there was no way he could go on without her impish company.

Suddenly, he stopped in mid-air. Movement had caught the corner of his eye and he dived down for a closer look. In a moment, the jungle opened up to reveal one of Venus' many quicksand pits, and there, right in the middle of one, was Jane, frantically waving her arms.

Nick flew down until he was just over her head. "I don't know why I let you talk me into letting you come along on this expedition," he said sternly.

Jane frowned in anger. "Just get me out of here before the quicksand ruins my hair!"

Nick grunted and lowered himself still further. "Grab hold of my legs." Jane did, and in a minute, both were clear of the bog and headed back to the spaceship.

Gateway to the Future
by Guy DeMonde

The last snow of the winter had barely melted from the sidewalks before Guy began to spot bicycles being pedaled around the neighborhood. He had a firm personal code: he'd never take his bicycle out before the very first day of Spring at least. But walking to school that sunny morning, he could hardly tell that it was still winter. It was so warm outside that all he needed to wear was a light windbreaker.

"Hey, Guy," called out a voice suddenly from the street. "Where's your hat?"

Guy looked up and just caught David Claudette's grin as he sped by on his new bike, roaring up West Sixth Street to school. A Christmas present from his married sister, it was a sleek red stingray bicycle with high handlebars and banana seat that was the rage that year. Dave's older brother, in on the secret, had likewise given him some accessories: a sissy bar, rear signal lights, and headlight.

"Hi Dave," said Guy, waving feebly and ignoring Dave's jibe about his hat. Everyone knew Guy loved his old green watch cap that he kept pulled down over his ears from the first chill of night late in the summer to the very end of May. Usually, he'd make some kind of disparaging reply to taunts about his old hat, but this morning, he just didn't feel like it.

He wasn't in a very good mood and as seemed to be the case more and more often in the past year, the problem was Noël.

Why that should've been, he still hadn't been able to figure out. On one hand, she continued to mock him for his interests in comic books, science fiction, and monster movies while on the other, seemed to treat him with a kind of special attention, getting angry only with him, when Jiff and Mike were involved in all the same things. He didn't need that kind of attention, but it did strike him as odd that she seemed to single him out. Not for the first time he wondered if there was something about him that attracted her, even with their differences? But that was just too far-fetched! Whenever he looked into those angry gray eyes, the only thing he saw in them was scorn.

And now here she was again, complicating his life.

The position of class librarian became available the week before when Shirley Beauxterre left school. It was the opening Guy had been waiting for and he decided to make the office his own. After all, wasn't he the acknowledged class bookworm? Didn't everyone know how he loved books? Reading them, handling them, categorizing them? In fact, his greatest dream (which he'd never told anyone before), aside from some day becoming a big name science fiction writer, was to start his own bookstore. The way he saw it, he was a natural for the job of class librarian and all he'd need to do to get the position was to give a short speech about why he'd make a good one. The vote that followed would've been only a formality. He'd expected no trouble.

Then Noël entered the picture.

She'd been absent the day the class learned that Shirley was leaving so she didn't find out about the opening until the next day when she placed herself in nomination. Later, after discovering that Guy would be running for the same office, she claimed that personal pride and responsibility to those in class who supported her prevented her from withdrawing from the race. Guy knew all that because he'd tried to get her to do it. After refusing to back down, a showdown between he and Noël before the whole class had then become unavoidable.

What he really wanted to do was to withdraw his own name from the contest and crawl under a rock some place. He just wanted to go off by himself and get away, but that was impossible now because he couldn't just back down. What would his friends say? That he let a girl scare him off? If Noël had her pride, then so did he; heck, even if he could back out he wouldn't, not to Noël of all people!

And so, confused about his own feelings and trying to get his speech straight in his head, he walked gloomily behind Trece and Marie as they gabbed away with Noël, who didn't seem to have a care in the world.

A few minutes later, Guy was sitting at his desk and surrounded by classmates talking excitedly about the special meeting of the class officers. Although everyone welcomed with enthusiasm any interruption in the regular class routine, this time anxiety prevented Guy from sharing in it.

As usual, Deni was the center of attention for both the boys and most of the girls. Guy couldn't help feeling jealous; even though he knew they were distant cousins, he could never warm up to Deni. He seemed too perfect: tall, good looking, popular, top grades, and the fastest runner in school. Everything that Guy wasn't. Oh, sure, Guy had his friends but that still didn't keep him from being regarded as a little strange because of the books he read or his writing.

More than once he wondered how he could explain to those who didn't understand, why he had to write. How could he, when he wasn't sure himself? All he knew was that after reading a really good book or watching a really good film, he felt himself bursting with ideas and an uncontrollable urge to express them. As a result, he'd been writing his own stories since the fourth grade and even sent some out to professional science fiction magazines like *Analog* and *Amazing Stories*, but they'd all come back, rejected. He'd been disappointed, but lately his creative energies had been centered on his most ambitious project to date: a science fiction novel.

Guy hadn't quite realized that he'd been daydreaming until he was yanked back to reality by the sudden sound of Sister Domicile's clicker. Instantly, his nervousness returned, and in full force.

"Mr. President, will you call the meeting to order?" asked Sister Domicile from the back of the room.

Deni rapped his desk with a small gavel and said, "This special meeting of the class officers will come to order. Will the class secretary please read the minutes from our last meeting?"

Sandra Reilly, the class secretary, started reading. She was sitting at the far end of a short row of desks that had been pulled out from the rest and reversed to face the class. On Sandra's left sat class treasurer Terri Larose and on her left sat Deni, the class president and after him was Nancy Bertrois, the vice-president.

Guy glanced nervously across to the girls' side of the room. Noël was sitting in her regular place, cool as a cucumber, as if she hadn't a worry in the world. Not for the first time he wondered how she did it; how on one hand, she could be considered by the rest of the class as a kind of snob because of her refined attitude and large vocabulary and on the other be accepted too. At home with every clique, she was outgoing, friendly, and knew what to say to anyone, no matter what their interest. In short, she seemed to have all the necessary qualities for popular acceptance; everything Guy didn't have. Idly, he began to wonder who the real Noël was: the cool, refined Noël of school or the fiery but more down to earth girl from Desrosiers Street?

"And now, new business," Deni was saying, the reading of the minutes finished.

"The position of class librarian has been vacated by Shirley Beauxterre," said Nancy Bertrois seriously, "and the class needs to decide on a new person for the job."

"Very well," said Deni. "We have two candidates who've asked to be considered for the position. Each will step up and tell the class his or her reasons why they want the job." He nodded to Nancy.

"You're first, Noël," said Nancy.

The rest of the class looked expectantly at Noël as she rose from her place and stepped before the class. Guy felt a drop of sweat begin to roll down his side.

"Mr. President," Noël began, bowing slightly to Deni and scoring points right away. More were quickly added when she turned, smiling sweetly, from the officers to face the rest of the class.

From where he sat, Guy could only fume in silence. How could a guy like him, lacking in all the social graces, ever match style like that? He was a clumsy clod next to Noël's refined manners. Just a science fiction nut while she read Emily Dickenson!

"Fellow officers and classmates," Noël was saying. "Libraries are the depositories of the accumulated knowledge of all mankind whose books have been painstakingly gathered sometimes over a thousand years.

The first real libraries were the prehistoric cave paintings in southern France; although they were crude, they contained all the knowledge that was thought important at the time. To their creators, they meant nothing less than survival itself.

"Modern libraries are no different. All the knowledge of the world is preserved in them for the same purpose: because those who don't remember the past are doomed to repeat it.

"Books are what connects our generation and countless others stretching to those men who drew those cave paintings. They're the most important possessions we have and I firmly believe that our own little class library is no less important than the Library of Congress or even the fabled library of Alexandria. It deserves just as much attention and will get it from me. If you choose me as class librarian, you can be sure that I'll regard it as a sacred trust. Thank you." She bowed again to the officers and returned to her place.

For long moments, Guy's mind refused to work and when it finally did, he realized that he'd forgotten his speech. And even if he had remembered it, it wouldn't have done him any good. Next to Noël's polished delivery, it would've been a pitiful thing. It's loss left an empty place in his mind that gradually began to fill with increasing dread. How could he follow the kind of performance that Noël had just given? But he hardly had time to worry about it before he heard his name called. Like a person in a dream, he rose and walked to the front of the class hoping that no one noticed the nervous trembling that suddenly came over different parts of his body.

"Mr. President," he said to Deni in a mumble.

"Could you speak a little louder, Guy, I need to take down what you say," said Sandra.

Guy was too much of a nervous wreck to be irritated.

"I--uh—I'd like to be class librarian because--um--because, well, I love books," he began, trying to find somewhere to put his hands. "Everybody knows that. Um, everybody I know thinks I'm crazy for liking to read so much, but, uh--well I'm not actually.

"Anyway, I'd like to be class librarian because I love books and I know I can do a good job of taking care of them and keeping track of them," he concluded, rushing through the rest of what he could think to say. "Thank you."

Hastily, he slinked back to his seat, thoroughly humiliated.

Back at his desk, Guy buried his head in his hands. How could he say such things in front of the whole class? That everybody thought he was crazy for reading so much? He could feel the burning flush of embarrassment glowing on his face as, angry and frustrated, he chanced a look at Noël only to find that she was watching him; but what was that funny look in her eye?

"All right," said Deni, "we've all had a chance to hear from the candidates, now we'll vote on which of them we want for the position of class librarian. Terri will hand out the blank forms. Write the name of your choice on it and fold it in half."

After the slips of paper were handed out the room fell quiet for a few minutes with the only noise being the sound of scratching pencils. At last, Terri collected the votes and deposited them on Sister Domicile's desk. The four officers then sorted them out and made the final count.

"The vote's been counted," said Deni after he and the other officers had double checked their work.

Guy held his breath. While the count was being made, he'd had time to think things over. Maybe the class had been unimpressed with Noël's cerebral approach and liked his simpler, more honest appeal for the librarian's job better? The notion seemed so plausible that by the time the officers were ready to announce the winner, he'd half convinced himself that he had a good chance of being elected.

"Five votes for Guy and twenty-three for Noël," came the devastating news.

Immediately, the class erupted with the sounds of happy congratulations for Noël. Surrounded by well wishers, her head bobbed continuously in thanks. As for Guy, he felt like slipping under his desk and sneaking out of the room.

The humiliation of baring his soul before the whole class to be laughed at when he wasn't around was too much for him. All he wanted to do was to go off by himself and maybe cry.

Only five votes. Was that the measure of what the others really thought of him? It meant that only himself, Ricky, Billy and Rocky voted for him and--who else? He tried to look around the room without raising his head. Then he remembered the look he'd seen in Noël's eyes. Had she voted for him? He caught himself softening toward her, but then decided she'd be considered by the others as a poor sport if she'd voted for herself.

And so, mired in self-pity, Guy somehow made it through the rest of the day and when he finally stepped out into the sunlight with the blue sky overhead, he thought that the world never looked better. It was still a fine day just as winter was giving way to spring and Guy felt an overwhelming urge to escape the bad memories of the morning and retreat to one of his favorite spots in the forest beyond Desrosiers Street.

An hour later, he'd done just that.

Warm in his worn but comfortable lumberjack's coat and his signature hat, Guy crossed the valley of ferns, brown and flattened over the long winter, and followed the trail on the other side. He skirted the base of Lookout

Hill before abandoning the trail and striking out through a thick copse of pine trees until he reached an ancient maple that leaned dangerously over Beaver Brook. The branches of the big tree hung low over the fast rushing stream whose waters, swollen from melting snow, rushed past on their way to the nearby Merrimack.

Directly over the water and nearly half way up the tree, planks had been nailed across a fork formed by two of the tree's branches. Guy had put them there years before. The original plan was to build walls and roof them over, but somehow, the work had never been completed. But that was all right, because he liked exposure to the sun and wind, to see as well as hear the leaves rustle overhead when a breeze came up. It was the perfect place to read or to just get away from things when he wanted to be alone.

He climbed the tree quickly, familiar with every branch and foothold from years of use. When he reached the platform, he didn't sit right away. Instead, as was his custom, he stood for a minute and surveyed his surroundings. In the summer, the platform would be completely swathed in leafage, invisible to anyone who didn't know it was there. But now, in late winter, the tree had been stripped of its leaves leaving Guy feeling exposed and naked. He shaded his eyes and held out a hand to balance himself against the tree. From his perch, he liked to imagine he could see for miles in every direction but the thousands of yards there must've actually been to the horizon was good enough. There was no one in sight. Not that he'd expected anybody to be; it wasn't the season. The woods were brown and drab and the ground much too wet and soft.

Satisfied of his isolation, Guy finally sat down, resting his back against one of the broad branches of the tree. He patted his coat pocket to make sure his book was still there. He'd intended to read some from Ray Bradbury's

Martian Chronicles, but decided he wasn't in the mood to read after all.

He'd been sitting there thinking for some time before he noticed a piece of paper caught on a branch just below the platform. He stared at it for a while before his curiosity finally reached a point where he felt motivated to pluck it from the branch. An instant later, he'd flattened the paper out on the platform and discovered that it was covered by a neat, graceful script, the kind of handwriting one would expect from a girl. It seemed to be a page from a diary. He grunted. He hadn't known that anyone kept diaries anymore.

"It's been harder to get along in school than I thought," Guy read. "Although I'm trying hard to make myself liked by the others, especially the girls, it doesn't seem to be working. But thinking about it now, I'm not sure I really want to try that hard anyway. After all, is it worth making friends if it means that I have to act like a stranger even to myself? What kind of friends would I have then? They wouldn't be friends of mine, just friends of some invention of mine, not the real me.

"It's a good thing that I get to be more myself at home. At least there, my friends are real friends who like me for my real self, not someone I'm forced to invent. Still, things aren't perfect even with them because none of them really understands me and it's hard to talk to them about the things I'm interested in--no, I've told myself before that if I'm going to keep a diary, I have to be honest with myself.

There is one person I might be able to talk to about things, but he can be so infuriating sometimes that it's difficult to imagine carrying on a meaningful conversation with him. But the thing that puzzles me the most is that I can't get him out of my mind. Maybe it's--

Guy flipped the sheet over, but there was nothing on the other side. His hands shaking, he folded it tightly and slipped it inside his coat. Suddenly he found that his heart was pounding faster, but he made no effort to ease the anxiety that had come over him. Instead, he leaned back against the bole of the tree and looked out over the forest, trying to make sense of his discovery and how he should feel about it.

A few days later, he was over at Ricky Poilette's house playing Battleship. It was after school and as usual, he felt funny being anywhere near the school when he didn't have to be. There was something about an empty school building where all manner of unpleasant things happened, from forced attendance to the consequences of missed homework assignments, that made Guy feel like dashing straight for the reassuring surroundings of home. But right then, sitting in Ricky's house across the street from St. Louis School, he managed to fight the feeling down and concentrate on the task at hand, namely, to sink the enemy fleet.

"B-12," said Ricky.

"Miss," replied Guy, placing a white game piece in the proper position on the board.

Then it was his turn. "A-10," he said.

From the hi fi in the other room, the voice of Sgt. Barry Sadler drifted into the kitchen singing one of the verses from *The Ballad of the Green Berets*. Ricky had received the album, along with the Battleship game, for his birthday and he and Guy had played them both over and over again ever since.

"I love this part," Ricky was saying.

"At home, a young wife waits," they both sang, hands pounding out the rhythm on the kitchen table. "Her Green Beret has met his fate/he has died for those oppressed /leaving her this last request/ put silver wings on my son's chest/make him one of America's best."

The song always sent shivers along Guy's spine and put him in the mood to read something about World War II (or even about the growing conflict in Southeast Asia, but he'd found that there was very little in print on that subject).

"Hit!" groaned Ricky.

"Yeah! What was it, an aircraft carrier?"

"I'm not telling!"

Guy smiled and placed a red piece on his board.

He was waiting for his friend to call out his next move when Ti Jean, the little kid who lived upstairs, pressed his face to the screen door and asked for Ricky.

"What do ya want?" growled Ricky, not in a good humor as he surveyed the damage Guy had inflicted on his once proud fleet.

"There's a girl out here says her friend's stuck in Greenhalge with their bikes. I told her you guys might help."

The two boys looked at one another and rolled their eyes. "Girls," they sighed. "Okay, we'll be right out."

Greenhalge was the neighborhood's public elementary school located right around the corner from, but still contiguous to, St. Louis. Surrounded by a ten foot high chain link fence, the portion of the school grounds that adjoined that of St. Louis near the Sisters' convent was the only part of the property not covered by concrete.

Stepping out onto the sidewalk in front of Ricky's house, Guy was surprised to find Polly waiting there with Ti Jean.

"What are you doing way over here, Polly?" asked Guy. It was extremely rare for anyone from Desrosiers Street to stray toward St. Louis, especially when school was out.

"Me and Noël wanted to go for a bike ride—" sobbed Polly, really upset. But Guy hardly noticed.

"Noël's with you?" he said. "She's the one who's stuck in the school yard?" Guy could hardly believe it.

"Yeah," said Polly, "she thought it'd be fun to ride in the school yard at St. Louis, and it was; there was a lot of wide open space. But then we decided to ride over to that school over there," she pointed toward the old Greenhalge building (which didn't have any of the architectural character that St. Louis had). "We were over there until it started to get late but when we tried to get out again, the gate was locked!"

"C'mon, Polly, it's not that bad," said Guy, attempting to comfort the girl whose tears, by this time, were flowing freely. He hated it when girls did that. "We'll get you out in no time," he said recklessly.

"How?" Polly demanded. "The gate's locked."

Guy didn't answer because by then they'd arrived at the gate and he could see Noël sitting on the ground where the uncovered part of the school yard ran up to the fence near the convent. Beside her, two bicycles stood on their kick-stands and the beginnings of a hole had been dug beneath the fence.

"Noël," called Polly, "I found Guy, he says he'll help us."

Guy saw Noël look up, then back down again as if she were embarrassed. Then she stood up and walked over to the gate.

Guy was shocked to see her condition: her face and hands were smeared with dirt, her clothes were filthy and one of the sleeves of her blouse was torn. Even Guy could tell that she wasn't in a very good mood right then and he struggled not to say anything he'd regret later. Instead, he determined to be all business.

"Oh, Guy, can you help us?" Noël was saying. "We can climb over the fence, but we don't want to leave our bikes behind."

"Wait a minute," said Guy, climbing the fence. There was a ringing as the chain links rattled against the supporting posts then Guy was over the top and dropping lightly to the ground on the other side. Polly followed, moving more carefully, then Ricky.

"We found a hole under the fence over there and tried to make it big enough to drag our bikes through," explained Noël.

"But it was taking too long and getting late so Noël told me to run home and get help," added Polly. "That little kid saw us and said he knew somebody who might help. I didn't know it'd be you guys."

"Have you tried going through the hole?" asked Guy.

Noël pulled at her torn sleeve and said "Yeah, but it was too small." It was hard for Guy to tell if she was blushing under all the dirt on her face.

"No kiddin'," said Ricky unkindly.

"There's no way we're gonna get these bikes under here," said Guy looking at the hole. Then he stood back, placed his fists on his hips and looked at the fence. "Ricky, do you think we can lift the bikes over the fence instead?" he asked his friend after a moment's consideration.

Ricky looked up at the fence, then at the bikes. "I dunno, let's try."

"Okay," said Guy, getting a hold on the fence. "I'll go on the other side near the top. Ricky, you climb up on this side. When we're ready, you girls hand up the bikes to Ricky one at a time." He reached the top, flipped himself over to the other side and clung there. "Ricky, from there, I'll help you pull them over the top. It's not gonna be easy handling these bikes so I'm gonna just let them fall to the ground on this side, okay?"

"At this point, I don't care what you do, so long as we get out of here with our bikes," said Noël.

It was a simple plan and in no time, both bicycles had been lifted over the fence. A few minutes after that, the four of them were standing together in the schoolyard at St. Louis.

"Thanks, Guy," said Polly, wiping away her rapidly drying tears. "And you too--uh, Ricky?"

"Yeah," said Ricky, putting his hands in his jeans, not used to being thanked by girls.

For that matter so was Guy, and especially not by Noël.

But he comforted himself with the suspicion that it was probably even harder for her to thank him.

"Thanks Ricky," Noël was saying. "And thank you too, Guy. I don't know what we would've done if we couldn't get our bikes out."

Guy shrugged and made it easy for her. "Ah, it's okay," he said, nervous at having Noël being nice to him. It was so much easier when she just criticized him, at least then he knew where he stood! "Besides, Polly would've just gotten somebody from home to come and help you."

"Maybe," Noël replied, straddling her bike.

"Bye!" said Polly as she and Noël pushed off toward home.

Guy watched them as they neared the street and noticed a wobble in Noël's balance. "Hey, are you guys gonna be okay?" he shouted.

"I feel so relieved that I could fly home," Noël called back, picking up speed as her bike made the turn toward West Sixth Street.

"Me too," echoed Polly as the two girls finally disappeared behind the cafeteria building.

Guy and Ricky stood for a while in the empty schoolyard watching after the two girls long after they'd vanished from sight.

Finally, Ricky said, "Who would'a thought that the girl who beat you for class librarian would end up owing you?"

"Ah, she ain't so bad," said Guy.

Ricky shrugged. "C'mon, let's finish that game before it's time for you to go."

Together, they headed back to Ricky's house, suddenly aware that something was absent from their lives that only an hour before, they hadn't even known was missing.

CHAPTER NINE

In which Noël learns that sometimes friends can be as dear as one's own family

June 23, 1968: School is out for the summer and it's hard to believe that it's been a whole year since we first moved here.

The nervousness I felt then seems so funny and trivial now. I've made a whole new group of friends, and not just sunny day friends, but real friends. Polly, Trece, Marie, Theo, Mike, Jiff, Guy, and even Don. They all have their quirks and idiosyncrasies, but I wouldn't take them any other way. It's what makes them who they are; without them, why, they'd be somebody else!

That year, after autumn had melted away in a fountain of color (as it usually did in New England), the winter started slowly but grew in intensity until there was so much snow on the ground that Noël thought it would never go away; but eventually it did and with the coming of spring the landscape blossomed into new life, bringing with it all the sights and scents that never failed to raise her spirits.

Like the seasons, the first year of school at St. Louis had also passed with a reassuring regularity for Noël. The year had grown in promise as she warmed to her subjects and discovered that Sister Domicile, though a hard taskmistress knew and, even more importantly, loved the lessons she taught. And Noël's relations with her classmates went from being chilly in the beginning to warm by the last day of school.

But sometimes the seasons could be deceiving; snow often fell in the spring and Indian summers could reach well into the autumn.

By the calendar, summer had definitely arrived as Noël, sitting on the backyard swing, reread *The Woman in White*, a novel she especially treasured. It had only been two weeks since school was let out for summer vacation but the flowering vines that crawled and drooped luxuriously over the fence, garage, and even the swing still displayed their white and pink blossoms. Even the tiny buds in the apple tree had still not developed into recognizable fruit. But it was summer for sure with all the bees gliding from blossom to blossom and creating a constant hum in the air.

Around her, the grass was in dire need of mowing but because of that, Noël was able to hear Polly coming across the yard long before she heard her friendly greeting.

Usually, she didn't like to be bothered when she was reading (except by Polly who, as her best friend, possessed privileges not given to anyone else), but this time she was kind of glad for the interruption. Thinking about her father's inexplicable behavior of the summer before (something she was spending more and more time doing lately), she hadn't been able to concentrate on her reading anyway.

"Hey, Noël," said Polly.

"Oh, hi Polly," Noël said.

"I should've known," said Polly coming to a halt by the swing. "When you didn't show up at my house when you said you would, I figured I'd have to come over and get you." Polly had placed her fists on her hips in mock indignation and continued, "Don't tell me: you started reading and forgot all about the parade."

That was true, but not because Noël had been reading. "Are we too late?"

"No, but you sure are lucky to have me to keep track of your schedule. C'mon, or we really will be late."

Noël stepped off the swing and, leaving her book on the porch, said "I'm glad you remembered the parade Polly, because I think I would've ended up missing it."

"Everyone else is already down the street," Polly said. "It wouldn't be the Fourth of July without going to see the Dracut parade."

The Fourth of July was a big deal in the small town of Dracut or so Noël's friends had been telling her for the past month. Forming up the street at Hovey Square, the parade would start down Pleasant Street and then make its way toward the high school a mile or so away. All of the town's fire engines and emergency vehicles were in it and everyone in town who owned a horse or antique car were allowed to take part.

Then there was the trolley.

The trolley was a kind of wildly painted bus in the shape of an old time locomotive that kids everywhere competed over for the chance of riding in. Finally, the parade would wind up with every troop of Boy Scouts, Girl Scouts, Cub Scouts, and Brownies bringing up the rear and marching to off key tunes played by the high school band. (After all that, Noël had begun to wonder if there'd be anyone left in town to act as spectators).

The two girls drifted down the street, joining an increasing flow of people as they went. There were the Jorgenson's, Mrs. Therrien, Mrs. Cardova, the Alors, the Laroses, the Agoulis', the Beaudoins and others that Noël didn't know very well.

At the end of the street, a thin line of people had already gathered along the sidewalk, some holding red, white, and blue balloons. An ice cream vender was pushing his cart up the street shouting "Creamsicles, fudgicals, popsicles, only 10 cents!" while an air of expectancy hung heavy over the crowd.

"This way," said Polly, weaving her way through people sitting at the curb and gathered around the front steps of their homes.

Noël followed as best she could until they reached a spot about midway along Pleasant Street which sloped upward to Hovey Square at the top of the hill. There, under two spreading maple trees, their friends sat or lounged on a carpet of thick grass. A couple of the boys were swinging from some of the trees' lower branches while Trece and Marie motioned enthusiastically for Noël and Polly to join them in the shade.

"You're just in time," said Trece from behind her horn-rimmed glasses.

"I would've been here a half hour ago but I was waiting for Noël," said Polly, sitting down next to Marie. "When she didn't show up, I knew she'd be caught up in a book or something back at her house."

"And was she?" asked Marie, looking at Noël.

"Of course," continued Polly, arranging her dress.

"I was reading *The Woman in White*, and I was just at the part where Marian is on the roof, listening in on her brother-in-law and the evil Count Fosco--"

"I tried to read that book after you raved about it once," admitted Trece. "But I couldn't finish it."

"Yeah, it was too slow," agreed Polly.

"No way," Noël protested. "It's a wonderful, tragically romantic book! All the great novels are, you know."

"Well, I don't know," said Polly. "When I tried reading it last summer, I found it pretty dull. Now it's spoiled me for summer reading for the rest of my life."

"Now that would be a real tragedy, Polly," said Noël quite seriously.

"If you girls want to read a really good book that's filled with romance and action too, you have to read *A*

Princess of Mars or even better, the first three Mars books by Edgar Rice Burroughs," said Guy, plunking himself down on the far side of the little group from Noël.

Noël wrinkled her face in distaste, making sure Guy saw it.

Trece laughed. "Your books are even worse than Noël's, Guy."

"Yeah, I saw some of the covers on those books," said Polly. "Four-armed green Martians and red skinned girls with hardly anything on--"

She hadn't finished what she was saying before the girls broke out in a fit of giggling. All except Noël, who thought books were too serious a subject to laugh about, even when they included Guy's ridiculous interests.

"You guys are so immature," Guy said, disgusted. "What's on the cover is only what the artist thinks the action in the book is like. Of course a picture of a four armed Martian is going to look stupid, even I'll admit that! But if you rely on your own imagination while reading one of his books, Edgar Rice Burroughs is such a good writer that he can make you believe in the most unlikely things." He shrugged and leaned back on his hands. "Anyway, if you can't even get by a book's cover then there's no hope for you."

"You've got to remember," added Noël, "that a cover's only for selling a book. A publisher is going try and make it as splashy as possible to get people to buy the book. It doesn't matter if it doesn't show anything from the story."

"That's right," said Guy, looking over to Noël in mute surprise. Was she agreeing with him?

Noël looked from Guy to the girls and suddenly realized the same thing. She blushed and turned away before anyone noticed.

It was right about then that Polly suddenly spoke up.

"Oh look, I think the parade's finally going to start."

As the attention of the others turned toward the top of the street, Noël raised her eyes to heaven and gave thanks for Polly's quick wits.

As the leading police car slowly rolled down the hill, siren blaring, Noël thought about her reactions of a moment before. Why had she felt embarrassed just because she spoke up in Guy's defense? And why did she feel such relief when Polly diverted everyone's attention from her to the parade? Did anyone even care that she had spoken up for Guy? What did she think it had meant to them? More importantly, what did she think it meant to *her*? Why should it mean *anything*? Frustrated by conflicting emotions, she didn't know which to follow for guidance; her heart or her head. Both seemed useless in figuring out what was going on inside her and the whole problem threatened to make her sick.

Luckily, however, her thoughts were interrupted by Jiff and Mike before they had a chance to become too morbid. Falling from an overhead branch, they hit the ground and rolled across the grass to the edge of a stone wall that ran along the sidewalk. Sitting up with their legs dangling over the edge, they waved to the policeman in the lead vehicle. Then, from nowhere, Don skidded on the slippery grass and thumped down next to Noël.

"Hi," he said, good naturedly.

"Hi," mustered Noël, trying hard to lighten her mood. Guy had moved down to the wall with Jiff and Mike and was cheering with everyone else as Old Glory was paraded past in the hands of a National Guardsman. The boys stood and saluted smartly as the flag passed and the girls placed their hands over their hearts.

Next came the Dracut High School Marching Band playing a slightly off-tune Stars and Stripes Forever. A dozen other groups followed, but if anyone asked, Noël would never have been able to tell them what they were because her thoughts started to wander again. When her attention returned to the parade, it was time for the antique cars to make their appearance. The boys marveled at all their shiny chrome and white walled tires and Jiff began naming the vehicles as if he actually knew their makes and models. "That's a Stutz Bearcat," Noël heard him say, pointing at a wood paneled station wagon.

Next, the town's two new fire engines wheeled into view, spraying the crowds with a light stream of water from their cannons. The boys stood, jumping up and down and begged for more in the hot July sunshine while the girls squealed in feigned shock.

At last, when the first engine had passed, it was replaced by the second and Noël felt something land in the grass beside her. As she reached for it, something else hit her on the head and fell in her lap. It was a tiny package of Bazooka bubble gum and, delighting in her good fortune, the somber mood that had slowly been dwindling within her, vanished completely. Around her, she saw that the others were scrambling to pick up all the gum they could find and all the time calling out for more. But all good things must come to an end, and the truck moved on down the street to dispense its largesse to other eager hands.

To Noël's friends, the climax of the parade had come and gone and, too busy searching the sidewalk and grass for stray pieces of gum, they paid little notice to the blue trolley as it lumbered past with its cargo of laughing children. It was followed by a troop of local horsemen who waved to the already thinning crowds. If there were still those spectators who didn't realize that the event was over, the arrival of the "pooper scooper," a little one-man vehicle that zig-zagged along the street scooping up the horse droppings, must have been a dead giveaway.

Noël had risen, ready to leave when she saw that the boys were still busily looking for gum along the street.

"For crying out loud," said an exasperated Polly, her hands on her hips. "How much gum do you guys need?"

"It's free," someone said with all the cold logic of a twelve year old.

Noël nudged Polly in the ribs and whispered, "Say, aren't we supposed to go over to Jiff's house for his birthday party?"

The expression on Polly's face suddenly changed, as if she'd received a revelation. Turning, she put an arm around her friend's waist and whispered into her ear. "That must be it. The other boys are keeping Jiff busy, while his mother rushes back home to get things ready."

Noël's eyes narrowed and she whispered back, "It doesn't look like they have to try very hard. It's good to see some boys who enjoy their work."

"Not so loud," cautioned Polly. "The party's supposed to be a surprise ya know."

"Let's leave now, maybe his mother could use some help."

"Good idea."

They were going to make some excuse about leaving, but saw it wasn't necessary; just then, all of the boys' attentions were focused on the wall where, theory had it, some pieces of gum may have been lodged between the rocks.

"Find anything?"

"Nope."

"Keep looking!"

"Just check your own section!"

"Hey, here's--nah, forget it."

"Don't say anything if you haven't got anything."

"There it ain't!"

"Huh? What? Awww, cut it out."

After listening to dialogue like that for a while, the girls were more than ready to take their leave.

"Let's get out of here, I think I'm gonna be sick," said Noël, holding her stomach.

Polly laughed. "That's for sure, let's go."

A few minutes later, they turned off Desrosiers Street and into the Jorgenson's lengthy driveway.

Being the nerve center of most of their activity, the Jorgenson's property was regarded by Noël's friends as the best place in the neighborhood to hang out. It had everything: a big, long front porch that had once frequently substituted as a spaceliner making the Earth-Mars run; a smaller, rear porch where Jiff kept plenty of comic books and the latest issues of *Mad* magazine for the entertainment of his friends when they were waiting for him to finish lunch; two apple trees whose sour tasting fruit always made them sick but were perfect for climbing; Mr. Jorgenson's sail boat which was stored deep in the backyard; a ruined chicken coop whose jumble of burned timbers and tree branches provided valuable material for everything from tree houses to sandlot villages; a garage with a sliding panel that could be used as a secret trap door when prisoners needed to make a "great escape;" a swamp that bordered the far end of the Jorgenson's back yard providing an endless menagerie of frogs, skunks, opossums, swamp rats, and wild cats and a whole selection of terrain features such as shrubs, hedges, trees, hillocks, walls and gardens.

Leaving the driveway and stepping into the back yard, Noël and Polly could hear hurried sounds of preparation. A long folding table covered with a brightly colored paper table cloth had been set up in the center of the yard with a small mountain of gaily wrapped gifts piled in its center. Mrs. Jorgenson was there, filling a number of tall glasses with pink lemonade.

"Do you need any help, Mrs. Jorgenson?" asked Polly, walking up to the table.

Mrs. Jorgenson turned, the pitcher still in her hand. "Oh thank you girls, but I think we've got everything under control."

"We?" muttered Trece. Everybody knew Jiff's older sister and brother were away for the summer and Mr. Jorgenson was working at his bakery.

"How's Jiff?" asked Mrs. Jorgenson, craning her neck to see up the driveway.

"The boys are keeping him busy down the street," said Polly, reassuring her. "Don't worry."

"Ah declah," said a heavily accented voice from the basement doorway. "Is that theah Polly Ah heah?"

"Morgan?" said Polly, as she turned toward the sound of the voice. "I didn't know you were here."

"Morgan arrived this morning," explained Mrs. Jorgenson.

"Jiff didn't tell us anything about it," said Polly.

"Ah'm part of the surprise," said Morgan, looking at Noël. "Ah don't think Ah know you."

"This is Noël," said Polly. "You didn't come up last summer so you weren't here when she moved in."

"Howdy," said Morgan, nodding his head.

"Hello," said Noël formally, finding that she liked the sound of Morgan's southern drawl.

"Morgan is Jiff's cousin from Alabama," Polly explained. "He lives in Huntsville, where they build those rockets the astronauts fly."

"Hi Morgan," said Trece and Marie together.

"Hi," said Morgan.

Then, before Noël could discover anything more about Morgan, the introductions were cut short by a cry from the driveway.

"Here comes Jiff!" Don called in an urgent whisper (if that was possible!) Seconds later, he came to a halt by the table. "Hey Morgan," he said as if no time had passed in the two years since Morgan was up last. "Jiff'll be here any minute," he told Mrs. Jorgenson, still slightly short of breath.

"Okay, everybody hide and as soon as I bring him out the basement door jump out with a great big 'surprise,'" instructed Mrs. Jorgenson as she returned to the house. She'd hardly disappeared before Mike, Theo and a handful of Jiff's school chums ran into the yard.

"Quick, hide! Jiff'll be out any minute!" someone warned, sending the newcomers scattering for hiding places.

Distantly, Mrs. Jorgenson's voice could be heard asking Jiff to come into the house for something then Guy's voice saying something about waiting outside. The next thing Noël knew, she'd been knocked from her hiding place behind a large shrub near the driveway. Her head was still ringing from where she lay sprawled on the grass and when her eyes finally focused again, she saw Guy crouching in her place behind the shrub.

"Why don't you watch where you're going?" she said angrily.

"How was I to know--Aw, forget it," he said. "Now hurry up and get back in here!"

Desperately, Noël looked around for some other place to hide but every place was taken. "Move over," she fumed, moving back behind the shrub and discovering too late that there was barely enough room for a single person.

There was no doubt at all that Guy knew she was angry; she made sure of that! Squeezing in beside him, she could tell that he was uncomfortable but she wasn't any happier about the situation herself.

"I need more room!" she growled, gamely snuggling in closer to him.

"You're stepping on my toe," complained Guy, his voice cracking.

"It's your fault, I was here first," Noël replied, hiding her own sudden discomfort quite well. Somewhere, in another part of her brain that wasn't occupied by thoughts of parties and books, she knew the reason for her sudden anxiety, but that still didn't help her understand why she felt that way in the first place. All she knew was that when she was angry, she could hide her weakness so it wouldn't show.

Beside her, Guy moved his foot and shut his mouth.

Time passed slowly and Noël began to find her anger shifting from Guy to Jiff. What was taking him? Her inexplicable anxiety at being in such close proximity with Guy was beginning to become unbearable. She'd become so distracted by her predicament that when the guest of honor finally emerged from the house, she didn't even notice it. Suddenly, the others were up and shouting "Surprise!" and, hugely relieved, she followed them quickly to her feet.

Springing from their hiding place at almost the same time, Guy made his exit with considerably less grace than Noël. Somehow, he managed to trip over his own feet and fell flat on his face with a thump loud enough to be heard by everyone, even over the clapping and shouting.

"What's the matter Guy," said Jiff, "can't wait for the food?"

Noël held her breath and was relieved again when Guy didn't say anything about having to share a hiding place with her. She paused mentally for a moment asking herself why such a revelation should matter?

"Yeah, when do we eat?" Guy replied, inducing general laughter.

Guy was brushing the bristles from his trousers when Noël caught him giving her a dirty look. She gave him a good stare right back, making sure he knew that the whole fiasco was his fault to start with.

Presently, everyone had closed in on the table where Jiff began to unwrap his gifts.

"This one must be from Guy," he said, holding up a mid-size package wrapped in the *Lowell Sun's* Sunday comics section.

"It's what's inside that counts," said Guy from the back.

The chuckling had died out by the time Jiff had unwrapped the gift.

"Hey, thanks Guy," he said, holding up the plastic model kit so the others could see. "It's that model of Superman I wanted."

"Don't lose the tube of glue I put in with it," warned Guy. His mother had given him a dollar for the gift and he'd used his last dime to buy the glue.

"This'll look neat next to my Superboy model."

A few minutes later, after all the gifts had been exposed to the ooohs and aaahs of the partygoers, Mrs. Jorgenson appeared just in time with the cake.

"You kids must be hungry by now," she said unnecessarily while a dozen lips smacked in anticipation of sampling the latest product from Mr. Jorgenson's bakery. (Smothered in creamy frosting, the cake could've fed a small army). Then, with Morgan handing out paper plates and Jiff pieces of cake, everybody helped themselves to a cup of lemonade and went to find someplace to sit down.

A half hour later, the guests drifted naturally into two groups. The boys stood around the end of the table that held the presents, plates in hand and speaking from around mouthfulls of cake or ice cream while the girls sat on the lawn furniture beneath a towering maple tree, their plates balanced delicately on their knees.

"Well, I think he's cute," Theo Agoulis was saying. The other girls giggled, all except Noël. But no one noticed.

"With those freckles and curly hair?" asked Denise.

148

"Yeah," replied Theo, standing her ground. There was more giggling.

"I do kinda like his voice," admitted Polly.

"You too?" said Denise, astonished.

"I didn't say I liked *him*," said Polly hurriedly.

"It's the same thing," teased Marie, munching on a piece of cake.

"Don't go putting words in my mouth," said Polly, blushing.

"Well then, who *do* you like?" demanded Theo.

Polly thought a moment. "Jiff."

The other girls gasped at the revelation. For some reason, it was the first time they'd flirted openly with such thoughts and Noël wondered why it had never occurred to them before.

"I like his blond hair," Marie was saying.

"Noël," said Theo, leaning forward from her perch at the end of a lounge chair.

"What?" said Noël suddenly, looking up and starting to chew on the cake she'd forgotten was in her mouth.

"I said, who do *you* like?"

"I don't like anybody," Noël snapped, surprising the others with the tone of her voice. "I don't know why you guys bother with such silly ideas."

Almost guiltily, Noël noticed the looks of doubt that suddenly clouded her friends' faces. Her intemperate remarks had had the unintended effect of forcing them to consider what they'd just been talking about. Perhaps for the first time in their young lives, they actually began to examine how they really felt and just what was it that had appealed to them about the conversation just ended. She couldn't be sure about the others, but Noël thought it would be a long time before they could trust each other enough to speak so revealingly about some of their most intimate feelings.

Adding to Noël's sense of guilt was the fact that she did indeed "like" someone but it was only after a great internal struggle that she'd come to admit it to herself. She hadn't wanted to believe it but how else to explain the way she felt whenever Guy was around? Desperately, she'd compared her feelings with those of the heroines of her favorite novels: in the company of their beaux, they would be overcome with an inexplicable anxiety, the same as her. But even then, Noël couldn't accept the logical conclusion; the thought of Guy with his comic books and jungle girls, his monster movies and the obnoxious, condescending way he and the rest of the boys sometimes displayed toward the girls made the whole idea just too outlandish. Not for the first time, she dismissed the whole troubling situation from her mind. How ridiculous!

With her conclusions fresh in mind, Noël broke the short silence that had settled over the girls' conversation.

"Anyway, the boys we know are too immature for any serious consideration," she said.

"Yeah, I even saw Jiff and Guy still catching frogs the other day," said Polly, anxious to follow her friend's lead.

"And Don told me he was trying to invent a new chemical with his chemistry set," added Trece.

"Boys are too silly to take seriously," said Theo, surprising everyone.

"Where are they anyway?" asked Marie, looking around.

The table was deserted, only a scattering of dirty plates and empty cups evidence that the boys had ever been there. Then, a sudden burst of muted laughter came to them from the front porch.

"They must be doing something with one of Jiff's presents," suggested Marie.

"Let's go see what they're up to," said Theo, who was always eager to mix with the boys. Getting up, she deposited her things on the table and led the way around to the front of the house.

"You know what Mrs. Jorgenson said to my mother once?" whispered Polly to the others as they rounded the maple tree to the front yard.

"What?" four voices asked together.

"That Jiff was her biggest firecracker when he was born on the Fourth of July."

The others laughed knowingly at that, even Noël.

"What're you guys laughing about down there?" asked Mike, leaning over the banister that surrounded the porch.

"Girl stuff," said Theo as the girls invaded the porch. At the far end, Jiff was sitting behind a card table with the others gathered around him. Bits and pieces of a dismantled Man of Steel lay across its surface and a partially constructed, blue plastic brick wall sat before him. A tube of glue was poised in his hand. "Is *this* what you're doing?"

"Uh--" Jiff was at a loss for words, not sure whether he should have been embarrassed or not. Noël had to smile at his predicament; no one could make a boy feel like he was all thumbs and left feet as easily as Theo could.

"This is a party," Theo scolded. "We're supposed to be having fun."

"We *are* having fun," said one of Jiff's friends whom Noël didn't know.

Theo pursed her lips and dismissed the boy's comments with a coquettish wave of her hand.

"C'mon, let's do something we can all play," said Theo.

"Like what?" Jiff demanded, the tube of glue still hovering in his hand.

"How about a game of fox and hounds?" suggested Marie.

The boys laughed at that idea.

"What's the matter with that?" said Polly, hands on hips.

"We'd slaughter you, that's what's the matter," said one of the other boys.

"How do *you* know?" demanded Trece.

"C'mon, we can outrun you guys any day."

"Wanna make a bet?" It was Theo and somehow, when she made a challenge like that, boys couldn't resist. Noël wondered why she'd never noticed it before.

"You wanna?" asked Jiff to the others.

"Why not?" said one of his school chums, "we'll get it over quick and shut them up."

"Okay, one game," said Jiff, getting up.

Immediately, the two groups burst into general laughter, kidding each other as to who would beat whom.

Ten minutes later, the boys had gathered on the porch steps in defeat. The girls, finding it difficult to keep the smiles from their faces, stood around them in a semi-circle.

"Another game?" asked Theo.

"Don't push your luck," said one of Jiff's friends. "We didn't really give it our best shot because we were sorry for ya."

"Sure you were."

"Yeah, we beat you fair and square."

"Want a rematch?"

It was the opening the boys were waiting for. "If you insist, but don't blame us if we slaughter ya."

What followed was a blinding series of games in which both sides managed to come out even. (Noël, with growing awareness, noticed how Theo proved the easiest for the boys to catch but the one they took the longest to return to base).

As the afternoon wore on, fox and hounds yielded to other games until Mrs. Jorgenson surprised everybody by reminding them that it was time for supper. Exhausted from a full day of hard play, everyone was happy for the rest and famished for the fat hamburgers and hot dogs Mr.

Jorgenson had prepared for them in the backyard fireplace.

A little while later Noël was finishing her second hamburger when the small contingent of Jiff's school chums bid him happy birthday one more time and started to leave. As they left, they didn't forget the new friends they'd made during the day and even had a wave for the girls. (Noël couldn't help but notice that though they waved to the girls in general, they all called after Theo by name).

After everyone who didn't live in the neighborhood had left, Noël and her friends found themselves sitting on the grass in the Jorgenson's back yard. The long day was finally winding down and before anyone noticed, twilight had arrived and the first stars began to wink near the eastern horizon.

Her eyes closed in delicious relaxation, Noël lay back against the grassy slope high up near the Jorgenson's house. A cool breeze that rose from the swamp below and bringing with it the strong scent of earth and plant life brushed her face. Around her, the trees stirred softly in the gathering dark and crickets began squeaking from the shadows. A feeling of profound contentment settled over her as she sensed the nearness of all her dearest friends and for a few minutes, Noël felt there were no other people on earth she'd rather have been with.

It was an altogether magical moment whose spell no one seemed eager to break.

But it couldn't last forever.

"It looks almost as if the swamp is glowing, doesn't it?" observed Mike, nodding to the rapidly darkening swamp.

"Where?" asked Jiff.

Mike pointed. "Don't look right at it, look to the side and you'll see it out of the corner of your eyes." Jiff tried it. "See what I mean?"

"Ohhhhhh, yeahhhhh--" said Jiff.

"I'll bet it's from swamp gas," said Don with assurance.

Surrendering to her curiosity, Noël lifted herself to a sitting position. She looked out in the way Mike had described and confirmed the effect for herself.

"How do *you* know, Don?" demanded Mike, swatting a mosquito.

"I read it once in a book on UFOs."

"What do they have to do with gas?"

"Nothing," Don replied. "It's just that swamps give off some kind of gas because of the rotting plants and stuff, and the gas glows at night for some reason."

"I don't know about that--"

"I think Don's right," said Guy from where he sat at the top of the slope. Noël hadn't noticed that she'd been lying right beside him. "I read something about that once."

"There goes a bat," said Morgan, pointing to a black speck that wobbled across the darkening sky.

"He's headed for the swamp," said Jiff. "That's where they hang out at night."

"You sure?"

"Yeah," Jiff said. "Peter and Louis and Don's brother told me they went down there one night with a broom and some tennis rackets and they were attacked by the bats and had to swat them away."

"Yuck," said Marie, looking around nervously.

"One got stuck in Butch's hair and they had a heck of a time getting it out," Jiff continued.

Marie and Trece moved closer together.

"I think we'd better be going home now," said Trece suddenly and got up.

"You don't have to go," said Polly.

"Well, I think it's late enough, my mother will be wondering about us," explained Trece as she and her sister retreated to the front yard and disappeared in the gloom.

"They don't like bats I guess," said Mike.

The others laughed lightly, but it seemed strange right at that moment. They were still feeling too relaxed.

"Well, I don't like bats either," admitted Theo.

"Aw, don't pay attention to Jiff, he'll believe anything my brother tells him," said Don.

"He said it was true," Jiff insisted.

"Butch is always pulling your leg."

"I've got a confession to make, fellas," said Polly, bringing her knees up to her chin and hugging them protectively. "Bats give me the creeps."

"Boy, you're easy to scare," said Guy, smiling.

"Well, what gives *you* the creeps?" challenged Noël, taking Guy by surprise. It was one of the few times she'd spoken to him all day.

Guy appeared to think for a moment before replying. "Weird movies I guess."

"Weird movies?" said Noël, skeptically.

"Sometimes, they give me the creeps," Guy admitted.

"Which movies?" Morgan wanted to know. He was almost invisible in the darkness because by now there only remained a thin line of fading pink in the west.

"Well, *Attack of the Crab Monsters* gave me the creeps once," Guy said. "I was alone one night and I had all the lights in the house off. When that part came where the two guys in the row boat pulled up the headless body from the water--well, *that* gave me the creeps!"

In the darkness, Jiff and Mike were nodding; the others just sat as if frozen, the mood created by the falling night had had its effect.

"What else?" Morgan persisted.

"I'm not sure which movie it was, but it was on *Fantastic Features* one night," Guy continued. "There was this scene where some guys are in a huge gravel or dirt pit, it was at night and all of a sudden, the sides started to dribble dirt and pebbles and somchow you knew

155

something was coming. It's kinda hard to explain, but sitting alone in the dark, that scene spooked me."

"Yeah, something like that happened to me too," admitted Jiff. "It was when we went to see *Planet of the Vampires* at the Strand last summer. Remember the scene when the astronauts come out of their graves on that haunted planet? It was in slow motion and they had to rip their way out of some kind of plastic bags. Boy, *that* was creepy!"

"I remember that," said Don, suppressing a shudder.

Even though she knew there was nothing to what the boys were saying, Noël couldn't help feeling distinctly uncomfortable and began to take reassuring glances over her shoulders.

"Ghosts are what scares me," said Morgan.

"There's no such things as ghosts," said Theo, but her voice lacked conviction.

"Ah heard this story once," began Morgan. "It was about this old woman in the back country of Alabama. One night, something woke her up and when she looked out her window, she saw a bunch of men dressed in the sheets of the Ku Klux Klan pulling a wagon with somebody tied up in the back. The next morning, she couldn't find any evidence that what she saw really happened but later, she found out that a tree way out in her back pasture was one of the places the Klan used to hang people at."

Polly gulped. "You mean, she saw the ghosts of the old Klan in her own yard?"

"Yeah," said Morgan, whispering now. "Ya'll see, once, her house was the home of a big Klan judge who died under mysterious circumstances as they say. And later--" The hesitation in Morgan's voice was for real. "--and later, the old lady was found hung on that same tree."

Without even realizing it, the others had begun to draw themselves closer together. They forgot that the house was right behind them or that the rest to the neighborhood was only around the corner of the yard. Right then, they were alone, and surrounded solely by the shapes of their imaginations.

An uneasy silence held sway over the little group. A bat flew overhead and an owl hooted from somewhere deep in the swamp; the sky had become thick with stars, but their weak light didn't help much.

"Did you ever hear the story about the crippled guy?" asked Jiff in a heavy whisper that made everybody jump.

"Why'd you do that for?" said Mike.

"What?"

"Scare the daylights out of us, that's what," said Don.

"What crippled guy?" asked Theo nervously.

Jiff leaned in closer. "Well, the way I heard it, he lived somewhere around here and what he used to do was lure people into his house where he'd murder them and bury their bodies in the woods."

"Why'd he do that?" asked Noël.

"Who knows?" said Jiff, irritated at being interrupted. "Does a crazy killer need to have a reason? Anyway, one night, he caught this guy by letting him into his house for some supper. He usually poisoned the food, but this time his victim woke up just as he was about to get killed. He was younger and stronger than the killer was and got the drop on 'im, cutting off both his arms and both of his legs."

"Yech," said Noël.

"Ugh," said Theo.

"Ooooo," said Polly.

"Gross," said Mike.

"When he was finished, the guy took the body parts and threw them into the swamp. But that's only half the story." Here, Jiff paused for effect. "Later that night, when the guy was going though the house, he noticed that all the crickets and frogs and birds that usually made a racket down in the swamp at night stopped all of a sudden. It was when he went out back to see what was up that he saw him. The crippled guy with his body parts jammed back together, coming up out of the swamp."

"Well, what happened?" asked Morgan.

"Nobody knows. The guy was never seen again. But from then on, whenever the crickets and frogs and things shut up, it meant that the ghost of the crippled guy was coming out of the swamp for somebody to kill."

"I don't know about you guys," said Polly, her voice trembling, "but I'm not sure I like it back here."

By now, Noël saw that she wasn't the only one checking over her shoulder.

"Hey, listen--" And everyone did.

"What?"

"I don't hear anything--"

"It's the crickets," observed Don. "I--I don't hear them."

"Ooooooh Yeahhhhh," said Jiff. "And I don't hear the frogs either."

It was true. The cacophony of night-noises from the swamp below did seem at that moment to have lessened in intensity. Was it only their imaginations? Noël wondered.

Gradually, everyone in the little group had drawn themselves so close together that there was no more room between them. They were nervous, afraid even, but somehow, they felt that staying together was preferable to breaking up. There was an unconscious desire at work, unknown to all, even to Noël, that kept them together there in the dark, a desire that overpowered any urge to flee.

"I think the noise is coming back," said Guy.

"Yeah," said Jiff, straining his eyes to see the crippled ghost that he'd created so vividly that he'd come to almost believe in it himself.

"Mike saw a real ghost once," said Polly, after the scare over the crickets had passed.

"You mean that light he said he saw in the Old House?" asked Theo.

"What about that house anyway?" asked Noël. "Polly told me about it, but she said nobody's ever been there."

"It was owned by an old lady everybody knows was a witch," began Theo, "she lived for nearly a hundred years until she died one night."

"What makes you think she was a witch?" asked Noël.

"Well, she had a black cat--" said Polly.

"'Cause everybody says so," added Mike.

"Anyway," continued Theo, "a year later, the police found a dead hobo in the parlor. They said he died from sheer fright."

Noël leaned back on her hands. She looked over to Guy and challenged him for the second time that night. "You don't really believe all that stuff do you?"

It wasn't so dark that she couldn't see Guy start. Noël smiled. She could guess what was going through his mind. Should he say what he really believed or stick to the old stories he and his friends had made up years before when they didn't know any better? For a moment, she felt a twinge of pity for him but it soon passed. He had to grow up some time and she would see to it that it was sooner rather than later. But then, what did that matter to her anyway?

For his part, Guy seemed to struggle for a moment, wrestling with the choice of supporting his friends or siding with Noël. "Of course I don't believe it," he said at last, shocking Mike and Polly. Belief in the story of the old witch had been a cherished memory from the old days when it was only he and Jiff in the neighborhood, before Don or Mike or Noël had moved in. "There's no such things as ghosts; or witches for that matter."

"Then what was the light I saw?" said Mike; he was two years younger than the others and still inclined to believe in the supernatural.

Guy shrugged. "I don't know. But there must be some kind of explanation."

"How often do you see this light?" asked Noël.

"I only saw it once," admitted Mike. "But I don't really look out for it. If I did, maybe I'd see it more often."

"How come no one ever went to check it out?" asked Noël. "Weren't you curious about the light?"

"Are you kidding?" said Polly. "Didn't you hear what Mike said?"

"Well didn't you hear what Guy said?"

"I say we go and explore it," suggested Guy. "But we need to plan it perfectly."

"Noël has a plan," said Polly, suddenly fearless.

"I do?"

"Remember? You mentioned something about it once."

"Oh, yeah," she turned to the boys. "I thought, what if Mike checks out his window every night until he spots that light again. And when he does, we can go to the Old House the next day before any clues disappear. Maybe we can figure this whole thing out."

"It sounds like fun," said Don.

"It sounds scary," said Theo.

"I'm for it," said Jiff.

"Me too," said Guy.

"Ah only hope Mike spots the light before Ah have to go back home," lamented Morgan.

"Are you kids still out there?" said a voice from right over their heads, scaring them all half to death. It was Mrs. Jorgenson, speaking from an open window. "I think it's late enough now, kids. Jiff and Morgan have to take their baths."

With real reluctance, they all stood up and moved out to the front lawn, now bathed in the yellow glare of a streetlight. Goodbyes were said and the little group broke up and headed their separate ways.

After that night, the summer drifted by in numberless, lazy days; all filled with fun and laughter and small adventures. For Noël, it was a particularly satisfying season with days spent in the nearby woods and playing with her friends in their new-found sense of togetherness, almost as if they were a new kind of family.

Meanwhile, the evenings were a dreamland of soft breezes, sweet scents and twinkling stars. Noël loved those quiet moments spent alone in her own back yard with only the fireflies for company or in the window seat of her room curled up in a fleecy nightgown with the moon in her face. At times such as those, it seemed she could never be touched by any problem or anxiety.

But she was wrong.

Near the end of the summer, on a day when the afternoon was just giving way to evening, Noël was walking through the tall grass around the house, picking the occasional wild flower and hoping to scare up a firefly or two. She found one and began to follow its erratic course around to the front of the house. She was so intent on not losing sight of the insect that she almost missed the dark figure standing near the front gate.

Startled at the unexpected sight, she stopped and determined that it was a man; a man wearing a hat and coat, even though it was still too warm for outer clothing. Any other detail about his physical appearance, including his face, was impossible to determine due to his having his back to the sunset. Briefly, the thought that she should be afraid entered her mind, but the reassuring sounds of her mother moving about indoors made her feel safe.

"Hello," the silhouette said.

"Hello," Noël replied, moving forward. "Can I help you?"

"You can if this is the residence of Vincent Archambault."

"He's my father, but he's not in right now." She was careful not to advance within the range of the man's reach, although he didn't seem at all threatening. "My mother's home though--"

"That's quite all right, young lady," said the man, holding up a hand. "It's your father I'd like to speak to. Do you know when he might be back?"

"An hour or so--"

The man brought up his arm and Noël could just barely make out the glow on the face of his watch. "Don't think I can wait around." He lowered his arm and Noël noticed for the first time that he carried a briefcase in his other hand.

"My father ought to be here around eight o'clock."

"That's okay," said the man. "Can you just tell him I was in the neighborhood and dropped by?"

"Sure."

"Thank you," he turned to leave then stopped. "Oh, and don't tell your mother anything about my being here. Just your father, okay?"

Noël was startled at the request but managed an "okay." The man touched the brim of his hat and disappeared up the street, leaving Noël with all the old fears and doubts she thought she'd long since banished. Then she realized that the stranger hadn't even mentioned his name.

Overhead, a shooting star streaked briefly across the heavens and Noël remembered how in ancient times, it could be interpreted as a sign for good or ill. But which, she wondered, did it portend for her?

The Old House

CHAPTER TEN

In which Guy looks for spooks but discovers instead something about himself

Nick Tropoli was marching at the head of the small column of space troopers as they hacked their way through the thick Venusian jungle. Up ahead, completely hidden from sight, was his second in command, John Moore, acting as point man for the force. Though Nick did not expect any kind of trouble as Venus was an unpopulated planet, there may have been survivors from the crashed alien space ship.

He looked over his shoulder at his tired, sweating men and grinned. They were the best the Inter Planet Space Force could offer and he had full confidence in their abilities.

Then his smile faded.

Immediately behind him marched Jane North. He didn't like the girl coming along on the whole mission, let alone this exhausting trek. The men believed it bad luck to have a woman on a mission and Nick was inclined to go with their instincts.

On the other hand, not only was Jane keeping up with the others, it had been her idea to find the crash site by using the ship's heat detecting probe. Nick had thought that there would not be any heat left, since the crash was at least a week old, but gave it a try anyway. It was the only way to make the girl shut up. His mistake. When the idea worked, she used it to constantly needle him and the crew. He shook his head. At least she let him stay in charge.

Gateway to the Future
by Guy DeMonde

Guy usually loved Halloween, but this year he was miserable.

First, it had rained all day, soaking everything and ruining he and his sisters' paper trick or treat bags. At one point, Trece's bag had burst open spilling her treats all over the ground and they lost a valuable half hour trying to find them all again. Next, he found himself stuck with having to chaperone his two little brothers around the neighborhood. Finally, no matter how much he tried telling himself that this would be his last year for trick or treating, (any longer and his height would give away the fact that he was getting too old for the holiday), deep down, he still couldn't help feeling like a fool.

And as usual, Noël was at the bottom of it.

Earlier in the month, she'd decided not to celebrate the holiday, deeming herself too old for trick or treating. By doing that, of course, she'd put everyone else on the spot, Guy included.

So he was miserable when he should've been excited. The problem was, he knew Noël was right.

Who knew? Maybe he would've called it off this year himself, but after Noël's declaration, pride wouldn't allow him to follow her example. He knew it didn't make any sense; that he should be independent enough to do what he wanted no matter how it looked to anyone else--but then he'd remember the fragrance of her hair that time at Jiff's party when they'd been squeezed together in the shrubbery. And when that happened, he got a little thrill down his spine that he was altogether unable to explain-- oh! He just couldn't stand Noël sometimes! He hated the way she always seemed to get his thoughts all mixed up until he didn't know if he was coming or going!

Angry, he shook thoughts of Noël from his mind and determined that he was going to have fun this Halloween night no matter what.

And if all went according to plan, that shouldn't be hard to do at all.

As soon as he could dump his brothers and complete his own rounds of trick or treating, he was scheduled to rendezvous with Jiff and Mike for their long planned revenge on Jonas Rondeau and Walter Lamont, two homeowners in the neighborhood who refused to cooperate with Guy and his friends during the year.

Both men wouldn't let the neighborhood kids cut through their property and whenever a ball would stray into their yards, wouldn't let anyone in to retrieve it.

Guy, Jiff and Mike had planned their revenge as far back as the summer when they'd buried a dozen eggs down in the swamp behind Jiff's house. Tonight, they'd dig them up and hurl them onto the well manicured homes of their nemeses.

But first, Guy had to get rid of his brothers.

"Okay you guys, it's time to go home," he said.

"Oh no, we're just starting," pleaded Joe, the four year old.

"Just starting," echoed Lou, his younger brother.

"Your bags are full and you'll be eating candy for weeks."

"I want more!"

"Want more!"

"I said you've got enough stuff, now c'mon," Guy said with all the authority he could muster. When he used that tone in his voice with them, it usually worked and a few minutes later, he'd deposited them back home.

With his brothers disposed of, Guy spent the remaining time until nine o'clock doing his own trick or treating (and struggling at each succeeding door with a growing sense of embarrassment). Despite his best efforts, by the time he'd finished and joined his friends beneath the streetlight in front of Jiff's house, he wasn't in a good mood.

"Is that you, Guy?" called Mike, squinting through the yellow cone of light.

"Who d'ya think it is, Tuesday Weld?"

"Okay, okay, ya don't have to be so touchy just because you had to take your brothers out instead of coming with us," said Mike through his hobo makeup.

"The Monster Man?" said Jiff, looking him over.

"What about it?" demanded Guy, not exactly thrilled about having to wear the same costume for three years in a row (his mother was an expert at extending the life of his wardrobe, but sometimes she went too far).

"Again?"

"So?"

"Oh, he's just kidding," said Mike, "let's get going before it's too late."

If anyone had been watching, they would've only seen a Monster Man, a hobo, and a pirate preceded by the beam of a flashlight as they headed across Jiff's yard toward the swamp. Minutes, later, having located the place where the carton of eggs had been buried, the three conspirators exhumed it and soon found themselves positioned behind a row of pine trees across the street from the home of Jonas Rondeau. A single dim light illuminated the back door and a jack o'lantern sat on the milk box.

Jiff patted Mike on the back and he and Guy watched him cross the street and make his way stealthily to within reach of the carved pumpkin. In a flash, he'd taken the jack o'lantern and hurled it into the street, smashing it to pieces. As Mike dashed back to the safety of the trees, the others covered his retreat with two expertly thrown eggs that struck the side of the house. Then, hidden in the shrubbery, they waited for a reaction, but none came.

"Okay then, three more," whispered Jiff. "On three." The others nodded tensely. "One, two, three!" At the final word, three eggs left three hands and thudded loudly against the house. "Bullseye!" cried Jiff.

"I got a window," crowed Mike.

"Mission accomplished," said Jiff. "Now it's Walter's turn."

Like three commandos, they made their way up the street. They passed through the Therrien's and the Cardova's yards until coming to the Caron's back yard. There, facing the rear of the Lamont's house, they were hidden in the deep shadows created by the Caron's home which had been darkened against trick or treaters. The situation proving perfect for the conspirators, Jiff once again handed out the eggs.

"On three," he whispered, wasting little time. The three boys spread out along the stone wall that bordered the Lamont property and held back their throwing arms. "One, two, three!" Again, the triple sound of thuds rang in the night. Quickly, Jiff handed out the remaining eggs saying "Fire at will!" This time there was only a single hit.

"Shucks, we must've overshot," Jiff lamented.

"I wish we could see what we *did* hit," said Mike.

"I guess we'll find out tomorrow," said Guy, surprised that he wasn't feeling more elated at the night's adventure.

"I think I ought to be getting home now anyway," said Jiff.

"Yeah, me too," agreed Mike.

"Okay, I'll see ya tomorrow," said Guy. "Hey Jiff, don't forget to take the egg carton with you."

"What do you think I am, stupid?"

Later that night, Guy sat before his bedroom window.

Behind him, Joe and Lou slept in the big bed. It was a pain in the neck to have to share the room with them, but Guy had no choice about that; glad at least to be able to fit in everything of his that was important.

His single bed was tucked in the corner opposite from his brothers'. Next to it was a high, drawered bureau that was reserved for his exclusive use. In its bottom two drawers, he managed to cram all non-essentials (such as clothing) freeing up the top two drawers for more important things like his comic book collection and writing materials.

Propped between the bureau and his bed stood a wobbly bookshelf he'd made himself from scrap wood. On its rough planks sat well thumbed volumes of Edgar Rice Burroughs, Maxwell Grant, and assorted science fiction authors (extra space was at a premium). A second shelf hanging on the wall over his brothers' bed held his set of classic Universal monster models: Wolfman, Dracula, Frankenstein, King Kong and the new, glow-in-the-dark Hunchback of Notre Dame (Guy hated the effect and it scared his brothers). Lately however, Guy found his interests shifting from the supernatural to the scientific and a second bureau in his room had become dominated by military hardware such as Huey Cobra Attack Helicopters and futuristic vehicles like the Jupiter II and the alien saucer from the *Lost in Space* and *The Invaders* tv shows. What other wall space that was still available in the room was given over to pin-ups of Spider-Man, the Fantastic Four, Thor, and the Avengers torn from old comic books.

He heard the big bed squeak and saw Lou shifting his weight. He turned back to his writing. He was sitting at a tiny desk shoved up beneath one of the windows in the room trying to work a little on his biggest project: a science fiction novel. He'd been writing stories and sending them out to magazines with no success since the fourth grade until finally giving up. The paperback was the trend of the future anyway so he decided it would be a more economical use of his time to concentrate on that market instead. Some days he was excited about his work, being greatly satisfied with it and at others, he'd read the same lines and think them terrible. Just now, he was in one of those moods and crossed out a paragraph he'd written only that morning.

Frustrated, he rested his chin in his hands and watched as the season's remaining insects dashed themselves against the window screen. Because of the glare of his desk light, he was unable to see anything outside. It was only then, after he'd turned it off, that he first noticed the signal coming from Mike's house next door.

Mike had been watching out for anything strange that might happen at the Old House ever since the summer but had never seen anything worth reporting. But now, Guy saw the shade in Mike's window being lifted and lowered in rapid succession. It could only mean he'd spotted something; or had a message of equal importance.

Quickly, Guy made sure his brothers were sound asleep then pushed the desk aside, lifted the window screen and eased himself out onto the shed roof. Replacing the screen, he was careful not to lower it all the way lest he lock himself out. Jumping lightly into the backyard, he climbed the fence and carefully lifted himself onto a trash can beneath Mike's bedroom window. From there, it was easy to clamber onto the overhang for the basement door and reach up for his friend's extended hand.

"What is it?" whispered Guy after his friend had pulled him inside.

"Ssshhh," hissed Mike, a finger to his lips. "I saw the light!"

"You did?" Guy turned to look out the window, but could only see the dark silhouette of distant trees. "Where is it?"

"You have to wait a minute, it's not too regular," whispered Mike. "I think the reason I couldn't spot it before was because of the leaves in the trees. But now that most of them are bare--there it is!" he finished, pointing.

Guy squinted and at first couldn't see anything; but then he saw it. A twinkling yellow light that bobbed around the dark bulge on the horizon that he knew had to be the Old House.

"See it?" Mike asked.

"Yeah," replied Guy, not daring to take his eyes away for fear of not being able to find the light again. Although it was fun to imagine what it might be, he'd never really believed the Old House was haunted; but seeing that ghostly light, he couldn't help feeling a chill run down his back and the short hairs rise at the nape of his neck. Then, almost to his relief, the light went out.

In silence, he and Mike waited for it to return, but it never did. "I guess it's gone for the night," concluded Guy.

"Now do you believe in ghosts?"

"No," Guy said with as much confidence as he could muster. "There must be an explanation for it, and we'll find out what it is tomorrow, just as we planned. It'll be Saturday, and everybody should be able to go."

"We have to go to church tomorrow," Mike reminded him.

"Right after church," Guy replied firmly, forgetting for a moment that the day after Halloween, All Saints Day, was a holy day of obligation. "We'll get the others and put the plan into action."

"I don't know," said Mike shakily. "That light gives me the creeps."

"Don't worry about it," Guy reassured him. "Meet me in front of Jiff's tomorrow morning; I'll tell Polly to get the girls and then go after Don. And don't forget to pack a lunch, we'll probably be gone all day."

Mike nodded and helped lower Guy from the window.

The next morning, Guy and Mike were sitting on the stone wall at Jiff's house when the milk truck from Shaw Farm pulled up alongside them. There was a jingling of bottles from inside and a moment later the milkman, in his pinstriped coveralls, stepped out the rear and deposited six quarts in the milk box on the Jorgenson's porch steps.

"Hey fellas," he said on his way back to the truck.

"Hi," they both said together.

"Got any ice today?" asked Mike, getting up.

"Sure, c'mon around back."

Guy rose and followed Mike to the rear of the truck. Inside, there were stacks of wooden crates filled with bottles of milk, orange juice, and cream among which rested chunks of clear ice. The ice helped keep the merchandise cool until the milkman could complete his rounds.

Tearing out some paper towels, the milkman scooped up two pieces of ice and handed them to Guy and Mike.

"Thanks," they said, sucking on the ice.

The milkman touched the brim of his cap, got in behind the wheel and moved down the street to his next stop.

By the time they'd finished their ice, the wall in front of Jiff's house was lined with the other members of the day's expedition. Only one person was still missing.

"What are we waiting for?" asked Theo, the latest to arrive.

"Jiff," everybody said at once, clearly impatient.

"He's always the last one," complained Polly.

Guy shrugged his shoulders.

"I think it's because he likes to make everybody wait; to show that he's in charge," said Noël.

It was a suspicion that had crossed Guy's mind more than once. But something he'd never admit aloud. After all, Jiff was his best friend wasn't he? It'd be disloyal to have such thoughts about him wouldn't it? But then he'd remember the times Jiff had abandoned him to go swimming at the Foisey's (but on hot days, could he really blame him for that?) or how sometimes he wouldn't come to the door when Guy called him even though Guy could tell he was only in the next room. Resentment as always, began to build up inside him at the memories but strangely, it wasn't aimed at the obvious target but at Noël for being so perceptive. Frowning, he looked at her out of the corner of his eye and couldn't help feeling admiration for her. Deep down, and so far buried within himself that he wasn't even aware of them, tiny tremors that warned of a coming earthquake began to rumble, but before they had a chance to make themselves apparent, Jiff came out.

"It's about time," said Mike, "we've been waiting out here forever."

Jiff was munching on an apple and trying to stuff his lunch in his jacket pocket. "I couldn't help it."

"Well, let's get going," said Don. "It's almost lunch time for cryin' out loud."

Thrilled with the prospect of mystery and adventure, they made their way down the street while all around them brown and yellow leaves, driven on the cold breeze, drifted earthward and gathered in thick carpets along the road. Although gathering streaks of clouds threatened to turn the day into an overcast one, the sun was still shining warmly, holding temperatures up. A perfect November day, it was Guy's favorite time of year when the uncomfortable heat of summer had given way to the cool of autumn.

Reaching the end of the street by Noël's house, they crossed the fence and entered the field beyond. The trees on the other side stood naked and black against the sky and the air seemed filled with their creaks and snaps as they bent in the stiff wind. They passed through fern alley, where everything was brown and dead until, reaching the foot of Lookout Hill, they made their way to the top. There, they had their first good look at the Old

House. It was still standing where it had always been; all gray and lonely.

"Well, there it is," said Jiff, unnecessarily.

"It doesn't look any different," observed Polly.

"I don't know," said Mike doubtfully.

"C'mon Mike, it's the same as it always was," said Don.

"Except now we know that it's not empty," said Guy.

"You think there's something in it?" asked Theo.

"Yeah, ghosts!" said Mike.

"Not some*thing*, some*one*," said Guy, ignoring Mike.

"Then we'd better make sure we stick with our plan," Noël reminded them. "We take our time, keep as quiet as possible and speak only in whispers."

"Right, if there *is* someone hanging around that house, there's a good chance they're up to no good so we don't want to give ourselves away," continued Guy. "If we know about them before they find out about us, it'll give *us* the advantage."

"What kind of advantage?" asked Mike.

"You know," said Jiff. "Either we can decide to stay and spy on 'em or skeedaddle out of there."

"You think there might be trouble?" asked Don.

"Maybe."

"If there *is* anybody over there, they're probably there to scare off anyone who comes around snooping," said Noël coolly. "It's the oldest trick there is, but it still makes sense."

For the second time that day Guy found himself agreeing with Noël. It *was* the oldest idea in the book, but that didn't mean someone wasn't going to keep on using it.

"Okay," said Jiff, shading his eyes and looking out over the woods below the hill. "Can anyone see a good place to start out?"

The tangle of trees and thorn bushes that lined the foot of the hill in the direction they needed to go seemed impenetrable.

"If we can get through this stuff and over to that line of pine trees," said Guy, pointing, "it should be easy to make our way to the house."

"Good idea, there's less ground clutter beneath pine trees," said Jiff. "But that still doesn't make getting through these thorn bushes any easier."

"They look a little thinner through here," said Don, carefully holding open a space between two shrubs.

"We'll have to double over for about twenty yards but it looks okay to me," said Guy.

"Well, there's no other way," said Jiff. "Don, you take the point, let us know if you spot anything out of the ordinary."

Don nodded and stepped into the forest.

"Guy, you take up the rear," continued Jiff, stepping down to the opening in the bushes, "and everybody else remember, be as quiet as you can."

After Jiff had disappeared into the thicket Mike and the girls followed. Guy brought up the rear and somehow wound up behind Noël, who seemed to be enjoying the whole adventure enormously.

Slowly, the seven youngsters wound their way through the dead and crinkly underbrush as quietly as they could (but not very successfully). As the morning wore its way on to noontime, the sun gradually became obscured in thin wisps of cloud and by the time they reached the green line of pine trees, the blue sky had become a solid slate-gray. Within the line of trees, a thick cushion of pine needles afforded them a means of making their final approach to the house as soundlessly as possible. When they at last reached the far end of the forest, they were delighted to find a scattering of tiny snowflakes falling all about them.

But just as the little group had reached the last of the pine trees, Don's sudden reappearance from farther ahead brought them to a stop.

"What is it?" asked Jiff.

"We've reached the end of the forest," said Don, jerking his thumb. "There's a street on the other side of those bushes."

"Okay," said Jiff, "everybody be extra quiet while we move up to the road."

"I'll check out the house," said Guy.

Then, as silently as they could, the seven friends covered the rest of the distance to the line of shrubbery bordering the road. There, they spread out in a line and crouched down so they couldn't be seen from the other side.

From his position on the extreme right end of the line, Guy had a perfect view of all his friends as they peered with varying degrees of success through the shrubbery trying to catch a glimpse of the Old House. It was just like the old days when they used to play army, he thought, except this time, it was sort of real.

Guy looked over to Jiff who was supposed to give him the signal to cross the street. But to catch his eye, Guy had to look past Noël who was right next to him in line. And seeing her just then, it occurred to him that she was really quite pretty. Again, he remembered the way her hair had smelled at Jiff's party and then, for the first time a whole new thought entered his mind: was he actually becoming attracted to her? Suddenly, for no reason, he found himself afraid and his mind quickly began reaching for a reason why there could never be anything between them: there was almost nothing they could agree on and the cold and aloof airs she sometimes put on infuriated him.

So preoccupied had he become with his thoughts that it was with difficulty that he finally noticed that someone was calling his name.

"Guy--Guy!" said Noël in a loud whisper.

Guy blinked and realized with horror that he'd been staring at her the whole time!

"Guy!" Noël was saying. "Jiff's giving you the signal!"

It was with greater relief than Guy had ever felt before that he rose and plowed through the bushes in front of him to the road on the opposite side. There, crouching behind a telephone pole, he noticed some bleeding from several cuts made in the passage. In his desperation to get away, he never even felt the thorns that had slashed his hands. *How long had he been staring at Noël?* he wondered. Had she noticed? He hoped desperately that she hadn't.

Whispering from the bushes behind him helped force the worrying thoughts from his mind as he remembered what the others were expecting of him. Looking around, he was surprised to discover the presence of other houses nearby: he'd always assumed the Old House stood alone out here. But he could see now how it really was. The Old House sat on a large lot at the top of a hill while the other, smaller, homes in the neighborhood were situated almost out of sight well below the crest.

Checking carefully in both directions, Guy crossed the street and peeked in the mailbox at the end of the driveway. It was empty, a good sign. If it hadn't been, it would've been an indication that the house might not be as deserted as it looked. Emboldened, he crept up the rutted driveway that bent around to the rear of the house. He was happy to note that it was bordered on either side by rows of heavily overgrown hedges that were choked in weeds and festooned with wild grape vines.

As he made his way along the driveway he could see that the house had once been gray in color but that over the long years most of the paint had peeled away leaving the wood beneath exposed to the weather. A large, enclosed porch ran along two sides of the house with many of its small window panes broken. The other two sides of the house, and much of the porch too, was covered with a thick matting of creeping ivy. The house had two floors with what looked like a roomy attic and a kind of cupola in the center of the roof. The cupola in turn, was crowned with an old weathervane fashioned in the shape of a rooster that'd long since been rusted into immobility.

By the time Guy reached the back yard, he was pretty sure the house was empty but felt obliged to continue with his inspection of the property. Like the house itself, the surrounding yard had fallen into complete neglect. The grass lay long and matted and the trees, with their branches sweeping the ground, needed radical pruning. Tangles of shrubbery covered everything, cutting off the property from the sight of any of the neighbors and almost obscuring a broken down tool shed in the corner of the yard. Satisfied that all was well, Guy ran back to within sight of the others and signaled for them to follow.

In a minute, they were all gathered in the back yard, looking up at the rear of the house.

"What now?" asked Mike.

"Let's explore the outside first," suggested Jiff, "starting with that shed over there."

The door of the shed was almost impossible to see with all the plant life that covered it, so it took some effort before they could reach it.

"Padlocked!" said a frustrated Mike.

"And it's brand new too," observed Guy. "See how shiny it is?"

"Then it must mean the place isn't deserted after all," said Jiff.

"Hey, look at this," said Don, waving them over to a grimy window.

The others crowded up to him and peered into the dark and dingy interior. Inside, they could just make out a mess of rusty garden tools and an old lawn mower. Crusty paint cans and moldy brushes lined the shelves against the opposite wall. "Nothing much in here," said Jiff, disappointed.

"I don't like that new lock," said Don.

"That doesn't mean anyone lives here," said Guy, still eager to explore and worried that the others might be frightened away. "There was a real estate sign out front; maybe someone just comes by once in a while to make sure no one's fooling around here."

"Yeah," agreed Jiff. "Look at this place, nobody's living here."

The boys stepped out of the tangle of weeds and vines and made their way over to where the girls had congregated around another curious find deeper in the back yard.

"Look at this," said Theo. She pointed at what looked like a huge mound of brush but which on closer inspection turned out to be two big cages covered over with ivy. "What do you guys think?"

The boys parted the hanging ivy like a curtain and stepped inside one of the cages. They were easily six feet high and about eight feet long.

"I don't know what to make of it," said Jiff, looking around.

"Maybe the owner was a mad scientist and he used these cages to keep the mutants he created in his lab," mused Mike.

"Cool!" said Don.

"No, no, they're meant for dogs," said Noël from outside the cages.

The others were incredulous.

"Dog cages?" said Jiff, but Guy knew Noël was probably right.

"Yeah, like for real big, vicious type dogs," she said. "Dobermans or something."

"That makes sense," admitted Don and everyone else seemed to agree, even Mike.

Approaching the house again, they found a set of concrete steps that led down to a basement door but inspection soon showed that it too was padlocked.

"Looks like we're not gonna be able to explore the inside," said Polly hopefully.

"Oh, yes we are," said Don from another spot along the rear of the house. When everyone turned to see what he was talking about, he grinned and pointed up to a broken window.

"You think we ought to try?" asked Guy.

"Of course, what else did we come for?"

"I don't know about this fellas," said Mike.

"Yeah," said Noël. "This house is obviously watched by someone, it's not deserted like we thought."

"Well, if you guys are too scared to keep going, you can stay here and keep a lookout," said Jiff.

Together, he and Guy knit their fingers together and gave Don a boost to the window.

"Hurry up," said Jiff through clenched teeth.

"I have to get these pieces of glass out of the window frame first," Don whispered. "Okay, it's clear; can you lift me a little higher?"

Guy and Jiff lifted him as high as they could until Don's foot left their hands and he hauled himself inside the house.

Everyone held their breath until he reappeared at the window, safe and sound. "It's okay, I checked around and there's nobody here. Who's next?"

Before either Jiff or Guy could speak, Theo said, "Me," and stepped forward, lifting a foot for the others to grab. Guy shrugged and bent to help lift her up to the window. In seconds, Don had dragged her inside.

"Anybody else change their mind?" asked Jiff.

"Okay, I'll go too, we couldn't trust you boys in there by yourselves anyway," said Noël.

Putting her foot in the boys' hands, she was quickly lifted the few feet to the window sill. Guy had tried to avoid Noël's eyes as she stepped up but now, with her leg propped against him for balance, he couldn't help feeling a thrill at the unintended contact. But more bothersome still, was the strange surge of jealousy he felt when Jiff had reached up to steady her. What the heck was happening to him, anyway?

When Noël had at last been pulled into the window, Guy felt both relieved and regretful at the same time, but had no time to ponder his conflicting emotions before he was needed to help Jiff lift Polly to the window.

"You're next," Jiff told Mike as he brushed his hands together.

"You guys go ahead," said Mike, obviously nervous about the whole enterprise. "I'll stay out here and keep watch."

"You sure?" Jiff asked.

Mike nodded.

"You'll miss the fun," said Guy.

"It's okay."

Guy and Jiff looked at each other, raised their eyebrows and shrugged.

A minute later, aided by Mike, Jiff had boosted Guy to the window. After that, Guy leaned far out and took Jiff's outstretched hand while Mike lifted him as high as he could. Jiff walked up the side of the house like a mountain climber until he could throw himself over the window sill. From there, it was easy for Guy and Don to drag him in the rest of the way.

Inside, it was dark with many of the windows covered against the sun. As their eyes began to accustom themselves to the weak light however, the explorers saw that they stood in a dingy, but roomy kitchen. It was all of an old fashioned design with many outmoded fixtures and the floor was covered with a worn sheet of linoleum that was all wrinkled and lumpy. Over their heads, a single bare bulb was fastened to the center of the ceiling; from it, hung a rotted length of string attached to a short length of beaded cord that dangled from the bulb's collar.

There were two doors in the room and Guy started for one of them.

"That goes to the cellar," whispered Don from where he stood near the other door. "Why don't we check that out last?"

"Okay with me," said Guy moving over to him. "What's out there?"

"Just a big room with the furniture covered in sheets."

Slowly the door was pushed open and they all moved into the next room. Shaded windows let in a feeble gray light that allowed them to make out the dim shapes of various kinds of furniture about the room. There were a few cobwebs in the corners near the ceiling but the room was otherwise tidy. Moving cautiously into the room, no one seemed to want to speak.

Then Polly cried out in sudden fright, bumping into one of the shrouded figures in the room. Leaping back in fear, she collided with Theo who lost her balance and fell back onto a second shrouded object. Confused and frightened, Theo reached out and filled the room with a booming noise that seemed louder than a cannon shot!

Immediately, unreasoning fear, like a prairie fire in the dry season, spread among them as first Polly, then everybody else ran from the room, through a foyer and then into a third room, hiding behind any handy object that afforded the least protection. Dust (disturbed for the first time in who knew how long), flew in the air, tickled noses and threatened to cause an epidemic of sneezing.

"What happened?" asked Guy, his head poking out from behind a sheeted chair.

"It was a ghost," said Polly.

"A ghost ? Are--are you sure?" asked Theo.

"I thought we agreed that there were no such things as ghosts," demanded Noël.

"I never agreed to that," said Theo. "Besides, if there's no such things as ghosts, why'd you run like the rest of us?"

"Noël's right," said Don with some firmness. "There's no such things as ghosts."

Slowly (and not without a certain trepidation), they all emerged from concealment as Guy led the way back into the first room.

"What kind of a room is this anyway?" asked Theo.

"It's a dining room," said Noël confidently, "see?" She knocked on a shrouded piece of furniture, shaped suspiciously like an ordinary dinner table.

"Now who started all that racket before, anyway?" asked Jiff.

"It was Polly," accused Theo, "she knocked me down."

"It wasn't my fault," pleaded Polly, "I thought I saw a ghost."

"Where?"

"There."

Jiff walked over to where she pointed and yanked the sheet off of something tall and thin. "It's only a lamp," he said.

"And this is a piano," said Noël, lifting a dusty sheet to reveal a row of black and white keys. "Theo slammed her hand down on the keyborad when she fell."

"Boy, it's like one of those old routines from an Abbot and Costello movie," said Guy.

"Does everybody feel as stupid as I do?" asked Don.

"Hey, Noël and Guy," called Theo from the room they had all run to for cover, "come over here for a minute."

"Why doesn't she keep her voice down?" grumbled Guy, trying to sound businesslike but more to hide the blush that he felt rise immediately to his face when Theo had mentioned his and Noël's names together.

"It's a library," said Noël breathlessly as she entered the room.

Although the room had only a single window, all the rest of the wall space was filled from floor to ceiling with bookshelves. Noël rushed to the nearest wall and began peering along the shelves while Guy made sure to choose the side opposite from her.

"They're all that dull classical stuff," said Guy.

"What do you mean, dull?" Noël demanded.

"All this stuff was written a hundred years ago," Guy said, suddenly aware that he was sailing into stormy seas.

"So?"

"So old books are usually dull," continued Guy. "Those old guys took ten pages just to say somebody sneezed." Somewhere in the back of his mind, Guy could tell Noël was speechless with mounting rage but couldn't help continuing on his dangerous course. "Did you ever try to read *Moby Dick*?"

"I'll have you know," said Noël, "that *Moby Dick* is one of the greatest works of art in American literary history. But you're probably more interested in the kind of hack writing Hemingway made popular."

"Who's he?"

If the room was any brighter, the others would surely have seen Noël's face turn red; as it was, Polly (seriously misreading her friend and speaking entirely too cavalierly) only said, "Well, we lost those two, they're never more content than when they're at each other's throats."

Noël was still lecturing him, but Guy wasn't listening, he was more concerned about what Polly had said. Was his relationship with Noël (or whatever you wanted to call it!) that obvious? Had something happened between the two of them that others could see but not themselves? Remembering the note of flippancy in Polly's words, Guy only hoped that whatever the others did see, they'd dismiss as nothing to be taken seriously.

"Let's keep exploring," said Theo, bored with Guy and Noël's exchange.

The remainder of the ground floor consisted of a large parlor and in a few minutes, the storm in the library having subsided, everyone was ready to move upstairs.

At the top of the stairs, the landing opened into a good sized sitting room and beyond that, a master bedroom at the rear of the house and two smaller bedrooms in the front. Back on the landing, Polly noticed that the stairs continued upward. "Where do those stairs go?" she asked, pointing.

The others drifted back one by one.

"There's a door up there," observed Guy, "so it must go to the attic."

"Then what're we waiting for?" asked Jiff as Guy started up the stairs.

Reaching the top, he opened the half size door a crack and peeked into the drafty room on the other side; a flutter of wings from somewhere inside indicated that pigeons had found their way in before him.

"Well, what're you waiting for?" asked Jiff, crowding him from behind.

Guy pushed the door open all the way and stepped up into the attic. In another minute, everybody else was with him and the pigeons had made a hurried exit through one of the broken windows up near the peak of the roof. The rest of the attic was disappointingly empty. Guy and the others gathered at the window in the front of the house and looked out over the way they'd come. Far out across the pine forest, they could make out Lookout Hill in the distance.

"Seems funny to look at things from this direction," said Don.

The others agreed.

All, that is, except Noël.

"Hey, where's Noël?" asked Polly, looking around.

"I'm up here," her voice said, but nobody could see where it was coming from.

"Where?" asked Polly.

"In the widow's walk," came the voice distantly.

"What's a widow's walk?" asked Theo.

"Over here," said Guy. He'd followed the sound of Noël's voice and found himself standing by a wooden ladder that led upward through an opening in the roof. Possessed by the spirit of adventure, he started up the ladder without a second thought and, reaching the top, discovered too late that there was only room for two in the cramped space of the cupola.

Noël had looked over to see who was coming up but when she saw it was Guy, quickly looked away.

Guy noticed the movement but said nothing. If she wanted to stay angry about their argument downstairs that was fine with him. But as much as he would've liked to return the frosty attitude, he couldn't. Instead, he found himself enjoying this little moment alone with her.

"Things sure look different from up here," he said after finding some of the houses on Desrosiers Street way off beyond the woods and fields that stretched out directly below them.

"Mm," was all Noël seemed able to muster, but Guy decided she wasn't being rude, just preoccupied. He followed her gaze and saw that she was looking farther off to the right where the hill upon which the house sat sloped downward and into a more urbanized part of town filled with tenements and shops.

But by the way she was staring, Guy knew that Noël was seeing something other than streets and houses.

"Hey, what are you guys doin' up there?" called Jiff from the bottom of the ladder. "Other people want to go up too."

"We'd better go down," said Noël, speaking for the first time since Guy had joined her.

"Yeah, sure--but Noël--look, before we go back, I want to say I'm sorry," Guy said, wondering where that had come from!

"Sorry for what?" asked Noël, looking as if she suddenly realized that there wasn't much room in the cupola for even two people.

"For getting you upset downstairs," explained Guy. (It was the strangest feeling; it didn't seem as if he was doing the talking, but somebody else!) "I really didn't mean to criticize things that way."

Noël stood frozen for a moment, as if not knowing what to say; then, just as she was about to speak, she was cut off.

"Well? Are you guys comin' down or what?"

Guy, increasingly uncomfortable with the whole scene, was only too glad to take advantage of Jiff's impatience and escape down the ladder. To his relief Noël, who came down immediately behind him, seemed uninterested in pursuing their interrupted conversation.

After everyone had a turn in the cupola, they'd made their way downstairs again and Don suggested that they finish exploring the house by checking out the cellar.

A few minutes later, they were all peering down into the dark basement. A set of rickety wooden stairs vanished in gloom half way to the bottom.

"Anybody want to go first?" asked Guy, kiddingly.

"Don wanted to go so bad, let him lead the way," said Theo, giving Don a nudge.

"I don't mind going first, but I need a light."

"There isn't any," said Guy. "You'll have to go by what's coming in from the cellar windows."

Don grunted in disgust but led the way down the stairs anyway.

As they descended the stairs, their eyes gradually became used to the dim light that filtered in from the window at the bottom. Although overgrown weeds outside the window and old, dusty bottles inside conspired to keep out as much light as possible, they eventually reached the basement's earthen floor. Everything smelled of mold and damp and the rafters overhead were filled with drooping cobwebs that the girls were sure crawled with spiders. As a result, every few minutes one of them would screech in terror and disgust placing everyone's nerves on edge.

"Will you guys cut that out?" scolded Don, trying to concentrate on his next step.

They passed among heaps of broken furniture, a massive plaster covered furnace, a rusty oil drum and dozens of decomposing cardboard boxes. And everywhere there were the tiny droppings of mice and maybe cats.

But finally, as the saying goes, all good things had to come to an end (although the girls claimed they'd be brushing cobwebs out of their hair for the rest of the week) and, reaching the far end of the cellar, Don turned and declared the house completely explored.

Thoroughly satisfied with the day's work, everyone felt the expedition had been well worth the effort and agreed that the house wasn't haunted after all, even Polly.

"Mike'll be glad to hear that!" joked Guy.

"Gosh, I almost forgot about him," said Noël.

"And our lunches," added Theo. "I'm starved."

"I'd like to take one last look at the library before we go," said Noël.

"Maybe we can get Mike to come in with our lunches and we can eat in the dining room at the same time," said Don.

"That's a great idea!" said Jiff heading for the stairs.

A few minutes later, while Guy and Noël were browsing in the library and Theo and Polly were clearing a place in the dining room for lunch, Don and Jiff had coaxed Mike back to the window.

"Are you sure it's okay in there?" Mike was asking as he handed up one of the lunch bags.

"Of course, now are you gonna come in or not?" said Don.

"I—" But Mike had no time to finish as a sound came from the front of the house.

"What's wrong?" asked Jiff.

"I heard something," said Mike. "Wait here."

He disappeared around the corner of the house while the others looked at each other. Suddenly he was back, skidding around the corner and obviously scared to death.

"Someone's here!" he said. "A car just drove up and I think they're gonna go inside!"

"Quick, hide," said Jiff as he and Don ducked back inside the house.

"What's the matter?" asked Polly from the dining room.

"Someone's coming, we have to hide!" said Jiff.

"Are you sure they're coming here?" asked Guy, coming into the kitchen.

"That's what Mike said."

"Quick, in the cellar," said Jiff, "there's no time to get outside." Then, like a small herd of elephants on the rampage, everyone dashed for the basement. When they were all safe behind the staircase, Jiff called from the door. "Everybody ready?"

"Yeah, hurry up and close the door."

They heard the door close shut as Jiff clumped down the stairs to join them. Tense minutes passed as their ears ached to pierce the enfolding silence. Finally, they could hear the unmistakable sounds of footsteps in the kitchen, then the cellar door opened and they all held their breath. A bright beam of light stabbed the darkness and swept the stairs, but whoever it was at the top didn't follow it down. He merely fiddled with something just near the entrance and then closed the door.

"That must've been the light Mike saw from his room," whispered Don.

"Ohhhhh yeahhhhhh," hissed Jiff.

Gradually the sound of footsteps fell away and after waiting for what seemed hours, they all moved out from their hiding place and inched up the stairs. Jiff pushed the door open a crack and looked into the kitchen.

"Hey, you guys; are you there?" It was Mike's voice coming from below the window. "The coast is clear, the guy's gone."

"Mike says it's okay," said Jiff. "C'mon, let's get out of here."

After their close call, it didn't take long before everyone squeezed out the window and were again gathered outdoors.

"C'mon, let's go home," said Jiff and began leading the way down the driveway, but when they'd almost reached the street, a sudden noise from the direction of the house froze them in their tracks.

"Someone's still at the front door!" whispered Jiff. Behind him, the others stood stock still like a line of statues.

"And we're stuck out here in the open like sitting ducks!" added Don.

"I know a place in the bushes over here we can hide in," said Mike. "That's where I was before."

"Okay, everybody follow Mike," whispered Jiff, "and for gosh sakes, be quiet!"

Step by step, they began backing away from the front of the house until they'd retreated beyond the corner, out of sight of whoever was at the front door. Then, more quickly, they all dashed for Mike's hiding place.

But once there, their courage began to return.

"I'd sure like to see who it is that's been shining the lights in this place all these months," said Guy.

"Me too," said Jiff. "Let's see if we can move up enough to see around the corner of the house."

"I'm scared," said Theo.

"Me too," said Polly.

"Stay here, you don't have to come," said Guy.

"I'm going," said Noël, suddenly moving ahead of the boys.

But the thick bushes and overgrown trees with their tangled branches made it impossible to move both quickly and quietly and so they weren't able to reach a point from which they could observe the intruder before they heard the sound of a car door being slammed shut. A moment later, the engine started.

Moving closer, they could just see a big blue car as it pulled out from in front of the house. Suddenly, Guy heard Noël gasp and dash from cover.

"Noël, are you crazy? What do you think you're doing?" cried Guy as he and the rest of the boys followed her to where she'd stopped at the end of the driveway.

Dust still lingered in the air as they all stood in the street and watched as the car disappeared over the crest of the hill toward the town on the other side.

"Noël--?" said Guy, but stopped what he was going to say when he saw the look in her face. It was the same one he'd seen when they were in the cupola and she was looking off toward that unfamiliar part of town.

"Maybe I am crazy—" Guy heard her say, so low that he wasn't sure he'd heard it at all.

CHAPTER ELEVEN

In which Noël joins Guy for a walk in winter

February 9, 1969: Spent the entire morning in the kitchen with Maman today. There wasn't much else to do as it was bitterly cold outdoors. We baked four apple pies, "the way Memere used to do it," as Maman says. Rolling and kneading our dough, peeling the apples, and placing the hot pies fresh from the oven on the back porch. We talked about this and that and generally caught up on what we'd each been doing the past few days. It isn't often we get to do that, just Maman and I, and I've learned to appreciate the times that we do. But later, when Maman had gone and I'd fetched a book to read (*Jane Eyre*), I felt depressed and no matter how hard I tried, I just couldn't concentrate on my reading.

I've thought about it often in the last few months and no matter how I turn things over in my mind, I can't escape the conclusion that these feelings are the result of what I learned when we explored the Old House last autumn. I've tried hard to find any other reason and to avoid recording my conclusions down in this diary, but I can't put it off any longer.

I remember the day perfectly: the sky was gray and it was snowing lightly. We'd explored the whole house (except the basement) and reached the attic. I found the ladder leading up to the cupola and when I climbed it, found a wonderful view spread out for miles before me. But it was when I turned to the west and saw all those streets and houses of a part of town that should've been strange to me that I realized that it wasn't at all. In fact it was familiar, like I'd seen it before! I'm afraid I must have stared for a while because I'd completely forgotten that Guy was in the cupola with me. The important thing however was that I recognized the neighborhood! It was the one I found myself in that night I followed Papa from the burning church!

But that wasn't all.

What I never told any of the others, even Polly, was that later on, when we were hiding in the bushes outside, I recognized the man who'd come to the house while we were there and who later drove off in the blue car! He was the same fellow who spoke to me last summer asking to speak to Papa! I didn't know what to think and for a long time, I'm afraid I was often so distracted that even Polly and Theo noticed. It took me weeks to control my thoughts enough to think clearly about those events. What did they add up to? What did it all mean? What was the connection between my father and this stranger? And why didn't Maman seem to know anything about it? Unfortunately, my imagination has been able to come up with possible explanations, but I still don't even dare believe them let alone write them down. My suspicions seem so preposterous that I can't even bring myself to mention them to Maman. What if I were wrong? I just couldn't bear the thought of being the person to hurt Maman in any way. Instead, I've decided to keep an even more wary watch than ever, distasteful though it may be. It's all like the kind of mystery I always wanted to have when I was little and reading Wilkie Collins novels, but now when faced with the real thing, it doesn't seem like so much fun.

I think I'll quit writing now. These last few lines have gotten me depressed again. I wish it were summer again--

Noël was curled up in bed with a thick comforter wrapped snugly around her legs. Outside, the snow that had begun to fall the night before was still coming down and the whole world it seemed, had been buried under a thick blanket of featureless white. Now, as the storm seemed to be winding down, howling winds took over, whipping the snow into curtains of dancing flakes and piling them into deep drifts that walled in buildings and snaked through open fields and highways. Outside her window, the trees had become a tracery of white ribbons and the streetlights, deceived by the mid-day gloom, still burned yellow.

But with all of the storm's activity outdoors, everything was silent. The heavy snowfall muffled every sound from the rumble of the occasional snow-plow to the cries of children at play. In fact, if it hadn't been for a loose pane in her window, Noël could easily imagine that she was the last person on earth, much like Mary Shelley's creature in the novel she was reading. (By coincidence, she'd just come to the part of the story where Frankenstein's monster, amid freezing temperatures and giant cakes of floating ice, found himself exiled to the North Pole). Shivering suddenly, she rose and went to the window.

Earlier that morning, when she'd been awakened by the sound of Dracut's emergency siren, she'd been in a much better mood.

Although the wail of the siren meant no school for her friends in the neighboring town, it didn't necessarily mean that Lowell would follow its example but it usually did, and this time had been no exception.

Like everyone else who heard the Dracut siren, Noël rushed downstairs to the kitchen radio and held her breath until the school cancellation announcements confirmed that there would be no classes that day for St. Louis. (Actually, Noël didn't mind school that much, but if she had a choice of going to classes or spending the day reading well, there was no contest)!

A cold draft at the window almost drove Noël away when she spied someone outside moving slowly across the street. She shook her head and smiled: what was Guy doing out in weather like this? From the looks of his determined steps, she guessed he had a definite goal in mind and whatever it was, it must have been important because everyone knew how Guy didn't like the cold.

On impulse, Noël put her book aside, pulled up the window sash and then the outer storm window. Immediately, she was met by a blast of cold air that swept into the room and sent the curtains rolling aside like the parting of the Red Sea. Snow-flakes struck and melted against her tingling skin as she leaned from the open window.

"Guy!" she called over the sound of the wind. "Guy!"

So much effort had it taken for Guy to make his way in the storm, that it took him at least three full steps before he could manage to stop his forward momentum. Then, holding his hand over his eyes, he looked up to Noël's room.

"Where are you going on a day like this?" she called.

Guy motioned with his hands that he couldn't hear her and began to come through the gate. Noël thought that it was a good thing it was already slightly ajar, because with the depth of the snow, he'd never have gotten it open.

Making his way through a deep drift that had formed in the yard, Guy finally hauled himself beneath Noël's window. Looking up, he said through his scarf, "What did you say?"

"There's a blizzard out there," said Noël with a smile in her voice. "What are you doing wandering the streets?"

Guy shrugged. "It's not so bad; in fact, it's kind of fun." He seemed to hesitate for a moment before continuing, "Besides, it's the day the new comics come out."

Noël groaned playfully (by this time, she'd become used to Guy's fanatical devotion to comic books and had even come to admire him as the only boy she knew who actually liked to read, but the things he wasted his time on still managed to try her patience; between his comic books and monster movies and ridiculous Martian princesses, she still had grave doubts that there was a serious thought in his head.). "You're crazy!" she finally said.

"Okay," he said and turned to go.

Noël watched him retreat to the gate and was inexplicably overcome with a feeling of sorrow for the small figure that suddenly seemed so alone in the desolate landscape around him. The scene helped strike in her a feeling of empathy for Guy that she'd never experienced before. For the first time, she saw him as very much like herself, isolated from others because of his interests, caught in a world of imagination he found difficult to share with anyone else. Now, Noël remembered those times she'd seen him riding his bicycle alone to the library where he disappeared for hours at a time and others when she visited with his sisters and saw him in his room hunched over a cheap typewriter.

It reminded her of the time, earlier in the year, when Sister Antoinette had suggested that the class start a newspaper and asked that those interested stay with her after school. When she joined the others after class, Noël wasn't surprised to find the usual faces: Deni, Terri, Nancy, Sandra, and Dennis Latour, the highest achievers in class. The person she didn't expect to find was Guy, who usually avoided group activities especially those involving such people as Deni and Terri.

Well, after telling them about the new printer the school had acquired that could be used to publish a newspaper, Sister Antoinette excused herself from the group and it was soon decided that they would all meet again at the home of Nancy Bertrois to decide who would hold editorial and staff positions and what features would be included in the paper.

When she went to Nancy's house the following Saturday, Noël really hadn't expected to see Guy in attendance, but he surprised her again by being there. It had created an awkward situation for her: in the neighborhood, she and Guy were friends and frequently did things together but at school, they behaved most of the time as if they were strangers. Noël found it hard to explain, even to herself, but it seemed that her high grades and his average ones kept them apart, just as it created cliques in the rest of the class. Often, the high achievers did things among themselves that the rest of the class didn't participate in. And the funny thing was, when she first came to St. Louis, Noël wanted to be accepted and now that she was, it was with an elite group that unintentionally isolated her from others in the class, including Guy.

Luckily, Guy seemed to understand the division among his classmates, and at that first meeting, didn't act any differently around her than he did around the others. Hovering around the fringes of the group as everyone gathered at the kitchen table, he mostly stood back and listened, making suggestions here and there in the conversation that to Noël's growing irritation, were regularly ignored.

"Why don't we run some fiction in the paper?" Guy had suggested.

"We could do a gossip column," said Nancy.

"Good idea," agreed Deni. "Write that down."

"Maybe we could make it a serial—"

"We could print the cafeteria menu for the coming weeks," said Terri.

"Put it down."

"--it could run as the last feature in each issue, leaving the readers begging for the next installment!"

"What about test results?" asked Dennis.

"I don't think most students would appreciate that kind of stuff being made public," warned Noël.

"She's right, better strike that idea," said Deni.

"Or maybe we can have some poetry—" Guy was saying, rubbing his chin. He was thinking aloud and Noël wondered if he even noticed that the others weren't paying attention. (She had liked the idea of poetry and herself had it included in the paper at a later time).

"I know, a comic strip!"

"What do you think, Noël?" asked Deni. "Got any good ideas?"

When they finally got around to voting for staff positions Deni, of course, was chosen editor, Terri became assistant editor, Dennis took over as copy editor and although everyone else became staff writers, Noël would eventually assume the duties of poetry editor. Guy hadn't received a single vote.

Noël remembered that by the time the business portion of the meeting had been concluded and Nancy's mother had broken out the soda and snacks, Guy picked a little at his food and tried one last time to sell his idea for fiction in the newspaper. Noël had spoken to him briefly and told him of her support for his idea but her time had mostly been monopolized by the others who insisted on including her in all their talk.

By the time the girls started playing records and the dancing begun, Noël noticed that Guy had quietly slipped from the house.

She shivered at the memory, feeling guilty at the treatment he'd received and her own continued participation in the paper afterwards.

Suddenly, the thought of going back to the isolation of her room, to the frigid wastes of the North Pole, wasn't as appealing as it had been only a few minutes before.

"Guy, wait a minute!" she found herself shouting from the window. "I'm going with you!"

Quickly, before she could change her mind, she gathered up her winter things and bundled herself against the cold. Tumbling down the staircase, she flew into the kitchen where her boots sat on the mat by the door.

"You're not going out are you Noël?" asked her mother from where she sat at the table sipping tea. The tone in her voice reflected Noël's own attitude of not three minutes before.

"Oh, ma, it's beautiful outside," argued Noël. "How can you expect me to sit indoors all day and waste it?"

Dashing outdoors, Noël felt as if she'd run into a solid wall of cold air as she made her way toward the foot of the driveway. Guy was waiting there and stamping his feet to keep them warm.

"It's about time," he said when she came within range of his voice.

"What do you mean?" Noël demanded. "I didn't waste any time at all." She was amazed at how quickly the old resentment toward him could begin to rise.

"Besides, there's no rush," she continued. "All you're going for is your old comic books."

As soon as she'd spoken she regretted it. It was a cruel thing to say, especially to Guy, and she'd immediately felt bad about it. His enjoyment of comic books meant nothing to her, but she knew how much he loved them.

"Well, if you don't care, why'd you want to come with me at all?" said Guy, angrily.

"Oh, I didn't mean anything by it," she said in the way of apology. "Which way are you going?"

"This way," Guy said curtly, turning toward the top of the street.

Slowly, they made their way against the wind with Guy in the lead and Noël bringing up the rear.

As they walked, Noël found the going easier by placing her feet into Guy's footprints and when she finally looked up to see what progress they'd made, she discovered that they'd reached Lakeview Avenue. There, she was struck by the complete lack of movement on the street.

"It's almost as if we were the only people in the world," Noël muttered.

The world at that moment, did seem utterly deserted; as if the earth had drifted from its orbit around the sun and fallen into an eternal winter, forever frozen under a blanket of snow.

At last however, a lone car broke the stillness and shattered the illusion. With huge cakes of snow still on its roof and hood, it swerved dangerously up the street.

"Are we going by the highway?" asked Noël, breathless from the exertion of walking through the deep snow.

"Yeah," said Guy.

"But why?" Noël said. "It'll probably be safer across the bridge among the mills."

"That way's too long, besides, we're not going all the way downtown."

"We're not? Then where are you going?"

"Dana's Fruitland."

"I never heard of it."

"It's just on the other side of the Lacroix Bridge on Bridge Street," explained Guy. "It's a neat place."

Noël had her doubts about how neat anyplace named "Dana's Fruitland" could be. "Is that anywhere near the Keith Theater?"

"Right across the street, on the corner, you'll see."

Struggling through the deepening snow, Noël decided to stop talking and save her breath. Soon, they were making their way along the highway and Guy led the way over to the island that separated its two lanes. On the far side of the northbound lane, the land sloped downward to the edge of the river where Noël could just make out white chunks of ice and snow drifting lazily on the slow current and through a fringe of snow-covered trees, the outline of old mill buildings. Beyond the mills, a snowy haze obscured the downtown and even the Lacroix Bridge that she knew spanned the river only a few hundred yards downstream.

A few minutes later, her body warm and accustomed to the cold, Noël followed Guy onto the bridge and began to cross to the other side.

Midway however, Guy decided to linger on the bridge, leaning over the railing and watching the chunks of ice float and crash against the span's granite-blocked pylons.

Watching one of them, it seemed to Noël as if it were the prow of some mighty sea vessel cutting its way through Arctic waters. The illusion proved so real that she had to push herself away from the sight to stop the dizziness that threatened to overwhelm her.

Beside her, Guy spat into the air and watched, fascinated, as the glob of saliva dropped down into the grayish waters below. Then, apparently satisfied, he turned and said, "Come on."

Stepping from the bridge, Noël found herself walking along the tall brick walls of the Boote Mills then past the curious sight of a railroad car that had been converted into a diner. Then, unexpectedly, the drab surroundings of white and gray collided with the incongruous colors of spring and Noël, looking though the glass of a large display window fogged with condensation, could hardly believe she was looking at the reds, greens, and oranges of fresh fruit and vegetables. Surprised at her delight, she looked up at the metal sign that hung over the window: *Dana's Fruitland* it proclaimed.

"Here it is," said Guy unnecessarily, stamping his feet clear of snow before going into the store. Noël followed him beneath the overhang at the entrance of the store (which faced out diagonally from the corner of the building) and stamped her feet too.

Inside the store, she was struck by two things: snow blindness kept her from immediately observing her surroundings and her nose was assaulted by a dozen different kinds of smells at once.

Maybe it was her temporary blindness that did it, but it seemed to Noël that her sense of smell was suddenly accentuated allowing her to divide the different scents in the store into two broad categories: vegetable and tobacco. Slowly, the different smells sorted themselves out: carrots, lettuce, corn, oranges, apples, potatoes, beans, and the earth from which they'd been taken from;

then the tobaccos, (whose brands she was completely unfamiliar with), but of which she knew she could smell at least a dozen different kinds.

Finally, as her sight began to clear, her nose picked a third, more familiar scent. Paper! The kind of paper books and newspapers were made from.

Looking around, Noël saw that a soda fountain with counter and stools stood on one side of the entrance and a row of wooden bins filled with fruit and vegetables on the other. Everywhere in the store's crowded interior, shelves and baskets of dusty groceries competed for room with cases of soda and refrigerated appliances. The overflow of merchandise was piled on the floor and arranged in such a way as to divide the store down the middle with wall space in the back devoted almost entirely to magazines. When Noël spotted Guy again, it was in that part of the store which, on stormy days, was apparently swathed in perpetual darkness.

"What are you doing?" she asked him anxiously; he had a pair of wire cutters in his hands and was busily snapping the copper strands holding bundles of comic books together.

"Getting at the comic books," he said. "Look out." There was an audible snap and a strand of wire sprung loose.

"Are you allowed to do that?"

"Of course, the store owner knows me because I come here all the time," explained Guy. "I can help myself to the comics if I count them up for him first and check them against the shipping list; I'll be done in a few minutes."

Noël had reconciled herself to the waiting when she spied a collection of paperbacks on a spinner rack behind a huge pile of empty boxes and shattered crates. Squeezing past the debris, she reached the other side and emerged before the magazine display area at the rear of the store. Slowly, she turned the rack, its squeaks loud in the close confines of the store. She was just about to turn away in disappointment at its sad collection of paperback romances and westerns when a gasp stopped her.

"Oh, wow," said Guy taking a couple books from the rack. "Two new Captain Future novels!"

Noël frowned.

Guy must've seen her, even in the gloom of the shop, because he seemed compelled to explain himself.

"They're by Edmund Hamilton," he said. "They call him the "world wrecker" because his science fiction stories are always written on a gigantic scale. He doesn't just write about space battles, he writes about exploding planets and dying universes. See?"

He held one of the books out for her to look at. But all she needed to see was the cover, which had some space-suited character blasting a monster with a ray gun while a woman screamed in the background. *Captain Future and the Space Emperor* it read.

"Guy, how can you waste your time reading stuff like this?" she asked, her exasperation overcoming her tact. "I know how smart you are and that you're capable of so much more so why don't you at least try to read more serious books?"

Guy shrugged, taking the book back.

"Because I find the books they make you read in school dull," he explained (not for the first time). "I'd rather read about stuff that isn't possible than about stuff that can happen any old time. I read because it's fun and reading about the real world isn't much fun.

"Besides," he said, turning to the cash register, "I do read more important stuff."

"I know," Noël sighed, "but there are other subjects besides World War II."

"Well, maybe when I get done with all the books I can find on World War II, I'll go on to World War I."

"I guess that's better than nothing," Noël said, wondering why she bothered so much about Guy's reading habits (it was only about the tenth time they'd had the same conversation).

Outside again, they found that the snow had finally stopped coming down. They recrossed the Lacroix Bridge and were half-way down the highway when Noël began to feel some fatigue from the long walk. Gradually, she started to fall behind Guy's more regular pace and was forced to ask for a rest. As morning wore on to noontime, they found themselves at the foot of Dean Avenue, which was blocked by a high bank of snow left behind by a passing snow-plow.

Guy threw himself over the bank of snow and tumbled over to the other side. Much too tired to follow his example, Noël opted to climb over the snow's crusty surface and jump down to the street, but when she landed, it was with a cry of pain.

Guy turned at the sound just in time to see Noël fall heavily to the ground.

"What happened?" he asked running up to her. "Are you hurt?"

"I think I sprained my ankle," Noël said, wondering at what sounded like concern in Guy's voice.

"Try to stand up," he was saying. "Put some weight on it and see how it feels."

Noël tried to stand, winced, and started to fall. If it hadn't been for Guy's hand under her arm, she would've found herself on the ground again.

"It's no use," she said. "I'll never be able to get home by myself; you'll have to go get my mother to come help."

"Are you kiddin'? We could be home in half the time it'd take for me to go back and forth to your house," Guy protested. "C'mon, put your arm around my shoulders and I'll help you walk home."

Noël did as she was asked and together, they struggled through the deep snow for a few more yards then stopped.

"This isn't getting us anywhere," said Guy. "Here, take this, and don't drop it." He handed her his bag of purchases and crouched down in front of her. "Get on, I'll give you a piggy-back to your house."

"You don't have to do that," Noël protested, embarrassed.

"If you want me to help you get home, then do it my way; now c'mon."

Feeling foolish, after all, she was over thirteen years old, Noël wrapped her arms around his neck while his hands took hold behind her knees. A few minutes later, as Guy lowered her on the back steps of the house, she had to admit carrying her piggy-back proved a lot more efficient than if they'd continued the way they started out. She reached out for the railing and handed the bag back to Guy.

Checking the contents, he said, "I hope you can make it inside, 'cause this is as far as I go."

"I'm not completely helpless," Noël protested, hoping no one found out about the episode. Imagining what Polly and Theo would say, she knew she'd never be able to live it down. Nevertheless, she owed Guy something and, swallowing her pride, she extended her thanks.

"Anyway, I appreciate the help, my ankle really does hurt."

"No sweat," said Guy, waving away the bother. "I only acted in the best heroic tradition; would John Carter have done any less for Deja Thoris? Or would Tarzan not have done all he could to rescue Jane from the clutches of Akut?"

Amazed, Noël didn't know whether to blush with embarrassment or flash with anger at Guy's bold comparisons. *What had come over him all of a sudden?* she wondered.

"Don't let it go to your head, Guy," she heard herself saying, quickly cutting off a situation that had every danger of veering off in a direction she wasn't at all sure she wanted to go--at least not yet.

She turned and began to hop up the four steps to the porch door. On the final step, her hand resting on the doorknob, she turned to look back at Guy's retreating figure. She could still feel her blush as it faded slowly from her face, but there was still something inside her that had taken pleasure in being, well--rescued, by Guy and for the first time, she actually wondered how things had turned out for John Carter and Deja Thoris...

Pollard Building

CHAPTER TWELVE

In which Noël falls victim to a practical joke

June 2, 1969: Another school year has ended (well, in a few days anyway) and it's time to look back and decide how it all went. When it began, I remember being a bit nervous because it was going to be the first time that our studies would shift from strictly grammar school subjects to those that we'd be concentrating on when we go to high school.

Although with all my reading I've been exposed to lots of different subjects, this year was the first time I'd taken real classes in literature, American history, and biology in a systematic way. Out of them all of course, I loved literature the best because Sister Alphonse actually led us step by step through such wonderful books as *Huckleberry Finn* and *The Scarlet Letter* for understanding not just pleasure. It was the best class I ever had and the most fun. (Even Guy had to admit that Mark Twain could tell a good story and how smug he was when the reading list included Jules Verne's *20,000 Leagues Under the Sea* and H.G.Wells' *War of the Worlds!*)

The funny thing about our American history class was how Guy revealed a whole new side to his personality that I never really suspected before. Oh, I knew he was interested in history, but I thought that only included World War II and such things, but he knew lots more about lots of different periods in American history. He was raising his hand so often, that Sister Louise stopped calling on him the third week into the school year!

But the subject that turned out to be a real surprise to me was biology. I never suspected that such a dry subject as science could be at all interesting (even when Guy pointed out that *Frankenstein,* one of my favorite books, had a lot of science in it), but when looked upon in the proper perspective, biology was fascinating. As Sister Jeanne told us, the ultimate purpose of science was to help us better appreciate the miracle of God's creation; and biology's in particular, was to seek out the mystery of life itself. Well, we only covered the first half of our textbook and according to Sister Jeanne, we'll be studying the rest after we get to the eighth grade when "we'll be able to handle some of the upcoming material." She never said exactly what material she meant, but everybody knew it was the reproductive system (sex). I know I won't have any problem with it nor any of the other girls in the class, but the boys are just so immature (Guy still reads comic books!) that I hope they teach us separately, otherwise I'm sure I'll just melt in embarrassment.

Looking over what I've just written, I've noticed how often Guy's name seems to pop up. I'm finding myself thinking more and more of him these days which is strange, because it wasn't that long ago when any mention of his name would drive me crazy! Maybe he's matured more than I gave the rest of the boys credit for in my last paragraph--or is it me that's matured? But of course, that's silly! I'm just the same as I've always been.

Noël dropped her plastic token into the cigar box and picked up a tray. It was Thursday, and according to the school cafeteria's weekly menu, that meant chicken salad sandwiches with spice cake for dessert. Most days Noël brought her own lunch to school, but on Thursdays, she made it a point to bring a quarter to buy a meal at the cafeteria. It was a bit of a strain on her budget (she'd only started baby-sitting for the Henderson's a few months before) but then, what was the money for?

She was standing in line right behind Nancy Bertrois and Terri Larose and could tell by their conversation that they were talking about boys again. Noël sighed, not knowing what to feel about a subject that seemed to be taking up more and more of the girls' attention lately. She'd tried once to recall just when the infatuation had begun, but hadn't been successful.

Just now, Terri and Nancy's romantic interest involved Deni Cardolet (someone Noël had to admit was attractive and intelligent, but somehow lacked an element of mystery that would make him interesting; there were no question marks with Deni). Other names that came up from time to time among her classmates were David Claudette and Rocky Fourchin. Generally speaking, Noël didn't care whom the others were attracted to because she herself wasn't particularly interested in anyone. Well, she had to admit that when Guy's name was brought up (which was hardly ever and certainly never in connection with any talk of romance!), she couldn't help feeling defensive. It was sort of a proprietary interest, as if Guy was hers alone to accept or reject as her whims dictated and everyone else better keep hands off! But why exactly did she feel that way at all? Tallying up all the things about him that drove her crazy, she came up with an impressive list, but paradoxically, didn't find them enough to completely dismiss him from her attention.

"Noël, stop day dreaming," said Sandra Reilly nudging her in the back. "I'm dying of starvation and you're just standing there."

Noël moved quickly up to the counter and looked around in embarrassment to make sure no one had read her thoughts. Luckily no one seemed to so she busied herself by filling her tray and moving over to the table reserved for the seventh graders. There, Sister Antoinette was directing traffic and waved her to a seat with the rest of the girls.

At the table, conversation among the students was already quite animated and Noël, slipping easily into the small talk, couldn't help noticing the good humor shown by everyone. And no wonder, there were only a few weeks left until the end of the school year.

Noël stopped talking long enough to start on her meal and, looking around, noticed how easily the talk among her classmates crossed gender lines. Had it been only a year ago, in the sixth grade, when the boys and girls generally ignored one another? It was hard to believe that over the past year, they'd formed mixed study groups (which frequently met at each other's homes after school), shared a portion of the school yard no longer divided between boys and girls and were allowed to pick their own places in class. (Curiously however, the sexes still sat separately at their cafeteria table even though it was no longer required). Gradually, any reticence between the sexes, and even between classmates who'd never really spoken to each other over the years, melted away. Now, as their final year at St. Louis Elementary School approached, they all seemed to feel themselves being drawn closer together.

"How'd you do on the biology semi-final, Noël?" asked Deni from across the table. They'd been talking together for the last few minutes, and Noël was not unaware of the jealous gazes of Terri and Nancy.

"I'm sorry, Deni," she said, swallowing. "What did you say?"

"I asked how you did on the biology test?"

"I got an A+, but it only covered the easy stuff; the hard part will be in the final," Noël replied, trying to sound interested.

"I got an A+ too, but—" Deni's voice seemed to trail off to nothing again as Noël's attention was drawn to the far end of the table where Guy sat with Billy Beaulois and Ricky Poilette. She couldn't help feeling kind of sorry for Guy, because it seemed to her that no matter what he did, he just couldn't mix well with the rest of the class. Of course, she'd noticed a long time ago that his personality was on the bashful, even introspective side and that he preferred going it alone sometimes. Did she really like him, or did she only feel sorry for him?

A spate of giggling reminded her that there was spice cake in her mouth that she wasn't chewing but when she turned to see what the laughter was about, Nancy handed her a piece of paper with what appeared to be two lists of names on it.

"Debbie Flynn is doing a survey," whispered Nancy. "Write down who you like in the class next to your name."

Noël looked at her, then at the paper. All the girls' names were there, and most of them had put down the name of the boy she liked. Of course it was a ridiculous thing to do, but Noël was trapped. To refuse to participate would make her seem a spoil sport to the rest of the girls and to place a name beside her own would open her up to gossip till graduation. Quickly, she came to a decision, wrote down Guy's name, and passed the list on to the next girl.

But she hadn't passed it along fast enough. Nancy, who'd been peering over her shoulder, saw whose name Noël had placed beside her own and passed along the information to Terri. From there, it was only a matter of seconds before all the girls knew. Their first reaction, predictably, was to gasp in disbelieving wonder, then cooler heads prevailed.

"Oh, Noël," said Nancy, "you're not taking this list seriously enough!"

"Yeah," added Debbie, disappointed. "You're supposed to put down who you *really* like."

"Well, you should've told me that before!" Noël replied.

Putting Guy's name down was the perfect solution to the problem; no one could possibly have taken her choice seriously and now, with the mood broken, the list had lost whatever legitimacy it might have had. But then, why did she still feel guilty about using Guy's name? It was a harmless prank, wasn't it? Okay, a bit cruel to Guy, but deep down inside her, something stirred. Feelings that...

Noël gulped hard and took a long sip of milk.

--feelings that she couldn't yet bring herself to consider.

To her relief, further thoughts along such dangerous lines were cut short with the ring of the dinner bell signaling the end of the seventh grade's lunch period and the beginning of the sixth's.

Somehow, the remainder of the week passed and Noël was able to get away from the school's gossip (part of which involved just who in the class she really *did* like) for the comforting routine of home and her neighborhood friends. Summer was drawing nearer and the days, growing longer by the hour, allowed everyone more time to spend outdoors. Fridays were especially precious as Noël and her friends, without the need of having to get up for school the next day, were permitted to stay out after dark. And so, a routine had developed in which the girls would find themselves gathered at one another's homes to talk and listen to records in the early evening waiting until dark to play kick-the-can with the boys. (The girls had no clear idea of just what the boys were doing while they

214

were spinning records but were sure it wasn't anything very interesting; Noël thought it peculiar how interests among the boys and girls had diverged in the last year or so until only the long-established ritual of kick-the-can remained).

Just now, it was one of those Friday evenings and Noël had joined her friends over at Polly's. A soft breeze ruffled the curtains in the window of Polly's upstairs bedroom as Theo switched records on the small portable phonograph that sat in the middle of the floor. The door was shut so as not to disturb the rest of the household.

"What're you gonna play next, Theo?" asked Denise Pomerleau from where she lay on the bed. Denise had moved into the neighborhood about six months before and her open, vivacious personality had won her immediate acceptance, especially among the boys. She and Theo had become quite close friends, much as had Noël and Polly.

"It's a surprise, see if you can guess who it is," Theo challenged.

"Is it a new release?" asked Polly, going through a record box crammed with 45s.

"This isn't twenty questions," protested Theo, pushing the black disc down the spindle onto the turntable. "But yeah, I just got it the other day." Lowering the playing needle carefully onto the spinning record, she sat back and an instant later, the latest pop tune to hit the charts filled the room. "Any guesses?"

"Uh, Donovan," guessed Denise.

"No," said Theo firmly.

"The Monkees," said Polly.

"You're bad," observed Theo.

"You're both wrong," said Noël. "It's the Cowsills' 'We Can Fly.'"

"That's right," said Theo, surprised.

"How'd you know that?" asked Polly.

"C'mon, anybody can tell the Cowsills a mile off," chided Noël. "Just listen to those harmonies."

Polly leaned back against the bed. "Well, I remember a time when you didn't even know who the Beatles were."

Theo and Denise looked astonished.

"It's true," Polly assured them.

"That was a long time ago," Noël protested. "When I first moved here."

"Yeah, remember that?" asked Polly. "We came over here while my sisters were playing Beatle records in their room."

Noël laughed at the memory. "That's right, we climbed up a ladder and peeked in their room while they were playing 'I Want to Hold Your Hand.'"

Life, Noël mused, could be strange sometimes. She remembered that day she and Polly had peaked in on her sisters. It seemed at the time that Anne and Lisette were so much older and farther removed from she and Polly and now, here she was with her friends doing the very same thing. Not feeling all that old, she realized just how young Polly's sisters had really been. It all made her wonder how she'd someday feel about herself looking back on what she was doing now. Slowly, with great deliberation, she took a good look at each of her friends, impressing in her mind the way they looked, so happy, so carefree, so sweetly and vivaciously alive. All of a sudden, she wanted dearly to remember them all as they were right then, to preserve them forever against a future when they might all be changed.

"Yechh," Theo was saying, making a face. "I never liked the Beatles' early stuff."

"Not me, I like everything they've done," said Noël, still sensitive to the fact that a unique moment was slipping away and eager to embrace it before it did.

Meanwhile, on another level of consciousness, Noël was aware that she probably wasn't being very critical about her enjoyment of the Beatles' music, but couldn't help it: she had a soft spot for the very first popular musical group that ever caught her attention. Before the Beatles, music to her had meant only Prokofiev and Strauss, but the talented British foursome proved to her that genius needn't be restricted to a single kind of music; that people of real talent could take any medium and make something grand of it as proven by her latest possession.

"And they keep getting better all the time," she continued, "Just like they say on this record." So saying, she pulled a colorfully designed LP from the paper bag she'd brought with her from home.

Polly and Theo gasped.

"What is it?" asked Denise, rolling over and looking past the edge of the bed to where the others were sitting. Then, she gasped too. "You've got it?"

"How could you afford it?" asked Theo.

"And you didn't even tell your best friend?" said Polly.

"I wanted it to be a surprise," explained Noël, pulling off the cellophane wrapping, and handing the album over to Theo to play. "I asked Record Lane downtown to reserve me a copy and then spent the next two months saving everything I could from my baby-sitting job to pay for it."

"Wow."

"I still can't believe you never told me—"

Despite their awe and delight, none of them by that time had not heard every cut from the Beatles' latest release, *Sgt. Pepper's Lonely Hearts Club Band*. It couldn't be helped, as every radio station in the country had been playing it constantly since it was released earlier in the Spring. But to actually have a copy to play for themselves had been a kind of freedom they could only have dreamt of.

Holding the album sleeve carefully, almost reverentially, Theo slipped the album out and placed it on the phonograph. Meanwhile, the others gathered around Polly as she opened the now empty gatefold sleeve and gazed upon the four uniformed figures inside.

"Aren't they adorable?" sighed Theo.

"I like John the best," said Polly.

"Not me," said Denise, "I go for Paul."

"Who do you like, Noël?" They all looked up at once. It was the second time in a week that Noël had been confronted with such a question.

"They're all good looking," she said carefully. "But I'd rather have a more down to earth sort of guy."

The others said nothing for a moment, looking at each other.

"Well, let's play it," said Polly at last, breaking the silence.

"I want to hear 'Within You, Without You,'" said Denise.

"Anybody ever tell you that you've got weird taste, Denise?" said Theo.

"Put it on 'She's Leaving Home,'" suggested Polly, "I think that's such a sad song."

"Just put it on at the beginning of side two and let it play through," said Noël. "I don't want my record getting scratched while you guys lift the needle back and forth."

The others had no complaints (they liked all the songs anyway) and contented themselves with listening to the music and taking turns dancing to the different rhythms. Unlike the others, Noël liked to close her eyes and let the music dictate her movements (almost like the meditation techniques she'd begun to read about in pop circles). But when at last the time came for 'A Day in the Life,' the climactic song of the album, she opened her eyes and sat back down on the floor. It was exactly the kind of number that convinced her of the Beatles' importance as musical craftsmen. It demanded to be heard and meditated upon rather than danced to.

After the album had been returned to its protective sleeve, Noël stood and excused herself for moment.

When she returned, Polly had a suggestion.

"Noël, do you want to go to the movies tomorrow?"

"We were just talking about it, and decided it'll be fun," added Theo, smiling.

"What's playing?" asked Noël, sitting down.

"*Yours, Mine, and Ours* I think," said Polly. It's supposed to be real fun."

"I've already spent all my money on *Sgt. Pepper's*," said Noël, "but I think I can borrow a dollar from my mother."

"Great, then we'll all meet in front of the Strand tomorrow afternoon at one o'clock then walk up to the Keith together, okay?"

"Why not go straight to the Keith?" asked Noël.

"Denise doesn't know how to get there yet."

"Oh, okay."

The next day, Noël walked downtown and arrived at the Strand shortly before the appointed time. She was puzzled at first when she discovered that none of the others were there but went inside anyway half expecting to find them gathered around the concession stand.

But they weren't there either.

Noël moved over to the velvet rope-line and tried to peek inside the theater itself. Maybe Polly and the others decided to meet at the Keith after all. Trying to catch a glimpse of the interior of the theater, all she could make out through the tunnel-like entranceway was part of the empty screen as it loomed over rows of red-padded chairs.

Puzzled, she began walking back down the long corridor to the street when she almost bumped into Guy who was coming in the opposite direction.

"Excuse me—" Guy began to say, then stopped. "Noël! What are you doing here?"

"I was supposed to meet Polly and the other girls here before going up to the Keith to see a movie, but they haven't shown up yet," said Noël. "What about you?"

"I was supposed to meet the guys here too, but unless they're inside, I think I'm the first one to show up."

"I just finished looking everywhere for my friends and didn't see any of the boys."

"Huh," Guy grunted. "Well, I guess I'll wait around awhile, they ought to be here any minute."

"Yeah, my friends too."

For the next few minutes, they stood around on the sidewalk in front of the theater examining the movie stills and posters in their glass display cases. When that lost its appeal, they moved past the ticket booth and sat down in the corridor leading inside. With their backs against the cool, veined marble that dressed the wall, they drew their knees up and watched other patrons (mostly those their own age) as they passed by.

"I wonder if I got the time right?" said Noël.

"I'm sure I must've gotten ours wrong," guessed Guy. "The guys have never been this late before."

Guy looked uncomfortable and Noël guessed it wasn't because his friends were late. She thought she knew what was going through his mind (he was probably wracking his brain to find something to talk to her about) and decided to help him out.

"Well, next year will be our last at St. Louis," she said. "We'll be seniors then."

"Yeah, and after that high school," said Guy, perking up immediately. "It's hard to believe things have moved so fast." .

"Too fast," agreed Noël. "It feels as if I just got here."

"How long has it been? Only three years?"

"Seems like it ought to have been ten, huh?"

"I--I wish it'd been ten," Guy said, but Noël missed the hesitation in his voice.

"Thanks Guy, we have had a lot of fun and it would've been so much better if we'd had all that extra time."

"What high school are you going to attend?" asked Guy hurriedly, nervous whenever Noël became too friendly.

"Actually, I haven't given it much thought," admitted Noël. "And you?"

"Probably St. Joe's downtown," said Guy. "I wouldn't want to go any place too far; having to rely on a bus and stuff would just be a pain in the neck. But you mean the Academy hasn't got a lock on you yet?"

Noël shrugged; St. Louis Academy was a girls only high school located over the cafeteria building at the elementary school.

"I like the Academy and St. Louis, but I don't think I want to attend a school that small," said Noël. "They only have about a hundred students there you know. On the other hand, St. Joe's has about five hundred; not too big and not too small." She hesitated a moment then added, "Besides, you won't want to be the only bibliophile at St. Joseph's would you?"

"Nah, I'd welcome having at least one person with some taste around," said Guy gruffly in what Noël suddenly realized was an obvious attempt to hide a fondness for her. But it was the fondness of one childhood friend for another; Guy doubtless felt the same for everyone on Desrosiers Street.

"Thanks," she said, "I think that's the nicest thing you've ever said to me."

Guy, who'd been looking at the passersby when he spoke, turned at her reply and their eyes met. Staring at each other for what seemed an eternity, Noël could plainly see that it was a struggle for him to keep from looking away.

221

"Well--maybe it's because--because of some of the reading I've been doing lately," said Guy, blinking hard.

"What reading?"

"You've heard of *The Lord of the Rings* haven't you?"

"By J.R.R. Tolkien."

"That's right," continued Guy more easily. "I read the trilogy last year and saw an advertisement in the back of the books for other fantasy novels so I went down to Prince's and bought *The Worm Ouroboros*, that's by E.R. Eddison, and that was great too. Ever since then, I've been doing some experimenting with different authors; I'll admit most of it's been tough going, but real rewarding. And do you know what the most ironic thing of it all is?"

Noël shook her head, somehow unable to take her own eyes from Guy's even if she'd wanted to.

"The books I'm finding the most interesting were written in the nineteenth century, books like William Morris' *Sundering Flood* or William Beckford's *Vathek* or George MacDonald's *Evenor*, the same period I always told you made for dull reading."

Noël smiled and leaned forward. "Didn't I tell you?"

Guy smiled too and even laughed. "Maybe what you should've told me was that there were plenty of monsters and fantasy in some of those books."

"Oh, like bait, huh?"

Then they both laughed, for the first time free of all self-consciousness.

When they'd stopped, Guy continued. "Take *The Sundering Flood* for example. It's wordy I'll admit, and the text is purposely archaic, but the reason for it was that Morris was trying to capture the feel of medieval times. He considered those years as a kind of simpler, golden age. Anyway, if you like older books like that, filled with romance and poetry, you've got to read it."

"What's it about?"

"Well, it may not sound too complicated but it's a story about a young guy who falls in love with a beautiful maiden named Elfhild; the only problem is that they live on opposite sides of a river no one can cross."

"Like a typical fairy tale."

"Right, but like I said, written for adults not kids and the important thing really, is the wonderful mood and atmosphere of olden days Morris captures in the story—what's the matter?"

"I can hardly believe what I'm hearing!" Noël gushed.

Guy shrugged. "I'm man enough to admit when I've been wrong."

"Well, as long as you're making admissions, I'll make one too," said Noël, lowering her voice. "Don't tell Sister Antoinette this, but I thought *Moby Dick* was so slow, I never finished it."

"What?" said Guy with mock surprise. "Little miss bibliophile didn't finish an assigned book?"

Noël shoved him playfully saying, "Don't you dare tell anyone, I've a reputation to think of."

They both laughed again and when Noël at last leaned back to catch her breath, she wondered why things couldn't have been this way with Guy from the beginning? For the first time, without any qualifications, she could admit to herself that, yes, she liked him, and wasn't it neat?

"And how about your writing?" Noël continued. "How's your novel going?"

Guy shifted his weight nervously. She knew he didn't like to talk about his own writing, but just then, she felt that they'd reached a kind of rapport that could overcome barriers that in the past may have seemed insurmountable.

"I've stopped writing short stories," Guy finally said. "I'm concentrating on a novel now; a science fiction novel. My cousin, who's taking secretarial classes, is typing it up for me."

"How do you feel about it?"

"To be honest, I don't really know any more. Science fiction just doesn't do it for me like it used to. I'm leaning more toward straight fantasy these days."

"You're not going to abandon the novel are you?"

"The thought has crossed my mind."

"Well don't do it, at least not before you let me read what you've got first—"

Guy straightened suddenly and turned to Noël, not just his head this time, but his whole body. "You want to what? Read my novel? A science fiction novel?"

Now it was Noël's turn to face away. "Like I said, maybe I was too hasty in judging your reading habits. After all, Jules Verne and H.G.Wells wrote science fiction and for all I know, your novel might be as good as one of theirs."

"Now I know your pulling my leg!"

"It was just a suggestion," said Noël, crossing her arms.

"Aw, I didn't mean it that way," said Guy. "I'm flattered. You can read it if you want to but on one condition."

"What's that?"

"You give me your honest opinion of it, no holds barred."

"You sure?"

"Yeah."

"Well, okay."

Conversation seemed to lapse a moment until Guy noticed the time.

"Wow! We've been talking for a half hour. The show's gonna start in a couple of minutes and the others aren't even here yet."

Noël looked around, dark suspicion beginning to form in her mind. "Guy," she said, "I think we've been tricked."

"Tricked? What do you mean?"

"I think it's my fault," said Noël (how could she tell him about her putting his name down on that silly list at school)? "It all has to do with girl talk at school. Somehow, Polly or Theo must've heard some of it and decided to set us up for a joke."

"It was Jiff's idea to come today, are you saying he was in on it too?"

"There was plenty of time for Polly or Theo to talk with him when we were playing kick-the-can last night."

Guy rubbed his chin, nodding. "Yeah, but that still doesn't explain why they'd pick the two of us to play the joke on in the first place."

"Why not?" challenged Noël, coolly. "It had to be someone, why not us, the two bibliophiles?"

"Why not?" echoed Guy, getting to his feet. "But let's make the joke backfire on 'em and go to the movies anyway."

Noël (who'd been holding her breath for the last five minutes) sighed in relief. "Good idea."

"Great," said Guy. "I'm positive that *Planet of the Apes* is gonna be a real cool show."

Noël didn't say anything.

"What's the matter?"

"Do we have to see that movie?"

"If you don't like *Planet of the Apes*, the second feature is *Island of Terror*, said Guy.

"Guy, those movies are just an insult to people's intelligence," said Noël, her sympathy of only a few minutes before vanishing like the morning dew.

"I thought I'd gotten through to you," Guy was saying. "I thought you'd changed your mind about things."

"*You* getting through to *me*?" said Noël, not knowing whether she should feel angry or insulted. "I thought it was *you* who was finally turning human."

"C'mon, you just finished saying you thought the classics weren't what they're all cracked up to be, if you gave it a chance, maybe you'd find that the same holds true for movies."

"With *The Planet of the Apes*? Fat chance!"

"Charleton Heston is in it," said Guy in the film's defense. "If a movie has a star as big as he is in it, then you know it's not going to be something stupid."

Noël snorted. "Charleton Heston can't act for beans; a piece of wood could do a better job."

"That's it," said Guy, obviously at the end of his rope. "If you can say that about a great actor like Charleton Heston, then you're more ignorant than I ever thought you were."

Noël didn't reply, but just turned around and began walking up the street.

"Where are you going?" demanded Guy.

"I'm not gonna waste my time on trashy movies, I'm going to the Keith to see *Yours, Mine, and Ours*."

"But it's probably already started by now."

"So?"

Guy stood on the sidewalk for a moment, scratched his head, and disappeared back into the theater.

Meanwhile Noël, still seething with an anger she herself found hard to explain (just what was it now that had set her off?), had almost reached the Keith. Everything had been going fine with Guy until they suddenly began arguing over nothing and now--now she was hurt and confused and didn't know what to think of him.

She was going over the distasteful scene at the Strand for at least the third time when she stepped beneath the Keith's marquee. She checked the displays to make sure *Yours, Mine, and Ours* was playing (although to be honest, her mind really wasn't on it) and moved over to the entrance. Because she and her friends usually went to

226

the movies at the Strand and had attended the Keith only a few times, she felt uncomfortable in its unfamiliar surroundings. In fact, she never noticed just how run down the theater seemed.

The whole entrance area was dirty and littered with candy wrappers and old newspapers and the glass display cases on the walls were cracked and grimy. Graffiti adorned the walls too and here and there, rough looking boys loitered about. (Didn't the boys say that they once had a fight with some roughnecks here?)

Cautiously, she stepped inside the theater looking for the ticket window and immediately caught the attention of some boys hanging around the doors. She was surprised when they began to whistle and smack their lips insultingly, but did her best to ignore their disgusting behavior.

"Hey sweet thing," someone said. "You lost?"

"Ain't she pretty with them curls and everything," said another.

"She's so precious, I'll bet she's never been kissed before," taunted a girl's voice.

"Oh, I'll bet she's been around," said someone else.

"How 'bout it, you got a kiss for me, princess?" said the first voice.

Noël began to feel warm and her hands started to shake. She held them together to keep anyone from noticing and joined the ticket line. She was just beginning to calm herself down, when she felt a hand on her shoulder.

"Hey princess," said someone from behind her. "I asked you if you've got a kiss for me?"

Noël spun about in surprise to face a boy at least two years older than she was, acne covered his face and a mop of greasy hair spread over his head. He stank of body odor.

Noël shrugged away from his touch. "Get away from me," she demanded. "Don't you dare touch me!"

"So she doesn't like to be touched," called the girl's voice from somewhere in back.

"It's okay, princess," said another boy who was almost as repugnant as the first. "Nobody wants to kiss Rod's ugly face anyway. But I'll give you your first kiss—" He leaned close to her, almost grazing her cheek with his lips.

Noël recoiled in horror only to find that the boy had taken hold of the waistband of her jeans. She twisted away and bumped into the wall amid general laughter.

"Playing hard to get? I like 'em that way—"

"You stay away from me," Noël warned uselessly and retreated hastily back to the sidewalk. She looked back to see that the two boys were following her and, shaking with real fear, she began to run back up the street. They were still following her when she reached the Strand. If she chose to keep going, they'd catch up to her for sure. Without a second thought, she ran up the corridor to the ticket booth, bought a pass for the show already in progress and plunged into the safety of the darkened theater.

Inside, it was easy to spot Guy. He and the boys always sat in the same place and usually propped their feet up on the seats in front of them. Noël followed the dim aisle lights and threw herself into the seat alongside Guy and sank down as low as she could. In her state of mind, she hardly noticed that Charleton Heston stood naked before a panel of distinguished looking apes or of Guy's sudden discomfort that she should've picked that moment to join him. But something of Noël's distress must have conveyed itself to him even in the darkness because after giving her a single surprised look, he turned slowly away again and concentrated on the movie.

A few hours later, they emerged from the theater, blinking their eyes against the late afternoon sunlight.

They walked together in silence while Noël cast an occasional glance behind them. Finally, his patience at an end, Guy spoke up.

"Well?"

"Well what?"

"What did you think of *The Planet of the Apes*?"

It was the last question Noël had expected to hear and Guy's asking it then very nearly set her off again.

"You think I came back just to watch that..." she hesitated (the movie had turned out to be more intelligent and interesting than she'd expected, but she wasn't about to admit that to Guy) and at the last moment edited what she was going to say. "...movie?"

"Well why else did you come back in such a hurry for?"

"You have no idea, do you?" Noël asked, impatient with Guy's blindness and too proud to explain the whole thing to him.

"What do you mean? If you didn't want to see the movie, why'd you come back then?"

Noël didn't answer.

"Well, if you're not gonna talk to me, then get lost," said Guy at length, giving her a little shove and storming off.

Cast adrift, Noël hesitated. Still afraid of running into the boys from the Keith theater and unwilling to chase after Guy, she decided to make her own way home. Warily, she scanned the nearby sidewalks and saw that they were rapidly emptying at this time of day. Making her way along Middle Street, Noël intended to find the railroad tracks and follow them out to the Ouellette Bridge.

She'd only been walking for a few minutes when, near the end of the street, she came across a familiar name. *Pollard Building* read the words incised in a slab of marble over the main entrance of a downtown office building. Noël thought a moment until remembering that her mother had once told her that was where her father had his office. The realization set her to thinking.

How many years had it been since she first noticed her father's strange disappearances and behavior? Ever since their family had moved to Lowell? And for most of that time she'd spent making up excuses for him in order to avoid having to face the possibility that he may have been up to less than honorable intentions. Suddenly, for the first time, she asked herself what had her father really been up to? Was it some sort of illegal activity? Oh, if only that were it! She could cope with that. It was the awful alternative that she was unprepared to accept: unfaithfulness to Maman--no! She refused to even contemplate such an impossible scenario!

A passerby bumped into her and she realized that she'd been daydreaming. Suddenly, the Pollard Building was in front of her again and on an impulse, she crossed the street and passed through its shiny glass doors.

A receptionist sat at a desk across the lobby from the main entrance.

"Can I help you?" said the woman from behind thick-lensed glasses. The afternoon sunlight streamed through a set of tall windows at almost a horizontal angle, splashing the receptionist's area in rich, yellow light.

"Yes, can you tell me if a Mr. Archambault works here?"

"May I ask who is inquiring?"

"His daughter."

"Well Miss," said the woman, "you ought to know if your father works here or not."

"Actually, I'm not sure if it's this building or another one—" Noël said, trying to sound confused.

"Oh, well then; yes, Mr. Archambault does work here. Shall I ring him?"

"Mr. *Vincent* Archambault?"

"Mr. Vincent Archambault," replied the woman, irritably.

"What company owns this building?" asked Noël on impulse. Her father was supposed to work for Cobalt Blue Technologies; if that company wasn't listed--

"There are a number of businesses in our directory," said the receptionist. "Are you suggesting that you don't know who your father works for?"

"Oh, I know who he works for, Cobalt Blue Technologies."

"They are one of our tenants. Their offices are on the third floor."

Relieved without knowing exactly why, Noël almost didn't catch the receptionist's next question.

"Do you want me to ring your father for you?"

"Oh no, that's all right. I was just passing by and thought I'd like to see where he worked. I've never been here before."

The receptionist merely looked at her.

"Well, good-bye."

The receptionist continued to look over the top of her glasses and said nothing.

On the way home, Noël had completely forgotten about the possibility of being followed and instead occupied her thoughts with worries about her father and frustration with Guy. By the time she reached Desrosiers Street, she had concluded only one thing: that life had grown a good deal more complicated than it'd been only a few years before and that it didn't look like it was going to get simpler any time soon.

CHAPTER THIRTEEN

In which Noël discovers that childhood does not last forever

October 27, 1969: For the first time since I began this diary three years ago, I've begun to feel a lack of interest in continuing to make entries. I guess it's because I've been feeling depressed lately although if anyone asked me why, I'd be hard pressed to point at one single thing. Maybe it's a bunch of things like the kids at school teasing me about Guy. Being in the eighth grade was supposed to be the best year yet at St. Louis (and it should be with all the new subjects and freedoms we've got) but it's just not turning out that way. Somehow, the girls in class found out about the trick Polly and Theo played on me with Guy at the theater (I suspect Billy Beaulois for spilling the beans but have no proof) and have been after me about it since school opened. But all that just doesn't seem enough to explain why I'm feeling so blue lately.

I was reading somewhere that depression is caused by a chemical imbalance in the brain. It would be nice if that was really all there was to it, then I could comfort myself with the thought that things aren't really as bad as they seem. Unfortunately, it would also be too easy an excuse. What I'm feeling is more complicated than that.

Things are changing too fast. I've never been good with time. Especially its passage. I've always found it easier to settle into habit than constantly having to adapt to new conditions. For instance, it was real tough moving here from New York and having to go to a new school. But since then, I've made Desrosiers Street my home and the friends I've made here are like my own family and if things didn't go the way I'd like elsewhere, I always knew that they'd be waiting for me here at the end of the day. But lately, I've seen signs that it might all be slipping away.

Maman says that sometimes, change can be good, that it builds strength of character. I'll be going to high school next year, but I can't see the good of taking on the responsibilities of being an adult if it means giving up my old way of life. I've been stopping at church on the way home from school to pray and I think it helps. At least, I leave feeling better, and not so alone. I've been reading more poetry too; sad poetry I'm afraid. I've been using Guy's old tree platform by the brook and have been retreating there when I get to feeling gloomy.

Noël was standing on the sidewalk along Lakeview Avenue just down the road from her house watching a huge iron ball suspended from a crane, swing slowly from right to left and into a half demolished wooden building. Instantly, the air was filled with the sound of splintering beams and breaking glass. With every swing of that giant ball, a little piece of her heart seemed to break apart too.

It was a late October afternoon and the sky was gray with low hanging clouds. A persistent drizzle had left the world soaked and dripping and even the fiery plumage of autumnal trees was only mushy pulp in the gutters. It was cold, and Noël, Polly, Denise, Don and Jiff stood on the sidewalk huddled in their hats, sweaters, windbreakers, and sweatshirts. None of them was saying much. It was as if the gloom of the day had seeped into the pores of their skin.

There was another crash and the big ball lay buried in the rubble of what had once been Bouchard's Market. It wasn't often that such a spectacular event happened in the neighborhood, and when it did, it usually inspired excited talk for weeks. But there was none of that among the assembled friends. *Did they all sense it like she could?* Noël wondered. That all around them, things were changing too fast, and not for the better? Did any of them suspect that this year would mark a turning point in their lives? Noël looked at the somber faces around her and thought they did.

"I'll miss going to Bouchard's," said Jiff solemnly, his face partially hidden behind the collar of his jacket.

"Yeah, me too," agreed Don.

"It was the only place around where you could still get a bag full of candy for only a nickel," said Polly.

"Yeah, there's no place to get that kind of stuff anymore."

"And they were just about to open their new soda fountain too," said Don, smacking his lips.

"Why are they tearing it down anyway?" asked Denise.

"Mr. Bouchard died and Mrs. Bouchard decided she couldn't run the store by herself," explained Noël, overcoming her lethargy only with effort. She remembered the times she'd come down to buy fried fish for her mother on Friday's and how Mr. Bouchard would let her behind the meat counter to watch him prepare it. Why, she could almost smell it now!

"Really?"

"That's what my mother said."

"I remember when me and Mike went once to buy some candy," said Jiff. "I took all the money I had in my piggy bank, about three dollars in pennies, and we went down and spent every one of them. It took us about four hours to decide what we wanted and Mrs. Bouchard just sat there behind the counter and waited until we'd made up our minds."

"Yeah," said Denise "I remember the time me and Theo stole a Planter's Peanut Brittle Bar from the store; I wish I hadn't done that."

"I'll bet Theo doesn't though," said Don.

"Where is Theo anyway?" asked Jiff.

"Didn't you know?" said Denise. "She has a boyfriend now."

"Why ain't I surprised?" said Don.

"Yeah, she's been fooling around teasing guys for the last two years," said Jiff knowingly.

"I think she's too young to be going around with a boyfriend," said Polly.

"Does her mother know?" asked Noël.

"Of course not," said Denise. "Theo meets him after school and when she comes home, she tells her mother that she's been with you guys."

"What about you, Denise," probed Jiff. "No boyfriend yet?"

"I'm working on it," Denise replied coyly.

"Mike told me once that Theo…"

"Why did Mike have to move, Jiff?" asked Don, switching subjects without a backward glance.

"His father works for a military contractor and they transferred him to Buffalo, New York," Jiff said. "Guy's been writing to him."

"It sure is gonna be quiet around here without ole Mike," said Don, unhappily.

Noël agreed with him. Mike had been an important part of their neighborhood family and she already found herself missing him. Now the day's gloominess, the memories of Bouchard's and the talk of Mike's leaving all combined to suddenly make her eyes water with tears. Quickly, she wiped them with the sleeve of her coat before the others could notice.

"Mike sent me his first letter last week," said Guy, gliding his bike up to a stop at the curb. A wet streak shown darkly up the back of his pale blue windbreaker where the rear tire of his bicycle had thrown up rainwater onto it. By this time, Noël hardly needed the evidence of the *Spider-Man* and *Fantastic Four* comics peeking from inside Guy's jacket to know why he felt the need to ride his bike on such a wet day.

Noël had begun to suspect that Guy felt the same way about the neighborhood family as she did. She couldn't be absolutely sure about it because their relationship hadn't progressed much since that day at the theater. What little warmth there was between them came more from necessity than desire. Their attitudes toward each other were just about where they'd been when they first met: chilly but proper.

Meanwhile, what conversation there had been while watching Bouchard's being reduced to rubble died soon after Guy's arrival. It simply could not be maintained amid the cheerless depression that settled over them when conversation stalled. They all left for home long before the wrecking crew had finished the job, even Don.

Later that day, after supper, Noël and the others began to drift over to Don's house for kick-the-can. There were still a few minutes until dark, (the proper way to play kick-the-can was after dark with only the spotlights on the corners of Don's house for local illumination), so they killed time in the Therrien's basement where Don was just putting the finishing touches on his latest project.

"What is it?" asked Denise.

"A robot," said Don matter-of-factly.

"A robot?"

"Yeah, a robot." Don fiddled with some wires in the back of the contraption and straightened.

It *did* look something like the robots Noël had seen on the more lurid covers of Guy's science fiction novels. It stood about five feet high and whatever mechanism operated it was safely hidden behind a crude skin of cardboard boxes stacked one on top of the other with the smallest at the top. That one formed a blockish head whose face had two tiny light bulbs for eyes. A pair of plywood arms hung on metal rods sticking out from where its shoulders should've been. Peeking out from beneath the edge of the bottom-most box, Noël could just make out a pair of old roller skates.

"Does it work?" asked Noël doubtfully. She still remembered the cardboard wings Don had designed the first time she'd met him.

"Of course it works," said Don indignantly. "It's gonna win me first prize in the science fair at the Lowell Technological Institute."

"You're in that?" asked Noël, impressed.

"Yeah, now watch." Don picked up what looked like an ordinary transistor radio and extended the antenna. He flicked one of the switches on its face, which Noël noticed had a good deal more buttons on it than a regular radio. Instantly, the robot swiveled on its hidden roller skates.

Everybody gasped in surprise.

They'd all become used to Don's wild schemes in the years they'd known him, but never had any reason to believe that he'd actually do something important. For the first time in their lives, the suspicion came to them that they might be in the presence of someone who was going to do big things. But if asked what sort of things, they'd have had no idea.

"What else does it do?"

"Watch," said Don as he began playing with his controls. Moments later, the robot suddenly jerked forward, turned, spun its arms up and down, traveled the length of the basement and came back again. All the while the display was accompanied by a myriad of colored lights that lit on and off including the pair of bulbs set in its head for eyes.

"Wow, Don, so that's why you wanted the transformer from my erector set," said Guy when he came in. "You're gonna win for sure."

"Of course I am."

"Hey, when are we gonna start playing?" asked Jiff from the basement door, unimpressed.

But they should've stayed inside with Don's robot for all the fun they had playing kick-the-can.

Everybody was cranky.

Don argued with Jiff, Guy with Noël, Denise with Polly, Trece and Marie with each other and when Theo finally appeared, she spent more time flirting with the boys than concentrating on the game. To make things worse, everything was still covered with rainwater and in no time, everyone was soaked, cold and miserable. Then it began to rain again and what interest there still was in continuing the game, petered out into desultory inactivity. One by one, the participants left for home until only the drizzly rain was left behind, turning the world into a wet, cheerless place.

A week later, it was still raining.

Oh, there'd been a couple of days during the week when it looked as if the sun would come out but hardly anyone noticed.

The gloom that seemed to have settled over the neighborhood still lingered with no relief in sight and Noël could see only endless days more of gray dreariness ahead. She tried to look forward to the bright spots of Thanksgiving and Christmas, but even the holidays didn't offer the comfort that they once did. She hardly imagined herself enduring the endless months of autumn if every day was going to be as depressing as these past few weeks. And the latest event in the neighborhood that had plunged it into even deeper depths of melancholy hadn't helped any.

It was still raining, but just enough to keep everything wet as Noël and the others huddled in the street in front of Mrs. Ginot's house. The only spot of color was from Don's yellow raincoat and the only movement was that of six pall-bearers as they maneuvered a casket out of Mrs. Ginot's front door and into the rear of a waiting hearse. Noël could see the shiny, rain-beaded casket through the hearse' curtained windows and hear the subdued voices of the members of Mrs. Ginot's few surviving relatives. The rear door was slammed shut and the black suited men began dispersing to other cars along the street.

"How did Mrs. Ginot die?" asked Theo brushing away damp curls.

At first there wasn't a reply. No one felt like talking. "In her sleep," said Trece. "When her daughter found her in bed, she was lying there as peacefully as if she were only asleep."

"Well, I'm glad she didn't have to suffer," said Polly, sniffing.

"Anybody know how old she was?" Don asked.

"My mother said she was eighty-seven," said Jiff, the most serious Noël had ever heard him.

There was silence again as they watched the line of cars pull away from the house and crawl down the street toward St. Therese' Church in Dracut. By the time they'd reached the end of the street, they were gray in the heavy mist of rain. Suddenly, the old house looked more empty than ever; like it had died too.

"She was a nice old lady," said Denise.

"Remember how she used to let us eat all the apples we wanted from her orchard?" said Guy. "Anybody else would yell at kids, or tell them to get off their property."

"Yeah, and I remember once how I asked her if I could have some old wood from her garage to build a go-cart, and she said to take all I wanted," said Don.

"Remember how she used to fill bags with pears and give them to everybody in the neighborhood?" said Polly.

"I do," said Noël. "It was only a few weeks after I moved here that we went over to get some."

"That's right," said Polly. "And other times she'd invite us over for tea just as if we were her friends."

"Her house was so neat, jammed with all kinds of furniture, knick-knacks, doilies, and old rugs."

"And it always smelled faintly of lilacs."

"The smell of lilacs will always remind me of her," said Noël.

There wasn't much more to be said after that and anyway, the rain began to fall harder obliging everyone to seek shelter indoors. The boys went over to Jiff's to help set up the latest object of his interest, a ten gallon tropical fish tank (there was no doubt that keeping tropical fish would soon become the rage among the boys). Meanwhile, Noël, Denise, Theo, and Polly retreated to Polly's house to play records and do some homework. Trece and Marie went home.

As the afternoon wore on, the clouds overhead grew thicker and the rain continued to fall until by the middle of the afternoon, it had become almost as dark outdoors as night. Even the streetlights had flickered on.

Later Noël, feeling some overwhelming need to be alone, made some excuse to leave her friends. At first, she thought she'd go up to her own room and spend the balance of the day there with a good book, but as she reached the end of the Rich's driveway, she couldn't help but look over at Mrs. Ginot's house. When she saw that no light shone from the kitchen windows, she was suddenly overcome by a feeling of sorrow and loneliness. She changed her mind about going home and instead, crossed the street to the old farm house.

The rain started to fall harder as she stepped into Mrs. Ginot's yard and the sound of it falling, running and dripping from the house and trees seemed louder than a roaring crowd.

Suddenly feeling alone in the world, Noël walked slowly along the side of the house toward what used to be a carriage house but which Mrs. Ginot had ended up using as a garage. Her old 1948 Ford had long since disappeared but it had been replaced by a sail boat that Mr. Jorgenson had been working on part-time for the last two years. When Noël reached the doorless garage, she could see the boat inside, sitting on a wooden frame with its bow poking out into the rain. All about it there was the sadness of a beached whale or a grounded eagle (she realized that she was mixing her metaphors, but just then she didn't care).

Noël sighed heavily and rounded the garage. Now she faced a gentle slope of land as it ran downward through the orchard to the swollen brook below. Everything looked as it always had: overgrown and unkempt with here and there, a piece of rusting farm equipment and by the time she'd come out from behind the house, her feet were soaked through with rainwater from the uncut grass. Finally, through the haze of falling rain, she found herself before the towering form of the old pear tree. It bore no fruit at this time of year of course and its leaves had been reduced to brown mush on the ground beneath it.

She looked up at the sky through naked branches and let the raindrops fall heavily onto her face. It felt good just to be standing there, alone with the rain. Then, opening her eyes again, she noticed something about the tree she'd missed on first approaching it. Studying its branches more carefully, she saw that many of them seemed all black and brittle. Reaching out, she snapped a twig free and broke it between her fingers with a dry snap. Thoughtfully, she gave the branch it came from a good shove and the whole thing fell away easily from the trunk. With growing surprise, she realized that the tree was dead.

And then she remembered what Mrs. Ginot had once told her, (was it only a few years ago?) that the tree would continue to bear fruit only "as long as I'm alive..."

That long month of October did at last come to an end, but November offered little relief. Rain continued to fall with monotonous regularity and Noël and the others shifted their activities accordingly. Then one day, during a break in the raining when the streets had a chance to dry, Noël phoned Polly to see if she'd walk up to the library with her. But Polly had gone to visit a school friend and would be gone for the balance of the afternoon.

Still intending to go to the library, Noël decided to see if Theo wanted to go. She found no one home at the Agoulis' but looking up through their backyard and across Mrs. Ginot's property, she saw Jiff, Guy and Don in the Jorgenson's backyard down by the swamp. Deciding that perhaps Guy would walk up to the library with her, she walked back up the street and entered the Jorgenson's yard.

Down by the tree line, near the swamp, the boys were gathered close together, laughing and pointing at something Jiff was holding in his hands. When Noël saw

Don look up, she waved him a greeting, but the reaction she received from the boys was hardly what she'd expected. Instead of waving back, Don nudged Jiff and said something to Guy.

Then something funny happened.

Immediately, the boys' hilarity ceased and, while Don approached her, the others began vigorously tearing up a magazine they'd been looking at and throwing the pieces off into the brush.

"Hi Noël," greeted Don, coming up to her.

"Hi Don," said Noël, sensing somehow that it would not be the right time to press the boys on what they'd been up to.

"What's up?"

"I'm looking for Polly."

"She's not here," said Jiff as he and Guy walked up.

"Why don't you check over Theo's," suggested Guy quickly. "I think I saw her going over there this morning."

"I already did, she wasn't there," said Noël, deciding suddenly not to ask Guy about going to the library with her.

"Sorry we can't help you," said Jiff.

"Yeah, well, thanks anyway...bye."

"Bye," the three boys said all together, ending the awkward moment.

Puzzled at the whole episode, Noël decided to head for the library on her own but when she turned back to look from the wall at the top of the Therrien's yard, she saw that the boys had gone back down to the swamp and were busy beating the brush as if trying to hide something. Frowning, she determined to investigate herself when she returned and find out what their odd behavior was all about.

Later that afternoon, when she'd once again crested the high ground in the Therrien's yard, it was drizzling again and the day was threatening to end in early dark.

Throughout the hours she'd spent at the library, memories of the boys' strange behavior kept intruding upon her concentration. The more she turned that morning's incident over in her mind, the more disturbed she became with the idea that the boys she'd known for so long and shared so many moments with had suddenly developed a secret life.

Sitting there in the library, alone except for old Mrs. Connor the librarian, Noël had plenty of time to think; and the realization that had come to her was that many of the boys' new interests seemed to coincide with those of her female friends' interest in boys only last summer. The suspicion began to grow in her that the changing dynamic among her male and female friends was to be a fundamental and permanent one. No more would they romp and play with as complete abandon as they once did only a year before. From now on, other considerations would play a part in their relations that would draw their wages in a certain loss of the spontaneity that had always characterized their friendship.

Reluctant to have her suspicions confirmed, but somehow unable to keep herself from facing the evidence that would make them impossible to deny, Noël moved stealthily through the Jorgenson's yard down toward the area of the swamp where the boys had gathered earlier in the day. There, she braved the dripping brush long enough to gather a few soggy pages of the magazine and spread them out on a piece of timber from the old chicken coop. Though torn and wet, she could still make out their contents and even though she wasn't surprised at what they held, she still couldn't help feeling disappointed.

It was the last straw.

The collected gloom that had been building up inside of her for the past few weeks burst out in an uncharacteristic display of anger and frustration as she scooped up the incriminating bits of paper, wadded them into a ball and threw them into the swamp as far she could. After that, she ran home, careless of who should see her emerging from the Jorgenson's yard. She was too busy trying to hold back tears whose significance even she didn't understand.

By the time she reached home, she'd managed to control herself long enough to make a cup of tea and retreat to her room. There, she curled up in the window seat and had a good cry. The rain that'd begun to fall again, complemented her feelings perfectly.

Hours later, she sat in the dark; it was night, and she'd come to grips with her tortured heart. Suddenly, she couldn't think of Guy or of the other boys in the same way she did only the day before. They weren't grown up yet, but sometime over the last few years, they'd progressed beyond childish concerns. It was a shock to Noël to realize that she couldn't remember the last time she'd seen them building plastic models or playing soldier or toying with their race cars and erector sets. They'd grown up (they'd all grown up, she corrected), without her even noticing.

She'd laughed silently to herself then; she'd always considered herself as being alert and observant, but she hadn't seen any of it coming. It crushed the ego (Guy would've liked that, a paraphrase from *The Planet of the Apes*)!

Of course, she hadn't been completely blind! She'd noted, not without a strange mingling of fear and delight, the changes in her own body over the same period; but somehow it never occurred to her that her friends (both male and female) might have been going through similar experiences. When she'd finally realized that, it gave her a whole new outlook on life. Suddenly, the depression she'd been suffering for months lifted and a whole new world seemed to reveal itself to her. Filled with unexplored possibilities and unknown potentialities, it beckoned her with a promise; not that events wouldn't continue to change (or even spin out of control!) but that change itself would become part of the wonder and the surprise of life. Things would never be as predictable as they'd been up until now and wasn't *that* neat?

She turned on the light and picked a book. She'd thought it dull and slow, and had left it untouched on her night stand for days; but now, flipping through its pages, she found it fascinating and fresh and wondered idly why it hadn't appealed to her before.

The Lowell Sun Building

CHAPTER FOURTEEN

In which Guy comes to a new understanding with Noël

The world was all black and soundless until occasional blurbs of light began to wander about the darkness. Then the blurbs began to grow larger and to merge together, and presently, the black turned to a kind of white. Then sounds could be heard creeping from background to foreground. At last, Nick Tropoli came back to full consciousness.

His first sensation was that of pain; the pain of a terrific headache. But after a few minutes, he managed to get the pain under control enough to inspect his surroundings.

A blurred face swam into his sight as he tried with all his might to make out its features. As they began to make themselves apparent, he gasped. It was the face of an angel!

"Have I died and gone to heaven?" he asked.

The face grunted and then laughed. "I guess that bump on the head did hurt you after all."

He recognized the voice and soon, recognized the face as well. "Jane?" he asked, embarrassed.

"Yes, it's me," she said, pulling away.

"What happened?"

"Nothing," she said easily. "After we boarded that Venusian space ship, you got too far ahead of us and got caught by a dozen of the creatures all by your lonesome. When we finally caught up to you, you were unconscious on the floor. I..." She stopped suddenly and Nick felt instinctively what she had meant to say.

He held out his hand and felt hers slip into it. "Thanks," he said, but he meant a lot more than he said aloud.

She squeezed his hand and smiled. "You'll never get rid of me now," she said.

"Best thing I've heard in months," he said.

She stooped and kissed him.

Gateway to the Future
by Guy DeMonde

It was early Saturday morning; so early, that the streetlights were still burning, their pale light just beginning to be washed out in the coming dawn. Far up on the highway, Guy saw the first one wink out; and as he pedaled his bicycle towards the Lacroix Bridge, he saw others go out in succession all along the road. Behind the empty mills across the river, the sky was brightening from pink to yellow and the last stars were fading in the west.

Pedaling as fast as he could, Guy raced up the middle of the deserted highway, glorying in the complete absence of traffic at that time of the morning. Zig-zagging in wide curves across the yellow dividing line, he only slowed in order to make the big turn onto the bridge. He crossed it in seconds and coasted into the center of downtown Lowell where stood its tallest building. The fifteen floors of the Lowell Sun Newspaper Building shot like a pale arrow into the sky and was topped by six, huge neon lit letters reading *The Sun* that could be seen from anywhere in the city.

Guy turned quickly down the driveway used by the delivery trucks and rode down along the building to the loading dock. There, he dismounted and made a ritual spit into the murky waters of the canal that separated the Sun Building from the Rex lot on the other side. He pushed open a side door and hauled his bike to safety inside. A narrow stairway led upwards to the second floor where the paperboys paid their weekly bills and collected their profits.

Guy and his father had come down to the Lowell Sun two years before to sign up for a paper route near Desrosiers Street. The wait had lasted only a few months before Guy received one (46 papers) around St. Louis School. To Guy, it was exhilarating not to have to scavenge for bottles or ask his parents for money to cover his weekly comic book and occasional paperback expenses.

At the top of the stairs, Guy pushed open a heavy door and entered the circulation department, which was deserted at that time of the morning except for Mr. O'Flynn, the first collector on duty. That was the way Guy liked it; he'd do his business without having to wait or worry about his bike being stolen.

"Hi, Mr. O'Flynn," he said, making his way to the very end of the long counter where only a few hours later, hundreds of other boys would leave little room to move.

"Hello there, Guy," Mr. O'Flynn said good naturedly.

"Do I have to wait?" asked Guy, joking.

"First in line."

Guy stepped up to the counter and poured out some change and dirty bills from a cloth bank bag he kept rolled up in his pocket. When he'd finished counting out the money, Mr. O'Flynn double-checked him, poured the change into an automatic sorter and banded the bills. What remained was his own; usually about five dollars. He took the money and left.

Leaving his bike where it was (he still had about two hours before anyone else showed up), he walked over to Brooks Drugs to check out the books. It was too early for Prince's Bookstore to be open, but the drugstore seemed to be open no matter what time he showed up. It's selection of books however, wasn't much; mostly romance novels and weird science books about ancient astronauts, UFOs, ghosts, and rains of frogs, but now and then he'd be surprised to find some good stuff too. Once he found the new Conan novel by Lin Carter (the first of the series he'd ever seen).

Slowly, deliberately, he scanned the two long rows of wire racks that dominated one side of the store, checking each pocket carefully (sometimes the distributor would put two or more titles in each). Finished, he was the happy possessor of *Carnacki the Ghost-Finder* by William Hope Hodgson and an anthology of fantasy stories.

A few minutes later, he was on his bike again, heading for Henry's Self-Serve. Dana's Fruitland had closed suddenly the year before, forcing him once again to search out a new source for comic books. After weeks of desperate looking, he'd finally found one. Unfortunately, it was located in the middle of a section of town off Bridge Street that was crawling with juvenile delinquents who'd like nothing better than to have a chance to beat up on Mr. Softee's son.

As a result, in order to get in and out of the area of the store safely, he had to go early in the morning (JDs were notoriously late sleepers) after paying his newspaper bill at the Sun.

Crossing the Lacroix Bridge, Guy continued onto Bridge Street and entered one of the more run down parts of town. Here, the streets were filled with old tenement buildings surrounded by vacant lots and choked everywhere with litter and garbage. Why, there wasn't even a single tree.

At last, coming in sight of the store, he slowed to a crawl and scanned the surrounding area for signs of life, prepared at a moment's notice to speed away at the slightest hint of danger. He saw nothing however and so continued on to the store. Leaving his bike where he could see it, he stepped inside.

Henry's Self-Serve had a peculiar way of handling their comic books, unlike any store Guy had ever seen. Instead of displaying them on a magazine shelf or spinner rack, the owner liked to clip them to a string that looped across the ceiling with colored clothespins. The buyer would point out which comics he wanted and the owner would dig them out from a stack behind the counter.

Guy dragged his eyes across the colorful covers until he spotted the latest issues of *Daredevil (The Man Without Fear)* and *The Avengers.*

"I'll take those two," he told the proprietor, pointing.

While he waited for the store owner to pick out the two comics from his pile, Guy looked around the store until his eyes stopped on some magazines that were usually kept hidden behind the counter but visible nevertheless to a customer who was tall enough to see. Instantly, he recalled that day the previous autumn when Noël had come across he, Jiff, and Don as they were looking through a similar magazine. They'd managed to get rid of it before she moved too close, but he always wondered if she'd guessed what it was anyway.

Guy left the store, his purchases in hand but forgotten. Shoving off on his bike down the steep hill toward home, he tried to understand (for the umpteenth time!) why it mattered to him if she *did* know.

Thinking farther back to another problem he had with her, he remembered the time they'd been tricked into going to the theater together and how good it felt for a while there to be just sitting and talking with her. He remembered the feeling he had when he noticed the envious glances of other boys as they walked past. He'd long since admitted to himself that Noël wasn't exactly hard on the eyes; in fact she was pretty darn cute...but just when was it that she'd begun to dominate his thoughts? Did he like her or not?

But then, any further thoughts along those lines were cut short by the blare of a horn and the screech of tires on pavement.

Later, all Guy could remember of the ensuing events was being restrained by unseen hands and crying out for his mother.

It wasn't until much later that he found himself lying in a hospital bed with the upper end elevated, propping up his head and shoulders. There were two other beds in the room; the one in the middle was empty but the one near the window was occupied by a younger boy who'd been struck by a taxi only a few hours after Guy had had his own accident.

Guy didn't remember getting to the hospital or being in the emergency room or even in the operating room. His memories only began with the bed he found himself in when he woke up (from being anesthetized, he guessed). The first thing he discovered upon looking himself over was that his right leg had been tightly bandaged and that he was wearing an article of hospital clothing that was designed (or seemed to be!) to limit his range of movement. If he stretched too far in any direction, he risked acute embarrassment because the "jonny" hardly reached his knees and was open at the back; all he could do was sit very still, which gave visitors the false impression that he'd been hurt worse than he was…and that wasn't too bad, as far as he could tell.

The doctor told him that it was a fractured leg and that he could even expect to take the bandages off in another two weeks. He couldn't feel anything when he moved it, so his personal prognosis was that, indeed, the doctor might be right. And so, mostly he just laid back, watched some television, read (he felt worse over the loss of the *Daredevil* and *Avengers* comics than he did about his injuries; *whatever happened to them anyway?* he wondered), and enjoyed the food. The only thing that really bothered him besides having to wear the jonny was being in bed when visitors came.

Well, except maybe for his parents, who'd brought him *The Son of Tarzan*, which he'd just begun to read the day before the accident. He was happy to have the book of course, but happier still amid the alien surroundings of St. Joseph's Hospital to see their familiar faces.

The next day, he'd just concluded chapter twelve where Korak, Tarzan's son, bloody and exhausted, fails to rescue his beloved Meriem from the clutches of a native war party. Suppressing for a moment his eagerness to continue reading, Guy closed the book and looked again at its cover. Executed by his favorite cover artist, Frank Frazetta, it was the kind of cover painting that made defending the books he liked to read a challenge. It showed an angry Korak wearing nothing but a brief loin cloth, shouting defiance to a giant ape threatening the golden haired form of Meriem as she knelt helpless in the lush elephant grass. It conveyed perfectly to the reader all the savage beauty and action of a typical Edgar Rice Burroughs novel and, as he was finding himself doing more often lately, Guy couldn't help putting himself in Korak's place and defending the honor of Noël...

Suddenly there was a knock at the door and looking up, Guy immediately felt his face grow warm as he saw the object of his daydream step into the room.

"Hi," she said.

"Uh, hi," Guy managed as he self-consciously placed *The Son of Tarzan* face down on a little table by the bed.

"I came by to see how you were doing," Noël said.

"Thanks," said Guy, caught completely by surprise.

There was a short silence until Noël seemed to remember something.

"Oh, yeah," she held out a paper bag, slightly torn at the edges. "I found this where you had your accident and thought I'd bring it over."

Guy reached out for the bag, felt a draft, and immediately regretted it. Quickly, he leaned back, clutching at the edges of the jonny, acutely aware that from where she stood, Noël might've easily seen more of his backside than was proper (although she'd seen plenty of him last summer when everyone in the neighborhood went swimming in the Therrien's new pool). Somehow, things between them had changed and, as if seeing her for the first time, he became aware of just how pretty she really was. Why hadn't he noticed that before?

"I read one of the stories in the anthology," said Noël, backing away a little. "*The Hollow Land* by William Morris? I recognized his name from when you told me about him once."

Guy, lying as far back in the bed as he could, thumbed through the book. "William Morris? You remembered?"

"I remember everything you said that day." There was no need to say which day *that* was.

Guy reached over to put the books on the night stand. Then, thinking better of it, decided to hold onto them instead. "I really am grateful to you for this," he told Noël. "I was really worried about them...I know it sounds stupid to be worried about a couple of books when I could've been killed, but..."

"Will you stop making excuses like that?" Noël interrupted. "This is me you're talking to, remember? All these years and you still think you're the only one around here who loves books? You don't think that I could feel the same way?" She moved in closer again, and this time, the thought of needing to be embarrassed never even entered Guy's head. "I love books as much as you do and if my guess is right, we both feel the same way about them, like their...windows on other people's minds or...like time machines we can step in and out of whenever we want to. It's readers like us, bibliophiles, that authors need to keep their thoughts and their imaginations alive." She reached out, gripping him by the shoulder. "So don't ever say your love of books is stupid, not to me anyway."

Guy gulped. "Don't worry, I won't." Then, in a bid to change the subject, he asked, "How did you find out about my accident?"

"It was in the paper," Noël said, letting go of his arm. "Did you know the driver of the car that hit you was a minister?"

"You're kidding!" exclaimed Guy. "Now I'll never be able to live all this down."

"Don't worry about it," laughed Noël. "But getting back to Morris...you were right, he is a good writer."

"Well, I have to admit I find his style hard to take, but it grows on you." Guy felt that as long as Noël was giving in a little, he could too and meet her half-way. In fact, she'd gone so far in smoothing things out between them that he suddenly felt sure that this was the time to tell her of something that he'd had on his mind for a long time.

"Noël, do you mind if I ask you a personal question?"

He could see that she sensed his question marked a shift in the tone of the conversation. There was a break between her good humor and her new seriousness that lasted only a moment, but to Guy it was as wide and plain as the Grand Canyon.

"No," she said at last. "I don't mind."

And all of a sudden, Guy wasn't so sure he wanted to ask his question after all, but it was too late to back off now.

He swallowed and said, "Do you keep a diary?"

Noël blinked and for the first time, Guy felt that he'd taken her by surprise. She opened her mouth to speak but then, deciding against it, looked around instead.

"Can I draw these curtains?" she asked, cocking her head silently toward the other boy in the room.

With growing alarm at Noël's reactions to his question, Guy could only nod yes.

Noël reached over to the plastic curtain that hung from a track on the ceiling and dragged it around Guy's bed until they were completely cut off from anyone outside. Then, returning to the bedside, she folded her arms defiantly across her chest.

"Now, what was it you asked?"

Guy was perfectly sure she remembered his question, but repeated it anyway.

"Do you keep a diary?"

"So what if I do?"

It occurred to Guy that Noël never looked prettier than she did at just that moment, but he pushed the thought from his mind and forced himself to say, "Well…I think I found a page from it."

Noël looked up quickly, shock and worry in her face. "What do you mean, you found a page from my diary?"

Alarmed at her reaction, Guy could tell by the look on her face that she was reviewing the diary in her mind, going over it leaf by leaf in a desperate attempt to discover if the missing page might hold embarrassing information.

"I tried to convince myself that I didn't know to whom it belonged, but I guess I never did fool myself," explained Guy. "I knew it was yours the minute I found it, but couldn't bring myself to give it back."

"Did you…read it?"

"Of course, I…"

"I…I…wrote that before last summer," said Noël, not sure herself what she was trying to say.

"I'll give it back to you when I get out of here."

There was a long silence then while Noël looked first at the ceiling then turned to stare at the curtain. Then Guy heard her sigh and suddenly her shoulders straightened as she came to some kind of decision. When she turned to face him again, Guy could plainly see new determination in her sky-blue eyes.

"Now look, Guy, I think it's nuts to keep acting the way we have," she said, placing her fists on her hips.

"Huh?" was all Guy could muster. "How've we been acting?"

"Don't get facetious with me."

Guy shut up.

"We've been behaving at cross purposes ever since we first met." Turning, Noël slapped her hands to the sides of her legs and began pacing around the bed. "I don't know how we got off on the wrong foot...well, maybe I do." She stopped on the opposite side of the bed from which she'd started and stared directly at Guy. "I admit, I was partly to blame. I was a conceited little child who believed that only I was right and everybody else was wrong; especially you. I thought that the stuff you read was trashy and immature. I was so blind, that until only last summer I never saw that we both loved the same thing in different ways. And it was my own immaturity that provoked an argument between us at the theater just when we seemed to be getting along."

She stopped to catch her breath, then drifted to the foot of the bed. She dragged a finger along the safety railing and continued. "Maybe that scared me," she whispered. "Maybe I was attracted to you...I mean, maybe there's something about you that I like, I'm still not sure. But what was worse," she said, looking up suddenly and raising her voice again, "was that you were acting the same way, maybe worse. I've been blaming myself, but you're just as guilty and because of all that, we've made our lives a lot less happy than they could've been."

"Hey, quiet in there," said a voice on the other side of the curtain, "you're getting too loud."

"Behave yourself, mister," Noël called out over her shoulder, "unless you want some of this."

"No ma'am," came the mumbled reply.

Guy cracked a smile at the exchange, but quickly erased it when Noël turned the beam of her attention back to him.

"Well, maybe the kid's right," she said. "I think I've yelled at you enough, too much probably. But I want you to do me a favor, whenever you think I'm being obnoxious, let me know because I don't intend on giving another speech." Then she pulled the curtain back giving the boy across the room a glare that sent him beneath the covers. As she was leaving, she turned at the door and said, "I'll be waiting for that page when you get out; and if I find out you've shown it to anybody..."

"I didn't!" blurted Guy, anxious not to get on her angry side again. "Honest, I didn't!"

Then she was gone and he was straining to listen as her footsteps retreated down the corridor, and when they at last faded beyond hearing, he imagined her the rest of the way out of the building. Only then did he lay back again, wondering at the change that had suddenly come over her.

There was still the fiery temper and the blazing eyes he remembered from past years, but he was sure she hadn't been kidding when she'd spoken of maturity. Of course, she'd always behaved as if she were more sophisticated than anybody else, but now that all seemed as unimportant as the way any of them had acted. The question was, could the rest of them, including himself, keep up with her?

Looking again at the cover of *The Son of Tarzan*, Guy was suddenly sure of one thing at least, he'd no longer be able to imagine Noël hanging back in a fight; if there *was* ever another spear handy, the king of the ape tribe would have his hands full!

CHAPTER FIFTEEN

In which Noël learns that things are not always
what they seem

June 25, 1970: I've waited about a week to make this entry, hoping that I'd be able to approach the subject with more objectivity, that it would all seem less dreamlike, but nothing's changed. It still seems strange to think that with last week's graduation from elementary school the first, most important chapter of my life is over.

It took place in church and everybody was there. The boys were all in blue and the girls in white and although I've always told myself that it was my neighborhood friends that I cared about the most, by the end of the ceremony, I was wiping tears from my eyes just like Sandra Reilly! Oh, how I'll miss my friends from St. Louis! I hugged everybody, even Guy (that raised a few eyebrows, but it's a sign of how much we've all matured in the last year or two that no one giggled or even had a jokey comment).

I don't think it can be considered boasting if I mention in my own diary that I received the highest honors in class. English, literature, history, science and religion were my best subjects; music, math and French my worst. But I hardly have time to rest on my laurels because almost as soon as graduation was over, Papa took me to St. Joseph's High School to register for next year. St. Joe's will be close enough to walk to classes and will have a smaller student body than an average high school and besides, Guy will be attending classes there too as well as a few other of our classmates from St. Louis. A good indication that I've made the right choice is that when I signed up for my freshman year, I was given a summer reading list that's very impressive. I've read some of the books before, but others like Arthur Conan Doyle's *The Hound of the Baskerville's* and Harper Lee's *To Kill a Mockingbird* I'd always wanted to get around to but never did. As soon as I saw them, I wondered how Guy would react to them?

It's funny how Guy seems to have stepped into my thoughts as naturally as he has and the times I've stopped to think about it, I've always concluded that the best thing I ever did was to have cleared the air with him last year, just like Marian Halcomb in *The Woman in White*. I still remember how foolish I felt that day walking home from the hospital until I realized that a great weight seemed to have been lifted from my shoulders. I'm still not sure how it happened, but sometime last winter, I decided to change some things in my life, to stop behaving like a child and to begin seeing things more like the young woman I've become. It's funny, but before that, I could never seem to sort out my feelings (those for Guy being only some of them) in fact, I wasn't even aware that they even needed sorting! But at one point, I finally decided that I wouldn't let doubt cloud my judgment again.

Anyway, I'm glad that one of the first things I did was to straighten things out between Guy and I. I don't want high school to be cluttered with all the emotional baggage I've been collecting since moving to Lowell. And so, just like that vow I took when I first moved here, I'm going to make another one now. With high school, I'm beginning a new chapter in my life. There are going to be new friends to make and new experiences to have. The emotions I felt at graduation have showed me that, no matter what I think, I won't be able to prevent myself from forming new associations and new friends outside the neighborhood (although I'll always regard them with fondness as my dearest friends). I see now how fast time flies and I want to make sure that I broaden my horizons enough to prepare myself properly in four years to enter the adult world.

I'm confident now that I've come to terms with my feelings as a young woman should, and mastered them. There'll be no more petty squabbles that have spoiled friendships like the one I have with Guy.

Noël was sitting in the window seat of her room when she saw her father and mother walk out to the family car.

They stood close together for a moment, talking quietly before her father leaned forward to give his wife a quick kiss. Afterwards, he slipped into the car and, as her mother waved him goodbye, backed it slowly out of the driveway. She saw her father wave one last time from the window of the car before it disappeared beyond a fringe of trees. Her mother turned back to the house.

The little tableau enacted below her window only served to accentuate Noël's desire to get to the bottom of the mystery that had been plaguing her since her family's first arrival in the city. It was the kind of thing that she was beginning to feel more and more was necessary to give closure to a chapter of her life that had ended at her elementary school graduation. Now, having come to terms with herself the winter before and feeling a new confidence borne of her successful confrontation with Guy at the hospital, she determined to get to the bottom of it.

The only problem was that to do it, she might have to confront her parents, something she wasn't yet prepared to do. She felt certain that she couldn't raise the subject with her mother for fear of worrying her over nothing should her suspicions prove groundless and she felt it premature to confront her father in the same way for fear of upsetting the old trust between them.

She needed more definite information before taking any such irrevocable steps. Fortunately however, she had some ideas on how to do just that.

And so, right after breakfast, she pulled her bicycle from the garage and rode up to Hovey Square. She had two things to go on: recognition of the business district beyond the Old House as the one in which she'd lost her father the night she followed him from the church burning and the man in the blue car whom she saw at both the Old House and at home on that Fourth of July night a couple of years before. It was her intention to explore the streets of that neighborhood below the hill on which rested the Old House for any sign of the mysterious blue car.

Soon, she reached the point at which she'd abandoned her attempt to follow her father the night of the church burning. In broad daylight, with people moving about and traffic on the streets, the area didn't look as weird and threatening as she remembered. But after an hour of searching and turning up nothing, Noël decided to find the Old House instead. Perhaps revisiting the place where she saw the blue car would yield clues as to what she could do next. And so, following those streets that tended uphill, she left the business district behind and eventually struck open land that reached in from the countryside. Exhausted, she dismounted and walked her bicycle as the hill grew steeper and buildings became more scarce. Soon patches of forest began to break up the vacant lots, empty fields and overgrown pastures that formed the outer fringes of the wild area she used to play in with her friends.

At last, nearing the top of the hill, she looked up and saw the familiar widow's walk on the top of the Old House and in another few minutes the whole building bulked into view. Alone at the top of the hill, it seemed more isolated than ever with a group of quiet ravens perched atop a nearby telephone pole the only signs of life, and as Noël rolled her bicycle to a stop across the street from the house, even they flew off.

But now that she was here, what was she to do? She'd vaguely hoped to spy the familiar blue car in the driveway, but it wasn't there. She let down the kick-stand of her bicycle, walked to the center of the dusty road and placed her hands on her hips. Concentrating, she tried to force an idea into existence, but instead, only memories came up.

She remembered the day the whole gang, including Mike, had come up to explore the house. How they'd begun in the yard and moved indoors. Noël raised her eyes to the upper floors and in her mind, she was back in that widow's walk with Guy as snowflakes swirled all around them. Everything looked the same as it did then, nothing seemed to have changed.

Until she noticed that the real estate sign was gone.

It could only mean that someone must have bought the house.

There was something vaguely regretful about the notion that strangers would be walking that old property. Although she hadn't thought about it much lately, she'd come to regard the place as the personal possession of she and her friends. But then, suddenly, such thoughts were swept from her mind as a new idea took their place.

The real state sign! Was there some connection between it and the man in the blue car?

Quickly, she hopped on her bicycle and rode back down the hill to the business district. There, she wasted little time finding a telephone booth and, flipping quickly through the directory's yellow pages, found what she was looking for.

Minutes later, she was standing across the street from the Landmark Real Estate Co. and in the shade of the awning that hung from over its windows, rested the blue car.

It'd been a long shot, but she'd felt sure that she could recognize the name of the real estate company that had been on the sign in front of the Old House if she came across it again. And when she'd looked through the real estate section of the telephone book, sure enough, it'd leaped out at her.

Crossing the street, she leaned her bicycle against the storefront and pressed her face against the window. Inside, there was only a single room with two or three cluttered desks. Near the door, a woman sat at one of them. Polaroids of houses were everywhere: on the wall, on the desks, on the floor.

Noël moved out of sight and did her best to straighten her clothes and comb her hair. As presentable as she could be in clean pressed jeans and blouse, she walked to the door and went in.

The woman inside looked up at the sound of the door. "Can I help you, miss?" she said.

"Yes," replied Noël, trying to sound serious. "I wondered if you could tell me who owns that car?"

The woman craned her neck to see where she was pointing and nodded. "That's Phil Johnson's car."

"Does he work here?"

"Yes; he's one of our agents," the woman said. "That's his desk over there."

Noël looked over to where the woman indicated and amid the clutter on the desk, saw a card holder.

"Do you think he'd mind if I took one of his cards?"

"Help yourself."

Noël took one of the cards and placed it in her pocket without looking at it.

'Also, I was wondering if the house on Adeline Lane was still for sale."

The woman smiled, obviously wondering what interest a fourteen-year-old girl had in one of their properties.

"The Deschenes property? It's just been sold," the woman said. "By Phil as a matter of fact."

"Who bought it?" asked Noël, with altogether too much eagerness in her voice.

"I'm sorry, I can't say, that's confidential."

Noël nodded. "Well, okay, thank you."

Outside again, Noël waited until she'd ridden a few blocks before taking Phil Johnson's business card from her pocket. Studying it, she noticed an identification photo in the upper left corner. Looking at it more closely, she gasped. It showed the same man whom she first saw in front of her house and then driving off in the blue car! For the first time, things were beginning to make sense and to her relief, they didn't add up to any of the dire scenarios her imagination had conjured up over the years.

Later that afternoon, Noël was sitting on the porch swing waiting for her father to come home. She'd turned over in her mind a dozen ways to bring up the subject with either him or her mother, and decided in the end on the direct approach with the key player. It occurred to her that she ought to have been nervous but she wasn't. Instead, she was calm, just sitting on the swing and watching the late afternoon shadows lengthen toward evening. The sun had dipped below the tree line when her father finally arrived and she watched as he pulled the car up into the driveway and cut the engine.

She heard a door slam shut as she rose from the swing and walked over to the side of the porch. Her father was just heading toward the kitchen door when he saw her standing there.

"Well, hello, beautiful," he said, smiling.

"Hi," said Noël, offering her cheek for a kiss. "Pa, can you sit down here for a minute, I want to ask you something."

Mr. Archambault cocked an eyebrow. "Serious stuff?"

"Um hm."

He shrugged and walked around to the front steps. A moment later, he was leaning against the porch railing, arms crossed over his chest with his dark suit and tie making him seem taller and rangier than usual. "Now then..." he said.

Noël, once again sitting on the swing, cleared her throat and looked around. The front door was closed and so were all the windows.

She went right to the point.

"Pa, have you bought a new house?"

For a moment, the eyes of both father and daughter locked. There was an extended silence between question and answer that seemed to Noël to last forever. Then, just as she began to get nervous, her father spoke.

"And I thought I was being so smart," her father said, his face in shadow: but there was a smile in his voice. "How did you find out?"

"I went to the real estate office that represents the property on Adeline Lane and asked about it," Noël explained. "They said it was sold. That's when I was positive you'd bought it... Well, maybe not completely sure, but almost."

"Uh, huh," said her father. "But how did you find out about Landmark in the first place?"

"It's kind of a long story," she said, but went on and explained everything that had led up to that afternoon's discovery.

"For a long time, I was worried about you," Noël concluded. "At first, it was on and off, you know? I guess it was a child thing, not being able to concentrate on any one thing for too long. But I do remember the night the church burned down and crying myself to sleep because...well, to this day, I'm not sure why except to say that maybe I felt that you weren't the person I thought you were. Does that make any sense?"

Her father nodded.

"Sure it does. My inexplicable behavior seemed to you a betrayal of familial trust. When I acted in a manner contrary to what you'd grown to expect, I seemed to have broken that trust. I was no longer the man you thought I was. Suddenly the world, which you thought comfortably familiar, became unpredictable and chaotic."

"Yeah, that's it, I think." She paused. "And I think I still feel a little like that deep down."

"As you should," said her father. "You've graduated now and you'll be going to high school soon. You'll find that the world is unpredictable, but you need not let your part of it get out of control. That's what education is all about, the kind you get at school and the other kind you learn here at home. It'll be up to you how you use that knowledge to keep chance events from getting the best of you. Keeping the shocks to a minimum is one of the keys to happiness."

Noël rose from the swing, wandered over to one of the porch supports and hugged it. Peeking out from around it, she said, "Does Ma know about the house?"

In the orange glow of the approaching sunset, she saw her father's head lower in thought then he straightened, walked over to the front door and pulled it open.

"Cecile?" he called. "Noël and I are going for a walk. I know, we'll be right back." Letting the screen door slam shut, he turned and cocked his head, "C'mon."

Taking her hand, he led Noël toward the end of the street where the old path led into the woods and fields beyond. They stepped through and found themselves in the yellowish light of late afternoon that turned the long grass into burnished gold. Together, they made their way toward the line of trees in the distance.

At the treeline, her father veered off in a direction Noël had never taken before and plunged in the direction of what seemed an impenetrable thicket of thorn bushes. But as they approached, a path opened up that was invisible to anyone standing more than a few feet away. For that reason, Noël and her friends had never bothered to explore in that direction.

Noël's wonder increased as the path opened up into a broad lane through the forest with the trees, their branches hanging low overhead, crowding close to either side. Here and there, she saw evidence that the path may once have been paved for patches of red bricks could still be glimpsed beneath the forest floor. Presently, a huge earthen hump of mud and sticks blocked the trail and they were obliged to climb over it. It was the biggest beaver lodge she'd ever seen. On the other side, the trail narrowed to a kind of causeway that divided a large swamp whose water level was a good foot higher on one side than the other. It was then Noël realized that the causeway was actually a damming project built by the beavers.

They descended the lodge and walked along the causeway until, reaching the end, stepped into a big clearing in the woods. All around them stood huge concrete structures pocked with hundreds of holes.

"This is an old rifle range built before the First World War," her father explained. "At least that's what my friends and I were told when we used to play down here."

Noël was somewhat surprised to discover that her father had once played in these woods just as she and her friends did but had little time to pursue the thought as the trail suddenly straightened out like a highway in the forest. Then, in the distance, she spied a telephone pole poking over the trees and in another moment she was standing in the road before the Old House. The entire walk through the woods had taken only a few minutes!

She took her father's hand again as he led her across the street and up the driveway of the house.

"Pa, why did you keep your buying the house a secret?"

"What else? I wanted to surprise you and your mother." He allowed himself a chuckle. "But if you know all about it, then I'm sure your mother does too. It's really hard to keep anything secret from her. And here I thought I was so clever." He let go of Noël's hand and continued up the driveway to the backyard. "I don't suppose your mother ever told you about this house?"

Noël looked puzzled. "Should she have?"

Her father shrugged. "I guess not." He walked a few more steps, turned, and waved an arm at the house. "This house used to belong to some of your mother's relatives." He must have seen Noël's eyes widen, because he laughed and continued. "It's true. It belonged to her grandmother. Unfortunately, the old woman died owing a lot of unpaid taxes to the city. The city ended up taking it but because of its condition, hasn't been able to decide what to do with it. When we moved back here a few years ago, the first thing I did was contact Phil Johnson; did I tell you he and I went to school together at St. Louis? Phil started the ball rolling on the red tape, I made an offer to the city and they were happy to let me take it off their hands.

"But your mother is a very sentimental woman and it hurt her more than she'll say to have lost access to this old house. It holds lots of pleasant memories for her. Maybe that's why she never told you about it."

Noël didn't say anything. She just stared up at the big old house. Suddenly it seemed like a whole new building, not the old spooky place it had been just minutes before.

"C'mon, I want to show you something," her father said, gesturing for her to follow.

Leading her deeper into the backyard, in the direction of the old cages, he squeezed past them and into the thick undergrowth to the rear where she and her friends had never gone. There was a cascade of clinging vines, thick with flowers, draping the trees like a blanket making it difficult for her father to find the spot he was looking for.

At last, he found it and managed to force a way through by holding the tightly grown vines apart. He signaled for Noël to pass on to the other side. There, in a small glade, completely enclosed by a dozen vine-draped trees, stood a wooden gazebo. Noël laughed with delight and stepped up beneath its circular roof, admiring the small, white flowers that poked from the vines around the clearing and the straggly rose bushes that threatened to swallow up the gazebo.

"We never found this," she said, as her father joined her on the platform.

"It's no wonder," he said, leaning against the railing. "I almost didn't find it myself, and I knew where to look."

"It's beautiful!"

"This spot is pretty special to me and your mother," said her father, looking around.

"Why?" asked Noël, tossing her head and luxuriating in the moment. Crickets had begun to chirp from the shadows and frogs croaked from the other side of the trees. The season was advanced and the world was on the cusp of summer.

"Because this is where we shared our first kiss."

"Oh, that's so romantic."

Her father effected ignorance of such matters, as men would. "I guess it was," he said. "She brought me up here one afternoon to show me the house. Then she showed me this gazebo, much the same way that I just showed it to you. Come to think of it, I wonder if she had that kiss planned all along?"

Noël smiled knowingly.

"So, anyway, what do you think of the whole idea? Will your mother go for it?"

"I'm positive she will!"

"And you?"

Noël took a moment before replying. Would she like leaving the neighborhood? She'd outgrown the need for the security of familiar surroundings, even though she never wanted to forget her old pals and she remembered what her father had said earlier about learning to deal with the unexpected.

"Yeah," she finally said. "I think I will."

"Good, I'm glad," said her father. Then, putting his arm around her shoulders, he steered her back to the driveway.

"Pa?" Noël asked when they were back on Desrosiers Street again.

"Hm?"

"Do we get the house furnished?"

"As a matter of fact, we do; why?"

"The library too?"

He laughed and said, "I'm sure, I'm sure."

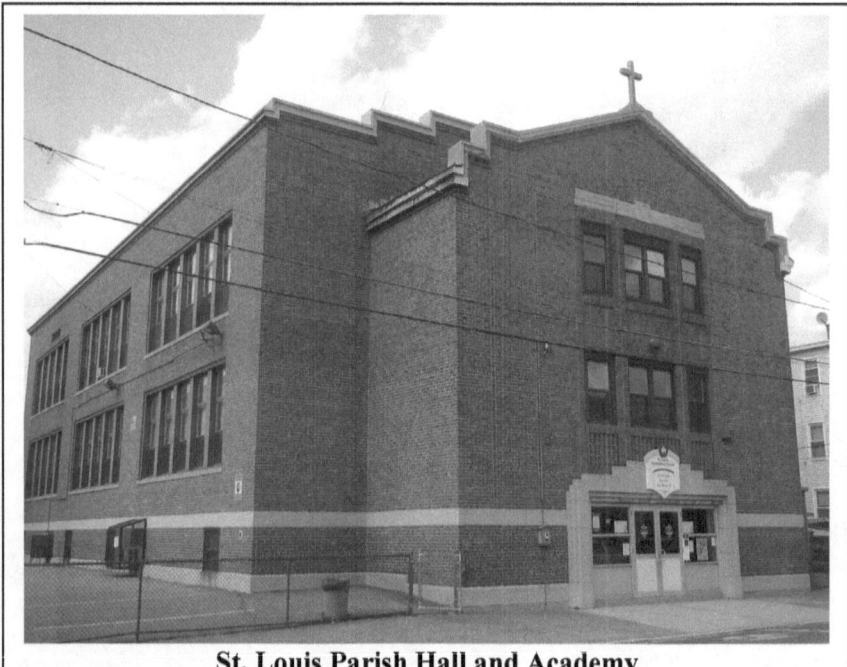

St. Louis Parish Hall and Academy

CHAPTER SIXTEEN

In which Guy takes dancing lessons and finds out it's not so bad after all

Nick Tropoli and Jane North were standing on the bridge of the USS Space Saucer *Marauder* watching the bright globe of Venus falling away. They were traveling at almost the speed of light, but couldn't feel it. And even if they could, they wouldn't care. Or at least Nick wouldn't.

Their brief adventures on the jungle planet had drawn them closer together and to Nick that meant something permanent. He was standing close beside Jane in the narrow confines of the viewport and it was the most natural thing in the world for him to slip his arm around her waist and draw her even closer to him. She didn't resist; instead, she fit herself more snugly against his powerful frame.

"Beautiful isn't it?" she asked, meaning Venus.

"It sure is," he replied, meaning her.

She sensed his meaning and looked up, but there was a smile on her face. "Is this what a girl has to do to get her hooks in you? Zoom through space to who knows where, trudge through uncharted jungles on an alien world, get captured by slimy Venusians, and almost killed by twenty foot long dragon flies?"

"It worked didn't it?"

"Sure did."

"I'm going to kiss you," Nick warned.

"Go ahead, I dare you."

So he did.

Gateway to the Future
by Guy DeMonde

Guy sat on the steps picking absent-mindedly at the remains of a strawberry sundae. It was just past noon and as usual on Sundays, everyone in the family was allowed to have whatever they wanted from his father's ice-cream truck. For Guy, that meant a banana split or strawberry sundae but this time, the weekly treat wasn't doing anything for him.

It was already August, the end of summer, and in another hour he was scheduled to attend a special "reunion" dance at St. Louis for all the eighth graders who'd graduated that year. He was terrible at such gatherings and knew it. Unable to make small talk, he spent his time fingering a soda until he could pick the right moment to make a strategic and silent withdrawal. And a dance especially was to be avoided at all costs.

This time however, he had no choice.

Of course, it was in his interest to go anyway as it might be his last opportunity to see his friends before they all went their separate ways; Ricky Poilette was going to Bishop Guertin High School a few towns away, Rocky Fourchin to Lowell High School and especially Billy Beaulois, who was moving to Northampton, a full five hour drive away in western Massachusetts. Kids going to high school had the knack of making new friends and suddenly finding no time for their old buddies of elementary school days; would that happen to them? Guy guessed it would and wondered idly what new friends waited for him at St. Joe's. Would there be any who collected comic books? Or read Edgar Rice Burroughs? Or did some writing?

Anyway, he had no choice in going to the reunion dance because he had it in no uncertain terms from Noël that he didn't. Ever since she'd visited him at the hospital, he'd been uncertain about just what the exact nature of their relationship was. Were they just good friends or...or what? He'd long since returned the page from her diary, and more than once he'd found himself regretting ever having read it. Because what she'd revealed on it was something that he wasn't sure he was prepared to handle. She liked him...heck, he knew he liked her, but what was supposed to happen next? The idea of, well, going steady with her, of being her boyfriend just seemed too much. It was one thing to imagine it, but the real thing scared him.

It used to be so easy! He'd known where he stood with her then: a kind of uneasy truce, a mix of like and dislike. But now, they couldn't pretend with trumped up arguments over books and movies anymore. She'd demanded a new, honest kind of relationship and expected him to act accordingly. But he'd since discovered that he wasn't ready and hoped to be able to gradually sort things out with her over the summer, but as things turned out, they'd hardly seen each other.

When he finally got back to school after leaving the hospital, he found the class caught up with graduation fever and in a mini-whirlwind of special activities from field trips to a religious retreat. And then, when graduation was finally over and summer begun, Noël had told him she was moving. Since then, he'd hardly seen her, let alone talked to her, as she'd been too busy helping her parents get their new house ready (it would take some time to get used to referring to the Old House as the new house).

As her family began to spend more and more time in their new home, it seemed funny knowing that Noël wasn't living across the street anymore. But Guy soon consoled himself with the thought that she wouldn't be far away (he smiled for the first time that day remembering how he made her promise him the use of the library in her new home; she said they'd both need it if they did their homework together).

It took him quite a while to discover that the main reason why he felt odd about Noël's moving away was his fear that she would find new friends; that there could come a time when he'd never see her again. After that, it took another few days before he concluded that such a development would be a disaster and consoled himself with the thought that he'd still be seeing her regularly in high school.

All of it made his mind go in circles and kept him from knowing what he really wanted. What was she to him, anyway? He'd always been a loner and hated being torn between desires.

Shaking off his thoughts, he went back into the house and tossed his empty ice cream dish into the wastebasket. It was time to get ready for the dance.

It was still early when Guy rounded the corner of Boisvert Street and came into sight of the St. Louis Parish buildings. There was the church, rectory, and elementary school on one side, and the parish hall with cafeteria in the basement and classes for the Academy girls above on the other. Just then, the lights were on inside the cafeteria and there was some activity at the entrance.

Guy pulled uncomfortably at the collar of his dress shirt and checked the knot in his tie. Then, quickly running a comb through his short hair, he stepped through the hall's entrance. Inside, a short series of concrete steps led downward and when he emerged into the cafeteria, he saw that most the tables had been cleared away and the walls decorated with multi-colored bunting. It was the girls' idea to hold a reunion dance and even though the boys had made a show of going along with it, Guy knew that some actually looked forward to it.

As he moved hesitantly into the room, Guy was surprised that the girls had actually hired a disk jockey. He sat behind a record player in a corner of the room where the cafeteria's old player-piano had been pushed aside. At the moment, the jaunty strains of the Beatles' *Get Back* filled the room making Guy feel a little better (he wondered if that was Noël's doing, although she liked folk-rock of the Barry McGuire/Phil Ochs variety, he new the Beatles were still her favorite). But even hearing the Beatles wasn't enough to help him get over his nervousness. He still hoped that at least Ricky Poilette or Billy Beaulois had shown up ahead of him so he wouldn't be forced to just stand around looking ridiculous.

Then he spotted Ricky standing by the punch bowl looking desperate (what had once been considered an asset in elementary school had by now become a liability: since Ricky lived right across the street from the school, he was invariably the first to arrive at any of its ceremonies or parties). Guy, walking swiftly over to him, tried not to look over at the thirty or so girls and handful of other boys generally standing around the perimeter of the room. "Hi, Ricky," he said, coming up to his friend.

"Am I glad you showed up," said Ricky not standing on formality. "I was worried I'd be the only one to come."

"I figured I ought to make an appearance," said Guy shrugging. "After all, this'll probably be the last time I see some of the others."

"My mother made me come," admitted Ricky, gulping punch from a plastic cup.

Watching him, Guy noticed that Ricky's hands were shaking and made a conscious effort to control his own by pouring himself some punch.

"Is Rocky or Bill here yet?" he asked.

"Uh, uh," said Ricky. "That's why I was thinking of sneaking out until I saw you."

"Chicken," said Guy with a twinge of hypocrisy. He was perfectly aware that if not for Noël's warning, he wouldn't even have shown up at all.

"You're darn right, I…"

"Hey, there's Rocky and Bill," interrupted Guy, waving his hand for them to come over.

As his friends crossed the room, Guy noticed that the cafeteria had begun to fill up as new arrivals joined together with friends to reform the groups and cliques they'd begun during the eight years spent at St. Louis.

"So you guys showed up after all," said Rocky.

"Sure, we're no wallflowers," said Guy, putting on a bold front.

"I found Bill hiding in the alley," laughed Rocky.

"I wasn't hiding, I was scouting out the joint."

"Sure you were," they all laughed (rather too self-consciously thought Guy).

At that point the music, which had shifted from the upbeat *Get Back* to more neutral numbers, changed again and Guy recognized *Sugar, Sugar*, the popular hit song from the Archies' Saturday morning TV show.

A few couples drifted to the center of the room, some hand in hand, and began dancing. Then, as the number's popular rhythm continued, more joined them. Most of those dancing seemed to be girls but there were enough boy/girl combinations to surprise Guy. Hadn't it only been a few years before that they all had no use for each other?

Then, seeing Noël for the first time that evening, Guy's heart seemed to constrict in his chest. She was dancing with Deni and his stomach felt as if it had just been tied into knots.

"Is it hot in here?" he asked no one in particular.

"The air conditioners are going," observed Billy, completely unaware of the true source of Guy's discomfort.

It came as a shock to Guy to realize that he was jealous! What had he expected anyway? That Noël would spend the night serving punch and cakes? Making small talk? He'd known for years that she was one of the sisters' favorites, liked by everyone and moved easily among the elite of the class. But that had all been knowledge in the abstract. Seeing the evidence for it right before his eyes was entirely different. What had he wanted, for her to be as shy and introverted as he was? To be bookish and nothing else? Suddenly more confused than ever, he managed to drag his gaze from the couple.

Grabbing up a finger cake, he bit it ferociously hoping that no one had noticed how he'd been staring at them.

The next few minutes seemed to stretch into an eternity as, trying to make small talk with his friends, Guy also felt compelled to steal sly peeks at Noël's dancing figure.

She seemed to him somehow transformed from her everyday appearance; more like an alluring stranger than the friend he'd played red light and kick-the-can with in the old neighborhood. She still had the same blond hair that curled inward at the shoulders (which tonight seemed to shine as bright as the sun), the same eyes that had often looked at him in cold fury (but now seemed to laugh as if they'd never known anything else) and her form was that of the girl he'd always known (except that now it seemed to move with more grace than he'd ever imagined possible).

Continuing to watch her, Guy felt a growing surprise, even shock. He had no idea that she could dance so well! Each motion, each step seemed to him to be as precise and exact as the rhythm of a poem while at the same time natural and unselfconscious. But all such cold analysis of dance style evaporated in an instant each time a chance movement of Noël's body brought up the hem of her skirt. Trying to control the pounding of his heart when such an occurrence revealed her legs a few inches above the knee, Guy couldn't figure out why that should affect him so strongly; after all, he'd seen much more of her when they all went swimming at the Therrien's hadn't he?

His increasingly desperate rationalizations were interrupted when Nancy Bertrois came over and asked Rocky to dance. As they retreated to the dance floor, Guy could tell that Ricky and Billy shared with him an unaccountable feeling of betrayal. Suddenly, it seemed as if everyone was dancing but the three of them and Guy, feeling somehow exposed, was seriously considering leaving the party when he noticed the looks on the faces of his two friends.

"What's the matter?" he asked.

But instead of replying, their eyes only widened. Then Guy, so tightly wound that he almost jumped, felt a tap on his shoulder.

"Would you like to dance?" said a voice and when he turned, saw that it belonged to Noël.

The moment had come upon him so suddenly, that Guy forgot about being jealous and almost about being nervous too; but in the end, his nerves didn't fail him and he soon felt his knees begin to knock.

"I asked if you wanted to dance," Noël repeated, slightly breathless and quite attractive in a skirt and vest combination.

"I heard you," Guy said defensively (the thought of exhibiting his stiff, gawky self on the dance floor beside Noël's obviously accomplished moves made him cringe). He swallowed. "Look, are you sure you want to...? I mean, I don't know how to..."

"Don't you think I know that?" said Noël in the same way she used to rebuke him in their literary arguments but this time she smiled when she said it. "But it's time you got some experience; we'll be going to St. Joe's next year and I don't plan on being embarrassed because my friend doesn't know a tango from the watusi. Now, c'mon."

Short of making a scene, he had little choice but to do as she said and to allow her to pull him from the safety of the refreshment area.

His body temperature continuing to rise the closer he was led to the action, Guy was sure the worst mistake he ever made was to come to this party instead of staying home to watch television. Again, his mind must have wandered because all of a sudden, he noticed that *Something* by the Beatles was playing and, as if from very far away, Noël was trying to tell him something.

"Don't worry, Guy," she was saying. "I made sure they played this song for us. It's a slow one so you'll have no problem."

As if in a dream, Guy felt himself propelled amid the other dancers. Briefly, he resumed control of his own actions by taking Noël boldly by the waist.

"That was easy," he joked. "What comes next?"

"I do this," Noël said, placing her arms around his neck.

After that, he found it hard to concentrate again. All he could see was Noël's smiling face as she looked up the few inches in height between them and all he could feel were the new, pleasurable sensations that suddenly seemed to course throughout his body.

"Hey, you've done this before," Noël said.

"Huh? Done what before?"

"Slow dance, silly!"

It was true. He looked down, and saw that he'd been naturally swaying and circling with Noël's movements.

"Didn't you know? I'm the house dancer for American Bandstand."

Curious, Guy glanced at the other couples moving around him, (it was like the times when he was a kid on an amusement park ride looking at his fellow passengers on the tilt-a-whirl) and was surprised to see that they weren't paying attention to him at all but only to each other. Then he saw Ricky and Billy still standing by the table, and felt a great sadness for them. He felt like a man who'd gone to heaven only to realize how miserable earthbound creatures really were.

"Deni asked me to dance before I could talk to you," Noël said. Had it only been a few seconds since his last comment? "I couldn't just tell him no." She giggled. "You should've seen his face when I refused the next dance and told him I was here with you."

"You didn't!"

"Of course I did; didn't I invite you to come?"

"You *told* me to come—"

Noël laughed. "It's so much easier when you just listen to me."

"Where'd you learn to dance anyway," said Guy, changing the subject. "I never thought you were the type to go in for rock 'n roll."

"Why not?" Noël demanded. "No one's dancing the waltz anymore and if we bibliophiles are going to have any fun, we're going to have to learn some more up to date steps."

"Granted, but that still doesn't explain where you learned those moves."

"Actually, I did it by watching Polly's sisters and practicing with Denise, Theo, and Polly."

"So that's it." *I could get used to this,* thought Guy, his earlier anxiety mysteriously vanished. It was something he'd scarcely imagined only a few minutes before, but here he was exchanging snappy dialogue with a pretty girl in the middle of a dance floor!

Suddenly the music ended and with it, the sense that time had been standing still. Had they been dancing for only the two minutes and fifty-nine seconds playing time of George Harrison's hit song?

As the beat of the music changed to the wilder notes of the Cowsill's *Hair,* the look on Guy's face must've registered the panic he felt because Noël decided to grant him a reprieve.

"Don't worry," she laughed, patting his arms. "I won't ask you to dance a fast one...yet!"

"What I'm really worried about, is your dancing with Deni again," Guy replied, surprising even himself. Did he just say that?

"Well, Mr. DeMonde!" said Noël, taken aback. "You're getting pretty bold in your old age."

She took a step back, placed her hands on her hips and made a show of looking him up and down.

Guy fidgeted from foot to foot, half expecting a burst of the old anger.

"As I informed you before, you're my only target for today," she said finally. "So be sure you're ready when I come by and don't let me catch you trying to sneak out before the party's over."

"No ma'am," said Guy, half seriously as he watched Noël cross back over to some of the other girls. He didn't know what to think about what just happened, but was sure of one thing, he was utterly delighted at the way things had turned out. What a great party!

After that, it seemed like he only had enough time to quiet the astonishment of his friends (Noël was considered by this time one of the prizes among the female population of the class), and drink a gallon of punch (he hadn't realized how thirsty he was!) before Noël summoned him to the dance floor again.

At last, after a flurry of dancing, laughing, and talking (Noël had insisted he stay with her as she visited nearly everyone in the class) the party was over and before he knew it, Guy found himself walking home, not sure whether his feet touched the ground or not.

Even after an afternoon filled with delightful surprises, he still wondered at the nerve he'd shown in asking to walk Noël home (even though he'd done just that a hundred times before when they'd been in school together; but that'd been different in a way he couldn't define). It didn't matter that she had to stay to help clean up or that she was expecting her father, it was enough to know that, if she'd been free, she would've done it.

He drew in a deep breath and exhaled. Was it his imagination or did the air smell sweeter to him? It seemed to him right then, that in that lungful of air, he could smell every individual flower and tree in the neighborhood and as he made his way along Lakeview Avenue, the woods that rolled up past the Merrimack River to the Old House…Noël's house now…called out to him with their promise of life and solitude.

At home, he'd hardly had a chance to change out of his suit before the inevitable questions arose: everyone in the family wanted to know what he'd done, how the party had gone, had he done any dancing, and as the barrage continued, the lure of the open fields next door, awash in the golden sunlight and lengthening shadows of late afternoon, seemed to him more and more attractive. Suddenly, he realized that the constant attention by his family threatened to overwhelm the good feeling he'd been experiencing since leaving the party and more than anything right then, he wanted that to last. As quickly as he could, he made his excuses and, leaving the house, dashed into the woodland at the end of the street with the vague intention of heading to the old tree platform by the brook.

He hadn't visited the platform for quite a while (he and his friends hadn't played in the woods for a long time and Guy realized with sudden regret that he couldn't remember when they'd stopped) and soon discovered that most of the old trails had vanished from infrequent use beneath fast growing grass and brush. Instead, he had to go by dead reckoning until he came to within a few hundred feet of the platform's location. Then, with the big maple tree in plain sight, he broke through a final barrier of undergrowth and emerged into an open area directly beneath its wide spreading branches. There, with the sound of the rushing stream close by, he reached out and tested the wooden slats he'd nailed to the tree's trunk those long years ago, found them still sturdy, and heaved himself into the tree.

The platform itself wasn't much, but the memories that hung about the platform were so thick right then, Guy thought he could cut them with a knife. He remembered the times he and his friends had met here in secret to plan raids on the kids who lived on Tilden Avenue, a dead end street across a stretch of meadow from Guy's house. Mostly, they were classmates at St. Louis (or former classmates some of them before Guy stayed back in the fourth grade) who made for convenient targets when he and his neighborhood friends had been completely taken by the spy craze that began with the James Bond films and then spread to television with shows like *The Wild Wild West, I Spy,* and *Honey West.* But the best of them all, the show that drove everyone wild with enthusiasm was *The Man From UNCLE!*

It was hard for Guy to imagine now how crazy they were about that show; how they fancied themselves UNCLE agents and went on missions spying on the Tilden Avenue kids. And they were somehow worth spying on because unlike the Desrosiers Street kids, they had a terrific two floor clubhouse, an upper entrance that led into a tree platform that in turn led to higher branches where a small crow's nest was located. Although the Tilden Avenue kids patterned themselves after the Hardy Boys, Guy and his friends always referred to them as THRUSH, UNCLE's villainous adversaries.

And the wars they had! Although no one actually fought to hurt each other, there was the capturing of each others' members and efforts to make them reveal their secrets. Wars usually began when Guy and Jiff had nothing to do and decided to sneak over to Bobby Toussain's house and poke about his clubhouse. Actually hoping to be spotted, they sometimes were and in no time, the Tilden Avenue gang would gather and catch up with them in some neighbor's back yard or across a fence. By then, of course, Guy and Jiff had assembled the rest of their own gang, Don and Mike and if he was available, Jiff's cousin Morgan. From there, action would proceed according to an unspoken code. First, there would be some taunting ("What were you doing in our clubhouse?" "Nothin'!"), then, there might be some jockeying for position by the parties as Don and Lester Beauchoin (who were about the same size) began to eye one another and move to the flanks. (Lester never came to those confrontations without something to throw; depending on the season, he might be armed with snowballs in the winter, green apples in the spring, chestnuts in the summer, or rotten tomatoes in the fall). When words failed, everyone paired off (Jiff and Deni; Guy and Bobby; Don and Lester; Mike and Deni's kid brother Normy) and soon there was general wrestling all around with mainly filthy and torn clothing as a result. When everyone had had enough or felt that the other side had learned its lesson, the melee would break up until the next time.

Suddenly, there was a loud caw of a big blackbird sitting in a dead tree and the memories began to break up; the youthful faces of his friends melting away like phantoms and Guy wasn't sure if he didn't prefer the comforting familiarity of the past to the uncertainty promised by the events of that evening.

Off in the distance, he could see the late afternoon sunlight flickering on the brook and the treetops swaying in the gentle August breeze. To his left, he could just make out the roof lines of some of the homes in the neighborhood as they indicated the way back to Desrosiers Street and not too far beyond that, the homes along Tilden Avenue. But those hadn't been what he was looking for as his eyes continued to wander northward to the newly painted widow's walk that gleamed in the sun from the top of the Old House. Still basking in the afterglow of the euphoria he'd felt upon leaving the party, Guy imagined Noël arriving home from the party and stepping from the car, laughing shortly, and talking easily with her father. She'd follow him into the house, greet her mother and maybe sit down for tea. Later that night, she'd put down her book and turn off her night light and the last thing she'd think of before nodding off to sleep would be him.

The strangely satisfying scene had taken such a strong hold upon his imagination that Guy never noticed the noise that came from the brush surrounding the base of the tree, nor did he hear the sounds made when someone began climbing up to the platform. So when at last the creak of a board did tear him from his daydream, it was with complete surprise that he saw who it was.

CHAPTER SEVENTEEN

An ending and a beginning

August 28, 1970: It's been an hour since I first sat down to make this entry and if I've started to write it once, I must've started a dozen times because I can count at least twelve pieces of crumpled pages on the floor. This final entry is turning out to be a good deal more difficult to write than I thought.

And I can't decide whether I'm happy about that or sad.

In my earliest entry, written in 1966 (it's hard to believe, even with the evidence of my own thoughts, that I could ever have been that young!), I wrote that the first obligation of keeping a diary was that the diarist should be honest. Well, I think up to now I have been, sometimes maybe even too much so and one of those times, the last time, is going to be right now.

This is to be my last entry. The end of my journal.

I'm not calling it quits because I don't expect anything of note to happen for the rest of my life; and I'm not fool enough to think that I don't have anything left to learn, far from it. I'm stopping because for quite some time now, I've been convinced that whatever help this diary has been to me (and it has helped a lot), it's proved to be increasingly inadequate in addressing new, more complex questions that have cropped up since I became a teenager (I'll be 14 next month). Once, maybe, working things out here for myself was a good idea, but these days the solution to some problems isn't as easy to find, sometimes there are even more than one! And for those, I really need to talk to a living, breathing human being: either Maman or Papa, one of my teachers at school, even my friends and yes, sometimes Guy.

In that first entry I also wrote that my life after moving to Lowell would be a blank slate upon which would be written new chapters and new adventures. How true that turned out to be! But now, even those chapters have become old ones and adventures that seemed fabulous and wondrous yesterday, no longer seem so. I sense now that it's time to turn the page again.

I'm sure the next part of my life will hold its share of problems, worries, and heartaches, but it'll have fun and excitement and fulfillment too. Already, I've felt my childhood friends begin to slip away as we all go our different ways, meet new people and leave our old interests behind. Soon, Desrosiers Street, even tired old Lowell too, will seem hopelessly provincial. This is the truth. This is being honest. What's also the truth is that I'm looking forward with all my heart to the future.

And the best part is, I won't be facing it alone, I'll be sharing all the hazards and the joys (and the first days in high school!) with a companion who, no matter how we might change, will always be my dearest friend.

The very first line I wrote in this diary was how I didn't take the news of moving to Lowell very well. I can hardly remember ever feeling that way, because looking back, it was the very best thing that's ever happened to me!

I remember how Maman once told me that life never turned out the way you expected it. And oh! I can see now how right she was!

What a fool I was! thought Noël again, seemingly for the dozenth time since coming home that afternoon.

Following the party, while cleaning up, her classmates had betrayed little of what they must've been thinking about Guy and herself, only bringing his name up once. And on the way home, her father had restrained himself from asking too many questions. Even her mother had little to say and nodded and smiled from over the rim of her teacup as Noël told her how things had gone (she'd only realized just how carefully her mother had listened when she suggested that Noël invite Guy over for supper one night). But since then, she'd gone up to her room and unbidden, the accumulated embarrassments of the reunion party came flooding back to her.

How could she have made such a fool of herself! she thought again.

Had she really said all those things to Guy? Practically telling him that he was her date, her...boyfriend! And what was anyone else, Guy included, to think, the way she paraded him around, holding onto his arm... *Oh, no!*

she thought, covering her face with her hands, she hadn't really brought him around to all her friends to make small talk, had she? But her memories were merciless and assured her that yes, she'd done exactly that.

Then she remembered all the little things: how she pulled him protestingly from his friends to dance, how she put her arms around his neck and brought him closer than she sensed he'd been comfortable with, how she had him participate in some of the faster numbers. And how patient he seemed through the whole thing, even cool! She remembered how he'd tossed off little jokes and assumed an air of tolerant amusement at the whole thing. Not for the first time that morning, Noël looked back and recalled her actions as having been as hopelessly immature, even giddy, as those she'd always disdained in other girls.

Oh, what must everyone think of me? How she must be the laughing stock of everyone at St. Louis! Then a new, more horrifying thought occurred to her: what if Guy told his friends about her behavior? In no time, it could spread into the neighborhood!

But instead of adding to her fears, the thought of that ultimate embarrassment seemed to act like a dash of cold water. Sitting in the window seat, she looked out to where the sun, hidden on the opposite side of the house, shone its light through the tree branches. What, after all, was there to be embarrassed about? Did she or didn't she like Guy? And if the answer was yes, why should she be embarrassed about acknowledging it in public? She'd be in high school next month and well past the age where such childish notions ruled her every move. She should be prepared to have friends that were boys as well as girls.

And besides, she liked Guy and enjoyed being with him at the party. He was nice and polite; funny and smart too. They had a lot in common. That didn't mean there'd necessarily be romance between them (even though there might!), they could be just really close and dear friends. And who cared what anybody else wanted to call it?

Feeling her spirits rise, Noël decided to go out for some fresh air and stepped into the back yard. Chancing a look over at the DeMonde's house, she saw no sign of Guy. It was just as well, she sighed. After all, just because she'd sorted out her own feelings about their relationship, it didn't necessarily mean that Guy had done the same.

Feeling oddly liberated, she wandered over to the rail fence at the end of the street wondering just how she should eventually approach Guy. The question couldn't be put off forever; and since the party, she sensed that things between them had fundamentally changed. Should she seek him out and risk scaring him off or avoid him for a while to show that she had no intention of pressuring him?

She was still debating on what to do when it occurred to her that whenever she had something difficult to think through, she always used to find it easier amid the bucolic surroundings of the woods and fields that stretched out before her. Hopping down from the fence, she stared off into the distance, remembering Lookout Hill and Guy's old tree platform. She recalled how she used to go out there by herself, to read some Emily Dickenson or write entries in her diary or just to daydream. High up above the woods, the platform had always been a perfect place to while away a sultry summer afternoon.

Slowly, she began walking through the tall grass toward the distant rise of Lookout Hill. She passed through the familiar fields and trees, plucking at stalks of grass gone to seed and, her thoughts preoccupied, not taking much note of her surroundings. Then, amid clouds of scattering grasshoppers, she reached the top of Lookout Hill. She lingered there only a little while before heading down the back slope in the direction of Beaver Brook, wondering vaguely if she'd still be able to find Guy's platform.

All the old trails had disappeared in the undergrowth (why was it that an abandoned playground where once children had laughed and played could seem like such a sad place?) so it took a while longer for her find the way, but at last, she recognized the big old maple tree towering over the rest of the forest and made a bee-line toward it.

It was difficult going, but at last she broke through the final tangle of brush and found herself at the foot of the old tree. Looking up into its branches, she seemed to feel something of Guy's spirit about it and she imagined all the times he'd come here to read his books and dream his dreams. Suddenly her throat tightened at the memories that flooded back. Memories of Guy, Mike, and Don, of Polly and Theo and Trece. Blinking back tears that began to water her eyes, she gripped the pieces of wood nailed to the tree trunk and began to pull herself upward.

Above her, the opening in the platform showed a square of pale blue sky criss-crossed in leafy branches and she could see the crude remnants of the railing Guy had nailed around it. It took surprisingly little effort for her to reach the top and as she took hold of the edge of the platform and poked her head through the opening, a board squeaked and she sensed movement near the bole of the tree.

There was a gasp.

"Noël!" exclaimed Guy, his hand hovering near his heart. "You scared the daylights out of me!"

Noël was as surprised to find Guy on the platform as he apparently was of her sudden appearance. She hadn't meant to see him again so soon, intending to think things through first, but it was too late to do anything about that now so she decided to take the bull by the horns and make the best of the awkward situation.

"Well, you did the same for me you know," she said at last, holding out her hand.

Guy didn't hesitate and took it, helping her to her feet on the platform.

"What're you doing out here?" he asked when she'd finished brushing herself off.

"Probably the same as you," she said. "I wanted to do some thinking and decided nobody would bother me out here."

"What kind of thinking did you need to do?" asked Guy.

Noël didn't answer right away, she just moved over to a railing made from a tree branch that'd been nailed in place at about the height of her waist and leaned on it a little.

"Look," she said at last, "you can see my house from here."

"Yeah, I know."

"Remember how we used to play out here?" asked Noël. "Remember the time you guys ambushed me and Polly?"

"Yeah, boy, were you mad!" said Guy, forgetting his earlier question.

"Do you blame me? You really scared the daylights out of us."

"Well, it seemed a good idea at the time."

"You're not going to believe this, but I miss it when you boys used to do goofy stuff like that."

"You do?"

"Yeah," said Noël, smiling. "Lately, it seems, we're all too old and stuffy to do anything fun or spontaneous, don't you think?"

Guy put his hands in his pockets and shrugged. "I know what you're talking about. These days all we seem to do is sit around playing board games or hanging out in front of Jiff's house talking. No one ever goes in the woods, just to go in the woods any more."

Noël swung herself down and, sitting on the platform, gripped the railing over her head and dangled her legs over the edge. "What've you heard from Mike?"

"He misses the neighborhood," said Guy. "And so far, it looks like he'll be able to come back for a couple weeks at Christmas."

"Remember how he used to be afraid of ghosts?"

"Yeah, and I think he still is!" laughed Guy, sitting down beside Noël.

"And how you used to be afraid of me," added Noël, continuing to look straight ahead.

"What?" said Guy. "Me, afraid of you?"

"Weren't you?" Now, she turned to face him.

"Of course not!"

Noël made a rude sound. "Right; you don't think I notice it when your voice gets all trembly when you talk to the girls at school? Or how you used to manage avoiding being on my team when we used to play games?"

"The girls at school don't think much of me and I don't think much of them," replied Guy, protesting too much. "And I never avoided any of the girls in the neighborhood."

"Except me; c'mon, admit it.'

"I...say, what was it you came up here to think about?"

"Remember that time we were caught behind the same bush at Jiff's birthday party?"

"What's that got to do with..."

"It was all you could do not to bolt out of there the minute you found out you had to share it with me," said Noël. "As a matter of fact, if I recall correctly, that was when you fell for me."

Guy's face suddenly went beet-red, but Noël couldn't tell if it was from embarrassment or anger.

"I did not! I tripped...*you* tripped me!"

"And what about the time you carried me home from Dana's Fruitland?"

"I didn't carry you all the way home..."

"Just like David Innes coming to the rescue of Dian the Beautiful." Noël knew that she was laying it on pretty thick by this time, but for some reason, she couldn't stop herself. She was enjoying it.

"Oh, come on! That's just too...hey, how do you know about David Innes and Dian the Beautiful?"

"Oh, I read *At the Earth's Core* years ago..."

"*Years* ago!"

"It was when I finally decided to get to know you better and the most obvious place to start was to read some of your favorite books. They were very eye-opening, let me tell you." Guy blushed. "Don't tell me you never noticed those books missing from your collection?"

"You read *my* books?"

"Sure," admitted Noël, breezily. "When you weren't home, your sisters let me borrow one from time to time."

Guy was temporarily flabbergasted. "What other books did you...?"

"Some of the titles are hard to remember," Noël teased. "The best guide I had were the covers. I picked the ones with the girls in the little fur bikinis on them..."

Guy, nearly bursting with frustration at the direction the whole conversation had gone, couldn't sit still. He rose to his feet and would've paced if there'd been enough room on the platform. Instead, he contented himself with leaning against the bole of the tree and crossing his arms over his chest.

"Well, what did you think?" he finally said.

Noël turned around to face him, propping herself on one extended arm. "They weren't very well written and the plots were horribly trite and predictable," she said.

298

"I'll admit, they were kinda fun in places, but they'll never replace real literature."

"And I'll admit they were never intended to be anything more than entertainment," said Guy, still a bit surly. "But the literature they grew out of, the dime novel and the pulp magazine, celebrated the individual. Whether the authors knew it or not, characters like John Carter, Conan the Barbarian or the Shadow were all extensions of the rugged individual that carved out this country from a raw wilderness."

"You're exactly right," agreed Noël. "But what I want to know is, have you learned anything from all this pulp style reading?"

"What do you mean?"

"Are you enough of a 'rugged individualist' to answer the question I asked you a few minutes ago?"

Noël saw that Guy was thinking carefully and guessed that he'd finally realized that she'd maneuvered him into just the position she wanted him. (Somewhere in the back of his mind, she was sure, he'd made a mental note never to play chess with her).

"Uh, what question was that?"

"That you've always been perfectly comfortable around any girl in the neighborhood except me," Noël said, getting to her feet.

Like a tigress moving in for the kill, thought Guy.

"I was the only girl you avoided, Guy; why was that?"

Guy licked his lips and put his hands in his pockets. "Okay, maybe I did try to avoid you. You made me nervous with your high grades at school and those big-domed books you were always reading."

"That's not the reason and you know it," said Noël, her eyebrows coming together.

When her hands went to her hips, Guy knew Noël was losing patience and decided quickly to cut his losses.

"Well..." he gulped. "Well..."

"Well, what?"

"I liked you!" Guy blurted.

"Liked? In the past tense?"

"I mean I liked you then…I mean now too…I mean, I just like you a lot, okay? I've been attracted to you almost from the first time I met you at the Dracut Library."

Satisfied, Noël smiled and lowered her hands.

"And what about you?" asked Guy, pushing himself away from the tree. "Do you like me or what?"

"It's getting late," said Noël, confusing Guy. "Are you hungry?"

"Huh?"

"Are you getting hungry?"

"Come to think of it, yeah; I guess we ought to be getting home…"

"Why don't you come to our house for supper?" said Noël.

"Your house?"

"When I told my mother about the party, she suggested I invite you over for supper some time, so how about tonight?"

"Right now?"

"Of course, right now," said Noël, beginning to lose patience again. "We can call your folks from my house to tell them you'll be eating over."

"Well, okay, I guess," said Guy, not being able to think of any other objections.

"Great," said Noël brightly. "Let's go."

A few minutes later, they were backtracking along the path blazed earlier by Noël. They followed it until they reached Lookout Hill then veered north toward the Archambault's house. When they reached the lonely stretch of roadway that passed in front of the house, Noël led the way across and into another field on the opposite side of the house.

"Why are we going this way?" asked Guy. "Why don't we head straight for the house?"

"I want to show you something," was all Noël said as she found another trail that led around to the rear of the property.

When they finally emerged into the open, the sun was low on the western horizon and had turned the sky all pink and rosy. In Noël's backyard (which still hadn't been completely cleared of brush) the evening shadows had begun to lengthen and darken.

"Where exactly are we?" asked Guy, recognizing the old dog cages but little else.

Noël didn't answer, instead, she moved toward a grove of trees and began pushing aside some hanging vines. "Look in here," she said at last.

Guy went over and poked his head in the opening she'd made. "Hey, there's a gazebo or something in here!"

"Go on in," urged Noël.

A moment later, they were inside and almost completely hidden from outside view. Noël sat down at one of the benches that ringed the gazebo as Guy continued to stand, looking around.

"Wow, this is really neat," said Guy, unaware that once again, he'd been thoroughly outmaneuvered.

"Why don't you come over here and sit down," suggested Noël.

Guy, suddenly nervous, couldn't think of any way to gracefully decline. He sat down (there was just room enough for two if they squeezed close together) and went on the offensive.

"You know, you still haven't told me what it was you went to the platform to think over," he said.

"I went to think about us, as you well know," said Noël, smiling.

Guy had never seen Noël's smile up close before. It was delightful and mesmerizing and...irresistible all at the same time. His heart began to pound so loudly that he was sure she could hear it as plainly as he could.

"What," he gulped, "what exactly do you mean by that?"

"I needed to decide whether we should have a... special...relationship, different from what we've already had, with each other and with the other kids in the neighborhood."

"How special?"

"That's up to you," Noël said. "I've decided to grow up and forget about what the others think. We'll be friends, real friends not just acquaintances. If I like you, then I'll spend time with you just as I do with my girl friends. The one thing I'm sure of is that I don't want to spend any more time wondering what you think of me; if I'm pushing too hard, tell me and if you think I'm not paying enough attention to you, let me know. What I'm most interested in is honesty, what about you?"

Still smiling, she gave her head a shake to clear a stray strand of hair from her eyes. She felt justified in congratulating herself on handling a tricky, sensitive situation rather nicely. Now, preparing for the coup de grace, she took Guy's hand in hers and said, "What about you, Guy?"

Now it was Guy's turn to smile for her, a smile that for the very first time, Noël was certain was not only genuine, but completely unaffected and devoid of self-consciousness.

"I've always thought that honesty was the best policy," he said, giving her hand an encouraging squeeze.

"Edgar Rice Burroughs couldn't have said it better," Noël laughed. "You want to hear another old chestnut?"

Guy nodded, laughing too.

"Before they were married, my parents shared their first kiss under this gazebo."

"Really?" said Guy in a voice that indicated he wasn't at all surprised.

The corners of Noël's mouth went up, revealing a pair of dimples that Guy realized were completely unnoticeable from more than a few inches away.

"I'm going to kiss you," Noël warned.

"Go ahead," Guy gulped. "I dare you."

So she did.

THE END